THE KITE

N.R. WALKER

COPYRIGHT

Cover Artist: Book Cover Zone
Editor: Posy Roberts, Boho Edits
Publisher: BlueHeart Press
The Kite © 2022 N.R. Walker

ALL RIGHTS RESERVED:

WARNING

This book is intended for an adult audience. It contains graphic language, explicit content, and adult situations.

TRADEMARKS

BLURB

Ex-Australian Specialist Response Group leader, Tim "Harry" Harrigan, has been running covert ops for almost a decade. A lone wolf, he's single-handedly taken down terrorists and national security threats, or so he thinks. He's been in the game far too long, and when he sees a familiar threat, he knows his time is up.

Asher Garin is a dangerous man. A man without loyalty, a man without a nationality, without a country, without a home. He's also a mercenary for hire to the highest bidder. His next job is a face he recognises, and after a tip-off, he learns he too is a marked man.

It's a different game now, and Harry and Asher have a better chance at surviving if they stick together. But it's not just the game or the rules that have changed. The stakes have too.

Because on their own, they had nothing to lose. Together, they do.

THE KITE

N.R. WALKER

ONE

GHARDAÏA, ALGERIA

HARRY LOOKED through the scope of his rifle and exhaled. It was midday, the Saharan summer sun was scorching hot, the air still and stifling. The desert city had narrow streets with sand- and mud-packed walls; a clustered oasis in the middle of a sea of baking sand. Somewhere nearby, children laughed, a baby cried, a woman yelled, cursing.

He was so far from home.

It had been so long since he'd set foot on Australian soil, he'd almost forgotten what home felt like. He longed for a life that wasn't his. Wasn't *this*. At first the longing was fleeting, no more than a whisper, but it sang a little louder now. In the quiet darkness of night or the patient wait for a kill.

Like now.

Harry had waited in the darkened room, at this window, for two days. His patience never waning.

He never moved. Stock-still, measured breaths.

Dirty sweat ran down his spine. He ignored it.

His mark appeared at the front of the building in the street below.

Harry took another breath. Deep, controlled. Patient.

This was it.

Confirm the mark.

It was him. No doubt. His intel had been spot on. It always was.

Harry inhaled. He moved his finger to the trigger.

The target turned around, as if he knew his time was up. Harry never much cared for the whys of his job. He was simply sent the information, photos, video if they had it. And he did whatever needed doing. Why that person was marked for removal was none of his business.

Their removal was.

The target turned to speak to someone. A small child, a boy, laughing as he ran.

Harry considered waiting but he couldn't miss this opportunity.

Another breath in, slow exhale.

He was going to lose his target at this rate.

Piss off, kid. You don't want to see this.

Another bead of sweat rolled down Harry's spine.

Somewhere off in the distance, a car horn sounded. Harry's mind threw him back to his teenage days of endless summers with mates, driving old cars and drinking by the river. The smell of possibilities and optimism floated in the hazy afternoon sunlight, memories of a simpler life . . .

Movement on the street below snapped him back to the dark and dingy room, to the blistering heat, and to his purpose. The small child ran ahead, disappearing inside a house. The man began to follow, alone and exposed.

This was his one chance.

The mark's head fixed in his crosshairs. The perfect shot.

Harry pulled the trigger.

MADRID, SPAIN

Harry pulled his coat collar up against the cold. He kept his head down, though he was aware of everything around him.

Always alert.

He'd needed to leave his apartment for bread and coffee and felt eyes on him the second he stepped foot onto the sidewalk.

Someone was watching.

Following.

He saw no one. Not even a shadow, but he felt them as if their breath was on his neck.

A class of young school children were on the sidewalk being ushered by teachers in lines of two. The children laughed and chatted despite the cold, and Harry considered keeping pace with them.

Using them as protection.

The people after you don't care if the kids die, Harry.

Harry crossed the street. No one crossed after him, but whoever was after him was closer now.

He could feel it.

That cold stab of dread, sixth sense, gut feeling. Like icy fingers down his skin.

And if someone was after Harry, it wasn't good. He was the hunter, never the hunted. If he was the mark . . .

Christ. He was the mark.

Harry ducked past two women, slipping through a narrow utility alley, and he ran. He was being chased now, silent and fast. At the end of the alley, he turned left and went through an open door, up a set of stairs to the roof, his heart hammering.

He ran along the roofline, exposed but faster than on the street. He heard footsteps chasing behind him but didn't dare turn around, and as the muted whirr of a bullet pinged past his head, he jumped.

He knew the sound of that gun. It was a SIG Pro 9mm with a suppressor.

French special forces, standard issue.

He landed on a first-floor balcony, using his momentum to leap again, this time to the ground. Pain shot through his ankle but he kept moving, down another alley, and through an open door and into a darkened hall.

Hands grabbed him, spun him and pinned his back against the wall as the door closed behind him. In half a disorienting second, Harry pulled his gun to his assailant's head at the same time he realised he had a pistol pressed against his.

Eyes flashed in the dark, familiar and close. A man's body pressed him hard to the wall, their chests heaving. A hand covered his mouth.

"Shh."

Harry didn't dare breathe, his finger on the trigger, still aimed at the man's head. The cold press of metal against Harry's temple told him to wait.

The sound of feet outside came running. The crackle of a radio, a French voice just outside the door. "I've lost him." The footsteps faded, and only after a long moment did the man move his hand from Harry's mouth.

Harry could see then who it was.

Asher Garin.

Asher fucking Garin.

Adrenaline exploded through Harry's veins and he started, pushing his pistol harder into Asher's temple. Asher gnashed his teeth. Anger and defiance flashed in his eyes. "Keep quiet or you'll kill us both," Asher hissed, barely a whisper.

His words didn't make sense.

Asher had saved him?

If there was anyone on the planet sent to kill Harry, it would be Asher. He was the only other man good enough. They were the top two government assassins in the world. Yet Asher had just saved him from the French?

Keep quiet or you'll kill us both.

Both?

After an eternity, Asher released him, though he kept his pistol aimed at Harry's head. "We need to get out of here," he murmured.

Harry's heart was thundering. His finger itched to pull the trigger. *Itched.* "The fuck?"

Asher held up his phone to show Harry the screen. "Sent to all agencies." An assignment, just like any other. Just like any of the thousand he'd received in the last decade. Locations, dates, names, and photographs.

Two photographs.

Harry's blood ran cold, and his eyes met Asher's.

Asher nodded, his stare intense. "You and me; double hit. They want us dead. You're a kite, and your government just cut you loose."

Harry grappled with his fight or flight instinct, his heart hammering, his ankle throbbing. But given two men had just tried to kill him and the fact Asher *hadn't* killed him—and the assignment on his phone screen—Harry could assume what Asher said was true.

Asher must have seen the realisation in Harry's eyes because he slowly lowered his gun. Just an inch. "We need to trust each other," he whispered. "The only chance we have is if we stick together. Can you do that?"

Trusting any other person went against every cell in Harry's body, but what choice did he have? If he said no, one or both of them died right here. If the assignment was sent to all agencies, there wasn't a country or government anywhere in the world that could protect them.

Harry had no choice.

Answering without a word, he took his finger off the trigger.

TWO

"WE CANNOT GO BACK," Asher said through clenched teeth.

"I have to," Harry replied. Going back to his apartment was high-risk, but if they were going dark, it made sense.

"They'll be waiting for you."

Harry met his gaze, their faces a little too close. "Let them come."

Asher growled and mumbled something in Romanian. Maybe it was Croatian or a mix of both. Harry thought he heard the word *suicide*, but it was hard to tell when Asher grumbled under his breath.

Asher held up two fingers. "Two minutes and I am gone, with or without you."

Harry gave a nod.

He was torn about trusting Asher, turning his back to him, giving him any kind of advantage.

If he was here to kill you, you'd be dead by now.

"My apartment is—"

"I know where it is."

Harry shouldn't have been surprised, but he was. Asher rolled his eyes and pointed to the door he'd come through, but Harry grabbed his arm. "This way." He led him to the other side of the stairs and cracked the narrow hidden door.

Silence. Empty.

Harry was about to open the door when he remembered he was no longer on his own. "It's a utility corridor," he murmured. "Fully enclosed. One hundred metres. Stairwell on your left."

Asher shrugged like he couldn't care less, and Harry slipped through the door. He crouched as he ran, past pipework, boxes, garbage, a clothesline. This city was full of back alleys, some open to the sky, some enclosed, and he'd chosen his apartment because there were three exit options, relatively hidden.

The stairwell was clear, though Harry knew his luck would have to run out soon. He took the stairs two at a time, ignoring the shooting pain in his ankle, and took his pistol in hand. He got to the door at his floor and stopped to listen.

More silence.

He cracked the door open and glanced down the hall.

Shit.

"You know," Asher mumbled, right behind him. "It would have been quicker if we'd walked up the main fucking street."

"Shh," Harry hissed. "My door's open. Ten metres on the left."

Asher sighed and stepped around him, slipping into the hall and into Harry's apartment. Harry had to hurry to keep up, but he'd heard the quiet pops of two shots fired before he'd even got inside.

Fuck.

One man lay dead just inside the door and another near the kitchen. Both wore French military boots, both armed with SIG Pro handguns. Both had headshots, not perfectly neat but effective.

Harry stepped over the second body just as a dark figure came out of the bedroom. Harry saw the pistol first and raised his, only seeing it was Asher a split second before pulling the trigger.

Both he and Asher stood there, guns pointed at each other.

Harry's heart was thundering, his adrenaline pumping. They were seeing each other in the daylight now. Asher was six-foot tall, dark buzzed hair, olive skin, and hazel eyes. He was dressed in black cargo pants, boots, a black shirt under a charcoal grey windbreaker.

He was incredibly good looking, Harry realised, and Asher could have easily been on some Milan runway if he hadn't found himself in the job of killing people. The fact he was pointing a gun at Harry's head didn't help. Harry shouldn't have found that so hot . . .

"Apartment is clear," Asher said, slowly lowering his gun. "Two minutes." He went and closed the front door before he went to the first dead French guy and began patting down his pockets.

Harry didn't wait to see what he was looking for, exactly —cash, ID, more weapons—and he went into his room and pushed his bed to the side. He lifted up the makeshift trapdoor and pulled out the backpack within it. He dashed into the bathroom and emptied the contents of the cabinet into his bag, and as he turned to leave, he heard a noise.

A thud, a stunted groan, and finally another muted ping of a suppressor. Harry pulled out his pistol, his heart thumping painfully, blood rushing in his ears, and he went into the hallway fully expecting to be met with a spray of fists or bullets.

But no, it was Asher, now standing over another body sprawled on the floor. A man in blue, a bullet hole in his left cheek. Asher waved his hand at the bodies. "No, please, take your time," he said sarcastically. "Did you want to freshen up some more? Maybe grab a bite to eat? Let me be a good host and take care of your guests." He gestured to the dead men on the floor.

His guests . . . Harry almost smiled. Until he actually noticed the guy in blue's face. He couldn't have even been twenty years old. "Christ. He's a kid."

"They're all kids," Asher grumbled. "Two French, one

Russian." He took the knife from one guy's thigh holster; it was a Russian army knife. "Fuckers get younger every year."

"Let's go," Harry said. He had no idea where they were going or just how much he should trust Asher.

He needed answers.

He walked out the door and straight into another young guy in blue who let out a startled curse in Russian and swung at Harry's head.

Harry took one hit to the cheekbone, grabbed the guy's arm as he swung through, spun him, took his head in his hands, and snapped his neck. Harry pushed the man's body into his apartment where it splayed on the floor next to the others. Asher gave Harry a curt nod, relieved the man of his knife and pistol, pulled the door closed behind them, and they walked back down the hall.

Harry's ankle protested, though he tried not to let on. "We need a ride," he said.

"I have one," Asher replied.

They went the way they'd come and, thankfully, encountered no surprises. After assessing the street, they walked quickly down the alley to the next block, where Asher pressed a key fob and a new model black Jaguar car unlocked. Asher drove, expertly manoeuvring them through traffic, heading south through the city.

"I hope whatever is in that bag was worth it," Asher said.

Harry unzipped his backpack. "Passports, weapons, about 60K cash in different currencies. And now four hitmen we no longer need to worry about." He pulled out a white pill bottle and threw back two tablets, swallowing them without water. "Where are we going?"

"Gibraltar."

Which meant next stop would be Morocco.

"Who put out the hit?"

Asher shrugged. "I don't know. Your people is my guess."

My people?

"Who tipped you off?" Harry pressed. "Who sent you the

assignment? And why would they send you an assignment when you're the mark?"

Asher gripped the steering wheel and he clearly debated whether or not to answer. Harry wondered whether he'd answer at all, but after a few blocks, he did. "I have . . . someone. An informant."

"Not your handler?"

Asher shook his head. "Sort of. What I showed you is a screenshot. My informant sent it to me and told me to get the fuck out of town."

"So you came to Madrid to warn me?" Harry was having a hard time believing that.

"I was already here."

Wait.

He was already . . .

Harry understood at the same time Asher snorted. "I was already here for you. I've been watching you for three days. Could have killed you a dozen times. You really should be more careful."

"You were here to kill me?" Harry asked. "I was your assignment? Three days ago?"

Asher nodded, almost cheerfully. "Yes."

"So why didn't you do it?"

Asher shot him a wary look and chewed on the inside of his lip for a second before he concentrated on the traffic for a moment. "Because it was you."

Harry stared at Asher, at his gorgeous profile, at the hint of a smile on his lips. "I never realised you were a fan."

Asher laughed, not entirely a happy sound. "Not quite. But I thought about it, what it meant that they wanted you dead. I knew you wouldn't have done anything wrong, which means they're cleaning house, and if they're getting rid of you, then I had to be next." He shrugged again. "Then my informant sent me the picture this morning. I can only guess they sent me to kill you so we'd be in the same place at the same time. Convenient to have us both taken out."

Harry thought about what Asher was saying. It made

sense. Except . . . "You knew I wouldn't have done anything wrong? So you *are* a fan."

Asher rolled his eyes. "We've been doing this a long time, you and me. I've followed your work. Keep-your-enemies-closer kind of deal. And anyway, there's a reason you're the second best."

"The second best?"

Asher looked right at him and laughed, and Harry hated that he found him attractive.

Christ.

"You never received an assignment for me?" Asher pressed.

Harry shook his head. "No."

"Shame," Asher mused. "I'm a little disappointed they never sent you to try and kill me. It would have been fun, no? To finally see which of us would win."

Was he enjoying this? He certainly looked like he was, like this was all a game.

Harry glared at him. He had more confirmed kills than Asher, and they both knew it. Asher was renowned for sniping, clean and efficient, from a distance; no one ever saw him. The man was an enigma. Harry was better on the ground, close combat. Oh, he could do stealth when he had to, but he had no problems backing himself in close quarters. "What's in Morocco?"

Asher shot him a look. His jaw bulged. "It's not Europe."

Both men were quiet for a while. Traffic was light as they left the city. The weather was good. Harry did his best to ignore the pain that was now radiating through his ankle and foot and up his shin.

"How bad is it?" Asher asked.

"How bad is what?"

"You're injured. You took pills before and you have sweat on your brow."

Goddammit.

He couldn't let himself be a liability. If he slowed Asher

down, Asher would simply rid himself of the deadweight. Harry knew this because he'd do the same.

"I'm sure it's just a sprain," Harry admitted. It felt worse than that, but he'd never admit it. Anyway, he'd endured worse.

"When you jumped off the roof," Asher deduced. "That was stupid, by the way."

"It was jump or be shot. I'd take my chances with the jump, thanks."

They were quiet again, the miles flying by.

"So," Harry said eventually. "What's your plan? You didn't just *not* kill me when you had a chance. You saved my ass. And I'm not buying the whole us-against-them bullshit." He waited for Asher to look at him. "What do you need me for?"

THREE

THE PILLS TOOK the edge off the pain in Harry's ankle, but they made him feel a little nauseous. He tried to ignore it. The nausea, the pain, the unusual mix of tension and ease with which he sat next to Asher.

Every fibre of Harry's body was against the idea of trusting him. Not just Asher, but trusting anyone. Especially Asher. But for a reason he couldn't explain, he felt comfortable with him.

Maybe it was because they were so similar.

They had vastly different upbringings, from the little Harry knew of Asher. But now as grown men, as assassins, they were alone, trained to be invisible, trained to kill, trained to never look back.

There was a solidarity in that.

When Harry had asked Asher what he really needed him for, what he'd saved his life for, Asher hadn't answered.

He'd just sat there, as casual as if they were going for a leisurely evening drive. He had one hand on the wheel, the other resting over his crotch, almost between his legs.

Harry hated how hot that was. He hated Asher for being so relaxed, so confident.

Maybe it was easy to be that way when he was the one

with all the information. He was the one with the plan, and Harry was just . . . doing what he was told?

He took a phone out of his backpack, causing Asher to cast him a wild look. "It's not traceable," Harry said. Like he would be that stupid. "This will ping my location as Paris. No matter where I am." He began to type out a message, then thought better of it. It'd be best if they thought he was dead. Although the four dead bodies in his apartment might tell them otherwise. But every hour, every mile they gained was a bonus.

Would they know he and Asher were working together?

All Harry had was questions.

"I need you to tell me what you know," Harry said.

"I know you were Australian Specialist Response Group. Highly trained operatives for the Australian Special Forces," Asher replied. "You were too good at your job and your particular skill set was put to better use. At the age of twenty-five, you were put into the field in Europe as an operative for the Australian government."

Christ.

"Not what you know about me," he shot back. Harry didn't even want to know how Asher had intel on him. "About this. About why you saved my ass and who you think wants us dead. And how you know any-fucking-thing about me."

Asher smiled, and good fucking lord, Harry hated him. "I want to put a gun to your head," Harry mumbled. "So fucking bad."

And what did Asher do? He laughed.

Harry pulled his pistol. "Tell me why I shouldn't put a bullet in you."

Asher didn't even flinch. In fact, his smile became a smirk. Unbothered. Unbelievable. He changed lanes and took the exit ramp. "We need fuel."

The tank was below a quarter. They'd been driving a while, but still. "Jesus. Why didn't you fill it?"

Asher cut him a glare. "Because I was too busy saving

your ass. Now put your gun away or you'll scare the locals. And give me some cash," Asher said as the petrol station came into view. He drove up to a bowser, took the money, and pulled a cap on his head. "And stay in the car."

Harry did a quick recon. It was getting dark now. Traffic was constant with workers heading home. The car at the next bowser was a woman with two kids in the backseat, the van at the end bowser was being refuelled by a man in his sixties, at least.

Harry kept his pistol in his hand down between his knees.

He also checked the glove box and centre console while Asher went inside to pay. He didn't know what he was looking for or expecting to find, but both were empty.

The next vehicle to pull up was a farm truck towing a horse trailer. It blocked half his view of the store, of Asher.

Fuck.

The driver, a man wearing farm clothes, got out and went to the petrol bowser and the passenger, a teen boy, went to check on the horses. Harry could see two horses in the trailer, but not much else.

Fuck, fuck.

Still holding the gun down between his legs, he chambered a round. Watching. Ready. Wondering what the hell was taking Asher so long.

Had he bailed? Was Harry a sitting duck? Was this a set up?

The boy at the trailer came around swinging a . . . window washer. He began cleaning his dad's windshield, and Harry's heart rate took a few beats to calm down.

And then Asher appeared, walking over as casual as anything, with a bag full of snacks.

For fuck's sake.

Asher climbed into the car and dumped the bag of purchases onto Harry's lap. "Are you fucking kidding me?"

Asher started the car and headed back to the highway. "Sandwiches, sports drinks, and water. There will be no dinner service on the boat to Morocco." He rolled his eyes. "You're welcome."

Harry rifled through the bag, pulling out a chocolate bar and a small tin of mints. "And these?"

Asher snatched the mints. "These are mine." He grinned. "And I don't share."

Harry looked in the bag. "There are three more packs of them."

Asher shrugged as he popped a mint into his mouth. "Some people smoke. I eat these. Would you prefer I smoked?"

"No."

"And I got ibuprofen for you. Reduces swelling. You're welcome twice now."

Harry hated that he felt gratitude toward him. "I'll say thank you when you tell me what the fuck we're doing."

Asher laughed and merged into the fast lane. "I'll take the pastrami."

Rage burned in Harry's chest. He wanted to punch that freaking smirk right off Asher's stupidly handsome face. Instead, he unwrapped the sandwich and handed it to him. "Hope you choke on it."

Asher bit into his sandwich and grinned around his first mouthful. "You've been alone too long. Your people skills are terrible."

HARRY HATED that he really needed the sandwich, and the water, and the ibuprofen. He hated that his ankle hurt, that his whole body hurt. He hated that Asher drove for another five hours and barely even blinked when he, the infamous Harry Harrigan, had trouble keeping his eyes open.

He hated that he felt comfortable enough to sleep in Asher's presence. He hated that he felt comfortable around him at all. Did he expect Asher to pull his gun on him at any second? Yes. Did he think he would?

No.

If Asher wanted him dead, he'd have been dead days ago.

Asher needed him for something. He'd tell Harry eventually. He'd have to. Or Harry could beat it out of him.

He wouldn't mind going a few rounds with him.

Gibraltar came soon enough, and Asher drove them down to the fishing docks. The night was dark, the water inky black. "I will do the talking," Asher said. "You try and not look so mean."

"You want me to smile?" Harry gave a fake toothy grin that probably looked worse by the dashboard light.

Asher looked aghast. "Christ, no. Just don't speak. And try not to look so big."

Harry would have rolled his eyes if he didn't spot a man approaching from the dock. "A friend of yours?"

"Not exactly. This is a transaction. He takes us to Morocco, he gets the car." Asher popped the boot of the car and got out. Harry quickly followed and regret flared through his ankle like a knife.

Fuck.

He took his backpack and saw Asher grab a duffle bag from the boot before he closed it. The man approached, a beanie pulled low, his face in shadow. Without a word, he got in the driver's seat and drove the car away, and Asher headed toward the darkened jetty.

Harry fell into step beside him. He was sure his ankle was only sprained. Badly, but not broken.

A face flashed in the dark from the back of one of the old fishing boats. Another man, older with grey hair underneath a beanie, a fishing coat. He unwound the mooring with no more than a nod, and Asher climbed aboard.

Harry followed, down below deck, into a small and dimly lit room that stunk of fish and saltwater. There were two long wooden bench seats. Asher sat on one, Harry on the other.

"How's your ankle?"

"Fine."

"Bullshit."

The engine on the boat rumbled loudly and the boat began to move. The noise, the rocking of the ocean . . . Harry couldn't decide if it was unnerving or comforting.

Asher slid his duffle bag up one end of the seat and lay down, using it as a pillow. He closed his eyes. "We've got two hours. Get some sleep."

Asher clearly had no issue in trusting Harry. Enough to close his eyes and sleep while Harry sat just two feet away. Well, it was either trust or Asher fancied his chances against him.

Harry was too tired to care.

Using his backpack as a pillow, he lay down, slowly lifting his foot up onto the seat. He hissed at the pain, and he knew that boot wasn't coming off for a while. Having it raised was a good relief though.

He'd never minded a little pain. He actually liked a bit of it. It reminded him he was alive. What he hated was being a hinderance. Being a liability. He felt like a wounded animal that needed to recoup in its den until it healed.

There was no safety of a den now. And no time to heal.

He tried not to think about how his handler had made no contact. Did they assume he was dead already? Had they really cut him loose without so much as a fucking word? Had they put a contract out on him? After all he'd done . . .

Knowing no answers would come tonight, Harry closed his eyes.

FOUR

ASHER WATCHED HARRY SLEEP. Much like he'd watched him these last three days. Much like he'd watched him these last eight years. Harry had been on the scene for two years when Asher started, and he'd known of him by reputation before he'd ever laid eyes on him.

He'd never forget when he first saw him. Six-foot-three inches tall, three-feet wide. The man was a mountain. A ruggedly handsome mountain. How he'd remained off-radar was beyond Asher. He wasn't exactly difficult to miss.

He had sandy blond hair cut short and blue eyes sharp enough to cut glass. His nose had been broken at some point. He had a scar above one eyebrow. His whole face had healed nicks and bumps, evidence of a decade of war.

It just made him more attractive.

Asher had considered, very briefly, in fulfilling his contract to kill Harry. Driving to Madrid, he was certain he could do it. Just another job. Safe distance, sight the target, pull the trigger. Easy.

Until he saw him.

What Asher had told Harry was the truth. The fact they wanted Harry dead meant Asher was also on that list. Of that, he had no doubt. Then he got the assignment screenshot. Seeing the French mercenary follow Harry into the street had put Asher into motion without him even realising it. His mission, his entire life, changed in a single heartbeat.

He'd wondered if Harry would try to kill him on sight. Sure, Harry had put his pistol to Asher's temple, but he was never going to pull the trigger. Asher's words had struck a chord. Not to mention the fact he'd saved his ass.

Seeing his eyes flash with recognition, with steel, had been unexpected.

Pressing him against the wall in the dark was another bonus.

Dangerous, exciting. Hot.

He looked like a different man asleep across from him now. Still annoyingly handsome but . . . smaller. Peaceful. That harsh set to his eyes was gone. The permanent scowl was softened.

It was almost a shame to have to wake him.

Except he didn't have to. The man driving the boat made the mistake of opening the door with a thud, and in a split second, Harry was on his feet, pistol drawn, aimed at the intruder. The poor man fell backward in shock and Asher couldn't help himself.

He laughed.

He motioned for Harry to back off, helped the man to his feet. "That's why I didn't want to wake him," Asher said. "He's a little grumpy."

The man backed away, mumbling something about ten minutes to land, and Asher turned back around to see Harry slowly sitting back down with his left foot slightly raised.

"You could have started with *good morning*," Asher said.

Harry shot him a filthy glare. Wow. He didn't even need the gun. He could just kill everyone with that look.

Harry snarled and put the gun beside him on the seat. Asher hadn't even seen the gun while Harry slept or where he'd pulled it from.

"We land in ten minutes." Asher relayed what the man had said. "How's your ankle?"

Harry replied with another glare. "It's fine."

That was a complete lie, but Asher wasn't about to argue. "We'll have to walk a fair way."

Harry levelled a stare at him before he blinked his anger away. "I'll be fine. I won't slow you down."

Asher raised an eyebrow and shrugged as if he didn't care. He hid the truth well. "We land near Ezzahra. From there we will be driven to Tangier."

"What's in Tangier?"

"A place to lie low."

If Harry was surprised, Asher couldn't tell. He tucked the pistol into the waistband of his jeans, took his backpack, and pulled out a chocolate bar. He looked at it, then offered it to Asher.

Asher smiled at him. "You have it. I have these." He took a tin from his pocket and tapped a mint onto his palm before popping it into his mouth. "I'll go up and check on the captain in case you gave him a heart attack. Bathroom, first door on the left."

Harry gave a nod and nothing else.

Asher took his duffle bag and left him to it. The captain of the ship was fine, if not a whole lot warier than he had been, and very happy to see the two stowaways get off his boat. The private jetty was covered by the jet-black night, not even moonlight to guide them.

It took a second for Asher's eyes to adjust to the dark as they made their way to the road. It was a bit of a walk, a rocky incline no less, and Asher wondered about Harry's ankle. He never complained though, never even made a sound. For a big guy, he sure was quiet.

Once on the road, a pair of yellow headlights up ahead flashed in the dark. On and off again. It was an older van, two figures sat in the front. The passenger got out and opened the sliding door and Asher knew, without even turning around, that Harry had his pistol in his hand.

"Calm down," he said quietly over his shoulder. Asher climbed into the van and Harry followed. He kept his backpack between his feet and his pistol, still in his hand, by the side of his leg.

Asher rolled his eyes, but not a word was spoken the entire way. Probably just as well. They drove into the city, past all the fancy hotels and expensive cars, and headed through the narrow streets, some lit, some not. The van pulled into a compound of sorts, the gate closing behind them. Completely enclosed, it was three sides of living quarters with a large courtyard.

"Jesus," Harry mumbled.

The two men got out and the first man opened the van door. He was in his sixties, had short, grey curly hair. He wore a faded black djellaba and a tight smile. "Mr Asher."

Asher gave him a warm grin. "Mr Sadik. Thank you so much for your hospitality. This is Harry."

Harry gave a nod, not any more relaxed.

Asher gave Harry a nudge to get out of the van, which he did, thankfully concealing the gun with his backpack. Mr Sadik watched as Harry unfolded himself from the van and stood to his full height, and Mr Sadik took a small step back.

Harry had that effect on people.

The man who drove the van, a younger man that Asher recognised, had gone to a door and unlocked it. Mr Sadik held his hand out toward it. "This way."

The room they were led to was more of a self-contained apartment, even if it was small. There was a daybed and small table, a television, a pile of square seat cushions in one corner, and a tiny washroom. The walls were whitewashed, the floor was old terracotta tiles, some broken, the curtain hung crooked across the window. Everything was old and there was a faint smell of some kind of spice.

It was perfect.

"It is adequate?" Mr Sadik asked. He stood alone, timid.

Asher went to him and put a reassuring hand on his arm. "Very much. It is good to see you again, Mr Sadik. Please tell me you've been well."

The older man gave a nod, keeping his head bowed. "Very

well, thank you, Mr Asher." He took a step backward. "I will leave you be. My wife, Malha, will bring you breakfast. Sleep well."

He disappeared and pulled the door closed. Harry dropped his backpack in the corner by the cushions, though he kept his pistol in his waistband. He began laying some cushions on the floor as a makeshift bed. "How do you know him? He's scared of you, yet obligated to help."

Asher chuckled. "No, he's afraid of you."

Harry stopped and shot him an annoyed look. "Do you ever answer any questions?"

Asher lay down on the daybed, put his arms behind his head, and sighed. "I saved his life."

That earned him another glance from Harry.

"Four years ago," Asher explained. "He's a pharmacist. He was delivering medicine to a not so nice part of town. There was gunfire, and I pulled him along with me and got him to safety. He'd have been killed for sure."

Harry raised an eyebrow. "Did you start the gunfire?"

Asher chuckled. "Possibly. The target had some body-guards who returned fire."

"You should have shot them first."

"And lost the mark?"

Harry grumbled something. "So you saved him but not before he saw you shoot them all dead. That's why he's scared of you."

Asher rolled on his side, facing Harry. He pulled a pillow under his head. Sleep was starting to chase him now. "Scared, perhaps. Indebted, yes. He promised to help if I ever needed it. This will see his debt repaid."

Harry lowered himself to his makeshift bed, grimacing at his ankle.

"You'll have to take your boot off eventually," Asher said sleepily. His blinks were getting longer. He'd only pretended to sleep on the boat; there was no way he was falling asleep in front of Harry Harrigan, being vulnerable and exposed like that. But now he had no choice. He wanted Harry to fall asleep first, but he didn't like his chances.

"Hm," Harry grumbled.

Asher studied Harry's side profile, watching his chest rise and fall . . . such a broad chest, huge biceps and forearms. He had barely an ounce of fat on him. The man was pure muscle. Honestly, if Harry wanted to kill Asher while he slept, with nothing but his bare hands, he very well could.

And so Asher closed his eyes and let sleep claim him, knowing if death was to meet him, he'd rather not see it coming.

———

DEATH DIDN'T WAKE ASHER. A knock at the door did, followed by a woman's voice. "Breakfast," she said, her Arabic strong.

Harry was already there and he opened the door as Asher sat up. A stern woman thrust a tray at Harry, not even trying to hide her disdain for him. Before he could speak, she was gone, cursing him as she walked away.

Asher couldn't help but laugh at the look on Harry's face. He turned and elbowed the door closed. "You have that effect on everyone," Asher said, still chuckling.

Harry snarled at him and put the tray on the table, limping slightly. Breakfast, as Mahla had declared, was pancakes and honey, eggs, bread with olive oil, and mint tea. It smelled incredible.

It tasted even better.

Asher couldn't help but moan as he ate. "I always loved Morocco."

Harry ate another mouthful of pancakes. "Come here often?"

Asher shrugged. "As good a place as any. What about you? The apartment in Madrid. You have one in Paris also, yes?"

Harry quirked an eyebrow. "You seem to know a lot about me."

Asher sipped his tea to hide his smile. "I was given a brief when I got your contract."

"Oh, right. When you were supposed to kill me. How's that working out for you?"

Asher chuckled. "I can remedy it for you now if you'd like."

Harry gave him a flat stare as a response. He finished his breakfast and sipped his tea, scrunching his nose at it.

"You don't like?"

"It's okay."

"Mint tea is very good for you," Asher said.

"It's not coffee."

Asher snorted. "Your brief never mentioned anything about you being so grouchy."

Harry put his tea down and sighed. "Well, I've been shot at, jumped off a building, been shot at again, had four school-boys come to my apartment to try and kill me, had you being a pain in my ass ever since. It's been a rough twenty-four hours."

"I'm a pain in your ass that saved your ass," Asher replied. "And they weren't schoolboys. Maybe college age."

"Lucky to be eighteen, any of them."

"When did they get so young?"

"When we got old."

Harry's gaze cut to Asher's. "Old? I'm thirty-six. How old are you?"

Asher shrugged. "Thirty-three." *More or less.*

"We're not old."

"That's retirement age in our industry."

"Is that why they're retiring us?"

"Probably." Asher sighed. "Been in the game too long. Know too much, seen too much. We don't move like we used to. We become a liability."

"That's bullshit. Instinct and experience will win over youth and reckless bravado every time."

"You'll get no argument from me."

Harry studied Asher for a long moment. "So in your grand plan that I'm not privy to, or that you refuse to tell me about, how long are we staying here for?"

"Until your ankle heals."

"My ankle's fine."

"Then take your boot off."

Harry scowled at him. "Compression keeps the swelling down."

Asher understood there was no point in arguing with someone so stubborn. "We'll be here for a week," he admitted. "Unless circumstances change."

"A week?"

"A week to keep our heads down."

"Shouldn't we keep moving? Get as far from Madrid as possible?"

Asher made a face, not sure how much to divulge. He knew he'd have to tell him everything at some point. He was actually a bit surprised that Harry was going along with him not knowing anything. But that wouldn't last much longer, and he knew it, so with a sigh, he relented. "I'm waiting for more information. Then I'll know which direction we need to go."

Harry's steely eyes lasered in on him. "Information on what?"

"On who ordered the hit on us."

Harry's brow furrowed, and he blinked. "From who? Who are you getting the intel from?"

"My informant."

"Your informant? Which agency do they work for? Which government?"

"No agency. No government."

"Who pays them?"

"The highest bidder."

Harry blinked, his confusion apparent before something clicked. "Like you."

"Yes, like me. No agency, no country." Asher glared at

him. His past really was no secret. Those who knew, knew. And Harry had to know. They'd circled around each other for almost a decade, and knowing your opponent's past meant knowing their weak spot.

The truth was, there wasn't much to know about Asher's history. There was no weak spot because there was no past. No country, no family, no nationality. No home.

"You said direction," Harry continued. "You said when you hear from your informant, you'll know which direction to go. You want to track someone down?"

"Yes."

"Who? The person who ordered the hit?"

"Not exactly. Not yet, anyway."

"Then what are you tracking down?"

"Information." Asher sighed and ran his hand through his hair. *Fuck it all to hell.* "I need proof."

"Proof of what?"

"Proof that you and I have been set up. For years, every job we took, every assignment, was for the wrong team."

Harry squinted at him. "Wrong team? What team? There are no teams—"

"The bad guys, Harry. We've been helping the bad guys."

FIVE

ASHER KNEW he'd struck a nerve.

Anger darkened Harry's glare. "My government—"

"Lied to you. Not just your government, but many countries. They tell you each assignment is a terrorist or war monger. But no. We've been taking out political chess pieces. Under-the-table deals to line the pockets of politicians and get rid of competition."

Harry recoiled, offended, hurt.

Asher had to strike while the iron was hot. "You wanted to know why they put a hit out on us? To get rid of evidence. They either kill you or they make you the scapegoat. If it goes public, they'll say you went rogue and carried out unsanctioned hits to justify your death."

"No." He shook his head, disbelieving. Asher saw him mentally flicking through memories, trying to piece it together, looking for proof to say otherwise.

"They used you," Asher said quietly. "And me."

Harry's jaw bulged, his nostrils flared. "What proof do you have?"

Asher took out his phone. "To start, this." He showed the screenshot of the assignment with their photos, names, locations. "Who knew you were in Madrid?"

He was about to answer, 'no one,' Asher was sure of it. But after a pause, he blinked. "My handler."

"No one else?"

Harry shook his head. "There isn't anyone else."

"So your handler knew you were there. They sent me to the same location, then put out a job on both of us, hoping to clean us both up in one fell swoop. They sent me there to kill you, and if your handler was the only one who knew where you were, it had to be them."

"Maybe they tailed me. Maybe they tracked me. Hell, maybe they're still tracking me. To here."

"No one followed you," Asher said quietly. "No one followed us here. They knew you were in Madrid because your handler either told them or he put the order out himself, Harry. I'm sorry."

Harry shook his head again. "No."

Asher opened a document on his phone and began to read. "Emir Yilmaz, shot to death in Turkey, four years ago. Waleed Sadeer, shot and killed outside his family home in Beirut, four years ago. Traeger Mayer, found with a bullet hole in his forehead outside his office building in Munich, three years ago. You've been very busy. Paris, also three years ago, Martin—"

"What's your point?" Harry snapped. "Yes, those are my assignments. What of it? Should we start naming yours?"

"Doctor Emir Yilmaz," Asher shot back at him. "One of Turkey's best biotechnicians had just released a study on petroleum engineering which saw the end of a rather large contract with Australia, Japan, and the US."

Harry was stock-still.

"Waleed Sadeer, financial business manager of National Bank of Lebanon, extensive oil finance portfolio."

Harry stared at him.

"German biotech genius, Traeger Mayer, was about to launch a renewable energy solution project—"

"Enough." Harry's voice was detached, quiet, and final. "I

don't ask for personal information on any assignment. I'm not
asking for it now."

"But these are not terrorists or bad people, Harry. They're
not brokering deals with terrorists or any threat to national
security. You can see that, right?" Asher scrolled the page on
his phone. "There's more."

"No. I said enough!" Harry stomped off into the small
bathroom and closed the door a little too hard, and the
shower turned on a few minutes later.

Asher wasn't bothered by the outburst. Or by the size of
him. Asher had met plenty of men as big as Harry. Some were
even almost as capable. And a few of them had even made
Asher wary, but not Harry. He didn't feel threatened at all.

Plus, he could understand why Harry was pissed off. He
had every right to be. He *should* be angry.

His government had lied to him.

Asher was sure of it.

With more time and more information, he would prove it.
He had a plan, and having Harry see the truth and on his side
would be incredibly helpful.

So Asher cleaned up while Harry showered. He stacked
the floor cushions back in the corner before taking the tray of
dirty dishes back to Malha and thanking her again for the
breakfast. She scowled at him, and Asher was certain he
heard a string of mumbled curses as he crossed the courtyard
back to their room.

He smiled in the sunlight, at the incredibly blue sky, and
went back inside. The bathroom door was open, so he
assumed Harry was done. "Moroccan skies are so blue," he
said, and he stopped dead in his tracks.

Harry stood there, wet and naked except for a very small
towel around his waist. It didn't hide much.

Holy Mary mother of God.

He was tanned, mostly. Huge muscular chest, not much
chest hair, defined abs, and he had a tattoo over his heart. A
series of stars in the shape of a . . . "Is that some kind of kite
tattoo?" Asher asked.

Harry, with his permanent scowl, looked down at his chest. "It's not a kite. It's the Southern Cross, the stars on the Australian flag. And I'm not a kite. For fuck's sake."

The Southern Cross made sense.

"You are a kite," Asher said. "Whether you like it or not." And then he noticed the scars shining silverish in the poor light. Some small, some not, mostly faded, some more recent. On his torso, his arms and what Asher could see of his shoulder. They looked like knife wounds, mostly. Scrapes, and maybe a bullet wound or two. "Jesus," Asher breathed. "Do you get paid per scar?"

Harry stood there a long moment, silent. "Are you done checking me out?"

Asher looked him over once more. "No. Damn."

Harry cocked his head. "You like what you see?"

"The fuck is not to like?" Asher waved his hand up and down, from his chiselled jaw to his . . . ankle. It was swollen and purple. *Krista!* He motioned to the daybed. "Sit down. I'll go . . . get something. I dunno what, but something."

Asher wasn't sure how Malha would receive his request for help, but he had little choice. He walked back across the courtyard and knocked on the door. His Arabic was a little rusty and she'd already accommodated them enough . . .

"Harry's ankle is not good," Asher told her. He held out his own foot and gestured it was like a balloon. "Swollen and bruised. Do you have anything? Bandages?"

She glared at him. A small child clutching her leg looked up at him. She ushered the child behind her and closed the door.

Okay then.

Asher went back to their room just in time to see Harry pull up a pair of boxer shorts. He got a very brief, very nice view of his muscular thighs and ass but was remiss that he'd not got a front view.

"Hm," Asher mused. "No scars on your back. Means you always face your enemies. I like that."

Harry grumbled something at him as he lowered his huge

frame onto the daybed. Asher picked up one of the floor cushions and laid it against the armrest and he patted it. "Lean back and put your foot up."

Harry glared at him.

"Quit your whining."

Harry snarled but did as he was told, and Asher knelt by his feet. He pulled his T-shirt over his head and began wrapping Harry's ankle. Harry tried to pull his foot away, startled. "What are you doing?"

"You need to keep this stabilised," Asher said, gently pulling his foot closer. "The sooner you get this right, the sooner we can leave."

"We could leave today if we had to."

"We could." Asher shrugged. "But we're not."

"You could," Harry said. "Leave at any time."

Ah, so that's what he was implying . . . "Yes, I could. I could have shot you three days ago in Madrid before you even knew I was there." He wrapped the shirt as tight as he dared and met Harry's gaze. "But whether you like it or not, we are better off together." He tucked the corner of the shirt into itself, which would, hopefully, keep it tight.

Harry inspected it, seemingly impressed. "I take it Mrs Sadik didn't have a bandage?"

"You know," Asher said cheerfully, "I don't think she likes us."

Harry snorted. "Who wouldn't want two contract killers staying in their home?"

Asher sat back on his haunches and smiled. "Exactly."

Harry's gaze went to Asher's chest, his abs, his thighs. Was he appreciating the view? *Was Harry checking him out?* "Not one scar?"

"My body is a temple."

Harry rolled his eyes. "Your body is a temple from a distance one kilometre away."

Asher laughed. "One point eight kilometres, thank you. Eighteen hundred metres is my best shot."

Harry frowned. "Thought it'd be better than that."

"With a ten-knot side wind, I'll have you know. Eighty percent humidity. You do better."

He smirked. There was no way he could do better than that, and they both knew it. "I prefer my ballistics lessons a little closer contact."

Asher raked his eyes over Harry's body, at the scars. "I can tell." He pointed to one scar in particular, about two faded inches long at the bottom of his ribs. "Knife?"

Harry shrugged, but as Asher moved his hand closer to touch the scar, Harry grabbed his wrist. Asher's gaze cut to Harry's, his heart racing.

Not fear. This wasn't fear.

This was something else.

Tension with sparks of excitement crackled between them. Threat of danger and daring flashed in Harry's eyes, sending jolts of desire through Asher that he was not prepared for.

"No touching," Harry said, his voice low.

Asher hummed in reply. "Threatening bodily violence turns me on."

"I didn't threaten you."

Asher's gaze went to Harry's hand, still gripping his wrist. "I never said you did. I was just letting you know for your future reference."

Harry dropped Asher's wrist and rolled his eyes.

Asher chuckled and was about to try and touch another scar when there was a knock on the door. Quick to his feet, he picked up Harry's backpack and gave it to him before going to answer the door.

"It is Idriss," a familiar voice said. "Uh, Mr Sadik."

Asher opened the door to find Mr Sadik standing there, holding a bag. "Malha told me to come. Said your friend has an ankle injury."

Asher grinned at him. "So she does like me." Mr Sadik was briefly confused until Asher stood aside. "Come in, come in."

He went to Harry, who was now sitting up, and knelt at his feet. He clearly wanted to unwrap the ankle but was too afraid. Asher stepped in and did it for him. "He looks scary, but he's not so bad," Asher said, unwinding the tee shirt none too gently. "Actually between you and me, Mr Sadik, I think he likes a little bit of pain."

Harry growled at Asher. Asher threw the balled-up tee shirt at him and Harry threw it back at his head five times harder. Asher laughed as he caught it and ignored the murderous glare Harry gave him.

Mr Sadik inspected Harry's purple ankle, gently feeling all around it. Harry could move his toes, which was a good sign. "I'm not a doctor," Mr Sadik said apologetically. "But I think it's not broken. Bad sprain, possible ligament damage. Impossible to know without imaging." He looked up at Harry. "You must rest it."

Harry sighed like a petulant child.

Mr Sadik produced two white packets of pills and showed Harry the first one. "For swelling." Then the second one. "For pain. Can make you drowsy. You must eat food with this one."

Harry shook his head. "No sleeping pills. Nothing that impairs my judgement. I have some pain pills." He produced the white bottle from his backpack, and after a quick read, Mr Sadik gave a nod.

He took a proper bandage from his bag and proceeded to bind Harry's ankle. "Keep it up if you can. I will bring you an ice pack and a special boot. Will help heal quicker."

Asher took some of Harry's cash and handed a decent sum to Mr Sadik. "For any supplies and food. And thanks to Mrs Sadik for cooking." Mr Sadik floundered momentarily. It was, after all, ten times more than he'd need. But he took the money, probably so as not to risk offending either man, and left with promises to return later in the day.

When they were alone once more, Asher closed the front door and went back to Harry. He fixed the cushion for him so he could recline a little and keep his foot up. He turned the TV so Harry could see it better and handed him the remote control.

The playfulness between them from earlier was long gone. Harry wore that scowl again, a dark expression on his face. Was he pissed about his ankle? Was he pissed that Asher had helped him? Or was he remembering the bomb Asher had dropped on him earlier regarding his own government lying to him?

"I'm going to have a shower," Asher said. He got to the door and stopped. He was going to say something compassionate or even meaningful to try and lift the dark cloud that now hung over Harry. But instead, like he always did, Asher went for humour.

"Uh, I don't expect to be long, so if you're gonna jerk off while I'm in the shower, at least let me watch."

Harry looked around for something to throw at him, and only finding a wad of money, he threw it at Asher. It was a left-handed backward throw, an awkward object with absurd trajectory versus gravity ratios, and it still managed to strike Asher in the chest.

He was a really good shot.

"Is throwing money at me while you perform sexual acts a tradition in your country? Which one of us does this make a prostitute?"

Harry pulled out his pistol and engaged the chamber. Asher burst out laughing as he ducked for the bathroom and locked the door behind him. "Just as fucking well," Harry yelled.

Asher smiled as he showered. The hot water and soap were a luxury he'd never take for granted. He hadn't expected to like Harry. All of his intel on the man had said he was stoic and cold. And he was grumpy and irritable. That much was true. But there was a decent man under the prickly armour. There was an incredible body too.

Asher tried really hard not to think about that while he showered. And afterward, Harry didn't speak much. He barely uttered a word for the rest of the day, lost in his thoughts. Asher would catch him with a deepened scowl or a blank, far-off look, and he knew it was best to leave the man alone.

He didn't joke; he didn't make any snarky or snide comments. Asher assumed Harry was trying to put together the jigsaw pieces of information he'd given him about his government, about the political games, so he left him alone. And later that night, when the room was dark and silent, Asher's assumptions were proved correct when Harry spoke.

"Tell me everything you know."

AUSTRALIAN SPECIALIST OPERATIONS COMMAND - SYDNEY, AUSTRALIA

Director Clive Parrish looked out his office window, lost in his thoughts, in the knowledge of what he was about to do.

The intercom on his desk buzzed, his receptionist spoke. "Gibson and Hull to see you, sir."

"Send them in."

Parrish ran a very cut and dry operation. Cut and dry, yes. But not black and white. It was a world of murky grey. A dark world of secrets and covert operations seldom few had the stomach for.

Gibson and Hull entered the room and stood opposite Parrish's desk. They were good soldiers. Tough, dedicated, and never questioned their duty. Even in civilian clothes, they stood with their feet apart, hands clasped behind their backs.

Gibson was a hard-ass. A mean bastard if Parrish was being honest. It's what made him good at his job. His short brown hair was greying a little now. His ten years in this division had hardened his blue eyes.

Hull was a yes-man. More brawn than brain, he and Gibson had been partners a long time and they made a formidable team. It was why Parrish had asked to see them.

He gave both of them a nod. "You know Harry Harrigan. I

know you trained together, served together. He was your CO. A good soldier."

Both Hull and Gibson nodded. "I know him," Gibson answered. He never agreed with Parrish's statement, and Parrish didn't care either way.

He didn't need to say that this would be personal. "We've lost contact with him and he's now acting on his own."

Hull gave a solemn nod. Gibson's gaze hardened. "Sir."

They understood. Parrish knew they would. "Last confirmed sighting was Madrid. His phone pinged in Paris, so start there. I want your feet on the ground. See what you can find out . . . Or take him down."

"Yes, sir."

"You should know," Parrish added, almost as an afterthought. "Independent contractor Asher Garin was assigned to neutralise him and hasn't reported in. He's probably dead. If he's not and you run into him when you're tracking Harrigan, take him down too."

SIX

HARRY DIDN'T SPEAK MUCH for the next four days. He had a lot to process, a lot to digest and internalise, analyse. And because he didn't fucking want to.

Asher spoke enough for the both of them anyway.

Although Harry had to give him credit. He seemed to know when Harry needed some space and time, and he gave it. Not that their small room afforded much space. He couldn't say the same about time.

So much time.

So much time for ignoring Asher. For ignoring the looks, the curl in his belly, the way his heart thumped a little too hard when Asher's eyes met his, when their fingers brushed. The way Asher looked after him, all still while maintaining all the space he could.

Maybe what Asher had said on day one was true: he had been alone too long.

Harry kept his foot up like a good boy, and he could tell his ankle was feeling better. Mr Sadik had delivered a boot to stabilise his whole foot, and Mrs Sadik had kindly kept them fed.

She'd even stopped cursing them.

Which probably had more to do with Asher trying to

charm her with his ridiculous smile and good looks than anything Harry had done.

Maybe she appreciated not seeing Harry much at all.

But by the end of day four, Harry had had enough of sitting still, of staying put. He felt safer on the move.

Especially if what Asher had said about his government was true.

Harry didn't want to believe it. He didn't want to believe the lies or that he was used as a pawn in personal political games that served no purpose to his country. He didn't *want* to believe any of it.

Yet he had a bitter, sinking feeling that it might be true.

Asher had joined some dots, yes. Convincing, too. But Harry wanted actual proof. He wanted to see his handler, look them right in the eye and see the truth for himself, face to face.

He didn't like his chances of that happening, but it was the only way he'd know for sure.

Asher had spent most of the last few days glued to his phone. Waiting on more information from his informant but also keeping an eye on any news out of Madrid.

The police had found the four bodies, which wasn't surprising. A quadruple homicide was always going to cause a stir, but what was remarkable was that as soon as it was discovered the deceased were French and Russian, and most likely military, the story disappeared.

Funny that.

But Harry had done as much sitting still as he was able. He put his booted foot on the floor and stood up slowly.

"Where are you going?" Asher asked, barely looking up from his screen.

"I'm taking a piss. Is that okay?"

Asher chuckled. "Need me to come hold it?"

"Shut the fuck up."

Asher's smile widened, as if being cussed at was his favourite hobby.

Harry made it to the bathroom, his ankle feeling a lot

better. When he was done, he went to the front door and opened it.

"Where are you going?" Asher asked, looking up from his screen now.

Harry pointed to the small yard in the compound. "To walk some laps and get some air. Some sunshine. I can't sit in this room any longer, listening to you mumble to yourself for hours as you look up god knows what."

"I don't mumble to myself."

"No, you have full conversations with yourself."

"It's the most intelligent conversation I can have in this room, present company included."

"Fuck you."

Asher sighed. "You keep promising but you never deliver."

Harry grumbled and walked out into the sun, opting to walk a few laps to get some kind of exercise. Even if it was wonky on his stabilising boot, even with the twinge in his ankle.

It had to be better than dealing with Asher and his sexual innuendos. Or maybe it was Asher's way of flirting? Harry wasn't sure. He hadn't done anything of the sort for so long, he couldn't even remember the last time.

He really had been alone for far too long.

Which was how he preferred it, if he was being honest. Alone, no one to annoy him, no one that never stopped talking. No one else to think about, worry about, and no one that made him irrationally angry, no one that he wanted to shoot several times a day.

The door to their room opened. Asher stood in the shadow and waved him in. Harry was just about to cuss him out some more—he'd only got in ten laps so far—but Asher's expression told him something was up.

His brow was furrowed, his eyes studying the screen he was holding, and there was no smile.

Harry had gotten used to the stupid smile.

He walked back inside and closed the door behind him. "What's up?"

"There's a woman we need to see in Algeria," Asher said, his tone flat and urgent. "We should leave tonight."

"Tonight?"

"Yes. We'll wait until after midnight and head southeast. Cross the border before morning."

"Who is the woman, where is she at, and why do we need to see her?"

"She has some information we need. She's in Algiers."

"See her? Or kill her?"

"Depends on her answers."

Harry nodded. "Fair enough."

"She's an academic. I don't expect her to be problematic. I can explain more on the drive there. How's your ankle?"

"It feels fine. I've told—"

"We'll need to do some walking. You up for that?"

Asher was all serious now, and if Harry had wondered how this smiling, sunshiny kind of guy had earned himself the reputation of being cold and calculating, he saw glimpses of *that* Asher here now. "Sure. You don't need to worry about me."

"I'm not worried about you. I'm worried about you slowing me down."

Harry bristled. "I won't slow you down."

"Good." Then Asher studied the screen for a few long seconds before turning it around to show Harry. "We've also got two visitors. I think they're friends of yours."

Harry leaned in to see the image. It was grainy and by no means a great photo. Then a second photo, same two guys, different location. "Shit." He didn't want to believe it . . . If those two were on the ground looking for him, all arrows pointed to the likelihood that the order came from Harry's boss.

Asher sighed, his full lips pressed into an unimpressed line. "You know them?"

"Hm." Harry scowled. "When was that photo taken?"

"Yesterday in Paris. Today in Madrid." Asher turned the screen back around and read directly from it. "Arrived in Paris from Sydney, Australia, the day before. Very interested in your apartments, apparently. I'm at a loss, actually, as to why you would ever keep permanent apartments. In Paris and Madrid."

"They're not permanent. I take a short-term lease in a dingy shithole that doesn't ask a lot of questions. Under a fake name, fake ID, fake history, fake papers."

Asher tapped the screen. "Not too fake though, huh?"

"They can't have known those names were me."

"Who are they?"

"Paul Gibson and Simon Hull. Last I heard, they were SRG . . . but that was years ago. Specialist Response Group, an Australian Defence Force special forces unit tasked with responding to counterterrorism. It's part of my old unit."

"You worked with them?"

Harry gave a nod. "We trained together, did ops together back home, and in Venezuela and Uruguay."

"Before you were kited."

God, Harry hated that term. "Yes. I don't know what division they are now; I haven't seen them in ten years. Who knows? Maybe they're private contractors now. A lot of high-ranking military go into private security, contract out for a few years and earn a fuckton of money."

"We need to find out who hired them."

"The assignment for both our necks went to all agencies, yeah?" Could Harry cling to the hope that it wasn't a home-ordered hit? That Gibson and Hull were hired by someone, anyone, else?

Asher conceded a nod. "True."

"So it could be anyone."

"Yes. But you said no one could know the apartments in Paris and Madrid were yours because you gave fake names. Did your handler know about them? Your address? Your aliases?"

Harry shook his head. "I don't think so."

"Yes or no?"

"I never told them!" Harry barked. "All fake passports and documents I've procured on my own over the years. They don't know any of that shit."

"So they're tracking you," Asher shot back. Not giving Harry the time to reply, he continued. "If we can confirm whose orders they follow, we'll know if your government ordered you dead."

Harry wanted to punch or kick the living shit out of something, preferably Asher, but he settled for a sigh. "Why are we going to Algeria?"

"Answers. My informant has a name and address."

"For what? Answers to what?"

"The contract you took six months ago. In Ghardaïa."

Harry raised his chin but said nothing.

How the hell did Asher know every single thing about him?

Asher met his gaze. "And who ordered the hit. And why someone would want a university professor of nuclear energy dead."

A university professor?

Harry's stomach soured. "Fucking hell."

Asher clapped his arm and walked over to his duffle bag. "We need to pack up and leave, tonight."

"Why the rush? I thought you wanted to stay put for a week. It's been four days. If our plans change, you need to tell me why."

"Because your two Australian ex-army friends were last seen heading south of Madrid, toward Gibraltar."

What the fuck?

"Why didn't you start with that?"

Asher zipped up his duffle bag and grinned at him. "Because it turns me on when you get mad."

Harry stared at him. He took the longest, calming inhale he could manage and exhaled just as slow. "You must be really turned-on," he mumbled. "Because I'm really fucking mad."

ALGERIA

The pain in Harry's ankle was a constant thrum. Both sharp and dull, with every step. When Asher had said there'd be walking, he wasn't wrong. It didn't help that the ground was rocky, sandy, and uneven.

They'd paid Mr Sadik handsomely for the old van, and after midnight, they'd driven east to the small town of Ahfir, made a very stoic exchange with two men, and were driven through mountain desert farmland through a checkpoint and were dropped off in the middle of freaking nowhere. Asher got out, Harry followed. Asher gave the men a nod, and without a word they turned around and drove away.

Not one word had been spoken throughout the whole ordeal.

"What the hell just happened?" Harry asked.

"We just entered Algeria without paperwork."

"Do I want to know how you organised this?"

Asher gave half a shrug. "My informant is well connected."

Harry shook his head and took in their surroundings, lit up by the almost-full moon and cloudless sky, thankfully. There were mountains to their north, open desert to the south, and not a road or a landmark in sight. Harry was never fond of the desert at night. Too many shadows for his liking. And the landscape played tricks on the mind, as did the wind, and it was far colder than it should be.

He fixed his coat and then his backpack. "What now?"

"Now we walk."

And so they walked; east for about five kilometres until, as the sun began to rise, they came to a quarry of some kind. The setting made Harry nervous, like they were walking into an ambush, but Asher seemed very familiar and his ease was a little reassuring.

In the quarry, they found a small and battered truck.

Harry took out his pistol, senses on high alert, but Asher just smiled and opened the driver's door. "Put your gun away and get in."

"It would probably help if you told me the details of the actual fucking plan," Harry grumbled.

On the seat was a large envelope, which a smiling Asher handed to Harry before he started the truck. The engine rumbled to life, loud in the still of the early morning, and Asher began to drive.

Harry peered into the envelope and couldn't believe what he saw.

Passports.

He pulled them out. Two for Asher; one Algerian, one Saudi.

And one for Harry. It was Australian; his photo with some random name and dates.

"How did you . . . ?" Then, answering his own question, he asked, "Just how well-connected is your informant?"

Asher grinned. "Very."

"So this is how you skip countries all over Europe and the Middle East?" Harry deduced. "You have some guy at an agency. Someone on the take."

Asher's expression became cold, his jaw clenched, and his eyes lasered into Harry. "Speak of him again that way and I will shoot you."

Oooh. A raw nerve.

And he dropped a pronoun. Speak of *him* again. Harry considered this. "So, is he a boyfriend? A lover?"

Before Harry could blink, Asher had his pistol pressed against Harry's temple, his other hand still on the steering wheel, smooth as silk.

Harry smiled at him, even chuckled a little and looked around the barrel of the gun. "Is that a no? Or a yes?"

Asher gnashed his teeth but pulled his gun away, and it was an interesting reaction, Harry noted. Normally cool and even aloof, this reaction from Asher was extremely emotive.

It told Harry a lot.

"Anyway," Harry said, playing it off. "I'm thankful to your informant. The passport looks good, even though I don't want to know how he got that photograph of me."

Asher glared at him.

"And you seem to know where you're going here," Harry added, gesturing to their surroundings. The small dirt road linked up with another dirt road, then a sealed road, and before long they were on the A1 headed to Algiers. The old truck rumbled and bounced along the highway.

"Do you think perhaps next time you could ask your friend for an upgrade in vehicle?"

"Do you think perhaps you could be grateful instead of an ass?" Asher retorted. "I liked you better when you didn't speak."

Harry smiled.

"And when you didn't smile."

THE DRIVE to Algiers took almost seven hours, given the speed of the truck wasn't exactly great. Asher had been quiet for about the first three hours and Harry had enjoyed the silence.

The rumble and the jostle of the truck became soothing, almost, and although his ankle didn't appreciate the vibrations, it sure beat walking.

They'd had to stop for fuel, and this time Harry bought them breakfast pastries and coffee, and Asher's mood seemed to lighten after he'd eaten. Because for the second half of the trip, he talked, and talked.

And talked.

Pretty much non-fucking-stop about Algerian history, trade and industry.

Clearly Asher was well educated in such subjects, but after three hours, Harry wondered if his ears might actually start to bleed.

"I always liked Algiers," Asher volunteered as they

finally came into the city. "The weather is great. The people, the food. So much history. Some very beautiful architecture."

"I've only been here twice, and never stayed long," Harry admitted, welcoming the change of topic. "Certainly not long enough to appreciate the architecture."

Asher glanced his way, smiled, and shook his head. "You've been to how many countries in the world?"

Harry tried to think . . . "Too many to count. Probably easier to list the ones I haven't been to."

"And you never appreciate the cultures?"

Harry looked at him as if he'd lost his mind. "Ah, no. I have assignments. I get in, make the target, and get out."

Asher sighed. "Which was your favourite? You had to like one more than the others."

Harry squinted at him. "The reason I like some cities over others, or whatever, is because of the anonymity. The ease with which I can hide, escape, go undetected, blend in. I don't look at the architecture."

Asher snorted. "In what city do you blend in? Please name one. You're six-foot three-inches tall, three feet wide, and angry."

"I'm not angry."

"You glare and scowl. Your size is intimidating enough without the death-stare."

"I don't have a death-stare."

Asher laughed now. "The way you look at me right now. The only reason I don't crap myself is because I'm not scared of you."

"You're not scared of me?"

He laughed and shook his head. "Not even close."

Harry sighed and decided to take in the passing scenery instead. On many trips to many cities in different countries, he'd kept his head down, only taking note of exit routes, landmarks, police presence.

But Algiers was a pretty city, he had to admit, as they headed toward the bay where there were palm trees and immaculate whitewashed buildings. "Hmm," Harry grumbled. "I just appreciated the architecture. Are you happy?"

Asher laughed. "Don't get any ideas. We're not staying in any of these."

Harry figured as much, but as Asher turned off and weaved through the back roads, Harry realised where Asher was taking him. "'Rock the Casbah,' huh?"

Asher shot him a confused look. "What?"

"Never mind."

The Casbah region of Algiers was iconic, yes. Bustling with tourists and locals, crammed, ancient buildings with narrow, winding and steep streets. Having never been there, Harry knew it by reputation alone, and the song, of course.

Asher pulled the old truck into a tight parking spot and killed the engine.

"Now what?" Harry asked.

"Now we wait."

"For what?"

"A guide."

Christ.

"How?" Harry asked. "How did you organise this?"

Asher gave him a sidelong glance.

"Oh right. Your informant."

"Don't speak of him."

Harry inhaled deeply and sighed on the exhale. "I'm very curious about you and him."

Harry was expecting another angry outburst, possibly another gun pointed at his head, but instead Asher raised an eyebrow. "Are you jealous?"

"Jealous? Of what?"

"You *are* jealous."

"I absolutely am fucking not."

"You wanted to know if we were lovers before." Asher hummed, though it sounded more like a purr. "Would you really like to know just how well we know each other? What he would do to me?"

"What I would really like to know is what your brains look like splattered on the window behind you."

Asher laughed. "You're so easy, Harry. So quick to anger. I'd have thought you had the patience of a saint, but you have such a little, teeny, tiny"—he held his fingers close together—"fuse."

Harry wanted to grab Asher by the throat and pummel his fucking head in, but that voice in the back of his mind, that voice of reason, his intuition that had kept him alive so far, knew what Asher had said was right.

Why does he affect me like this? Where is the patience and indifference I've prided myself on?

What is it about Asher Garin that rankles me so much?

"You are insufferable," Harry mumbled with a sneer. "And infuriating. You know you're annoying, right? You never shut up. Did your *boyfriend* ever tell you that?"

"You are equally insufferable," Asher replied. "If you ever run out of bullets, you could just growl at your next target. Maybe rip his arms off with all that pent up anger and beat him to death with the soggy ends. Or better yet, spend five days with them like I've had to, and they'll surrender."

"Well, just so you know, if sniping someone from a mile away is no longer an option for you, you could just kidnap them, give them a gun, and talk to them non-fucking-stop and they'd shoot themselves."

A knock on the window scared the shit out of both of them.

Harry pulled his gun and aimed it at the intrusion, but Asher deflected it, pushing the gun away. The intruder was a man wearing a traditional djellaba and a no-nonsense glare. He didn't even blink at Harry's gun.

"You want room or not?" the man said.

Asher turned on his high-wattage smile and charmed the man in both Arabic and English as they collected their bags from the truck and began walking. And he *was* charming, and the smile could soften even the hardest of souls . . .

Maybe even Harry's.

The man, who did not give a name, guided them through the spiderweb of narrow corridors and up the many, many steps. If it wasn't steps, it was cobbled stones. The walls got narrower the higher they climbed. Buildings jutted out overhead, powerlines, extension cords clung to exposed beams, and men herded donkeys along the pathways to collect rubbish. The streets so narrow, Harry could touch opposite side walls with either hand, and the buildings were in disrepair. Old, decrepit, peeled paint, crumbling walls, patched with whatever materials they could find. There was graffiti, tin bolted to walls instead of windows.

Yet it was strangely beautiful.

There were ornate doors in ancient and arched doorways, heavy wood with iron patterns whose age Harry would hate to estimate. The tile work was incredible. The steps and pathways were worn by thousands of feet over hundreds of years, carried along the air of danger, spices, and sweat.

And Harry caught himself . . . He was admiring the architecture.

Jesus H Christ.

He chastised himself, grumbling as he followed the two men ahead of him.

Asher glanced over his shoulder. "Ankle okay?"

"M'ankle's fine," he snapped.

His ankle was not fine, but he wasn't admitting that to Asher.

Harry hated that his ankle was sprained. He hated that Asher had hid them away in Tangiers to give him time to heal. He hated that Asher got them through three different countries without a lick of trouble, got new passports, transport, accommodation.

He hated that Asher was good at this.

That people warmed to him, fell for his charm and his disarming good looks. He hated that strangers liked him.

He hated that *he* liked him.

The man stopped at a blue door along one particularly narrow street. Well, it had once been blue. It was now peeled and rusted, but it had a decent lock. The man held out a key and Asher gave him the truck key in return, and without even a glance in Harry's direction, the man walked back the way they'd come.

Asher unlocked the door, but Harry stopped him from opening it. With a glance up and down the empty street, he took his pistol in hand and pushed the heavy door open and stepped inside.

It was dark, though his eyes quickly adjusted. The first room was small, the second room was clear too. No one was lying in wait for them, Harry determined easily, because there was nothing to hide behind.

The first room had a table and two chairs and an old sink basin in the corner. The second room had one single bed in it.

He turned around to find Asher standing inside, smiling.

"I'll take the floor," Harry grumbled.

Asher snorted but didn't say anything. Instead, he carried the chair into the bedroom, stood on it, and lifted the utility panel in the ceiling. "Give me your bag, and pass me mine."

Harry picked up the duffle bag, surprised at the weight of it. "Christ. What have you got in this?"

Asher lifted himself into the ceiling cavity, a space Harry could never squeeze through. Then he poked his head back down so he could see Harry. "I carry my friends with me. Barret and MacMillan."

Harry sighed and handed the bags up to him. A second later, two feet appeared, then two legs. "Catch me."

"I'm not going to fucking catch you."

"If I sprain my ankle, we'll both be useless."

"I'm not useless," Harry grumbled.

"So help me get down."

Harry knew damn well that Asher could manage just fine. But, resisting the urge to sigh again or to fucking scream, Harry moved the chair and grabbed Asher's legs. Asher lowered himself through the manhole just enough to put his crotch right at Harry's face height.

Deliberately.

On purpose.

Asher refixed the panel in the ceiling into place, then pretended to slip, gripping Harry's shoulders. Harry caught him, his arms around Asher's ass. He looked down at Harry and grinned. "You're so strong," he said.

Harry dumped him onto the bed, upending him with as much care as he'd treat a bag of rocks, and walked into the other room.

It had been far too long since he'd touched a man in a way that wasn't violent, and this was too much of a mindfuck right now.

"Being rough is my favourite kind of foreplay," Asher called out with a laugh. He appeared with that stupid fucking grin.

Harry glared at him. "Is everything a joke to you?"

"Not everything. I take food very seriously." He clapped Harry's shoulder. "Let's go get some lunch."

SEVEN

"I'M NOT GOING BACK DOWN ALL those steps," Harry grumbled. He was too tired for this bullshit.

"I thought you said your ankle was fine."

"It is." It kinda wasn't. "But I'd like to keep it that way."

Asher's eyes glittered with humour. "This way then," he said, going up to the end of the lane and turning left into what was kind of a tunnel. And it opened out onto a street. Like an actual street, with traffic.

Harry stopped. "Do you mean we could have driven up here instead of walking?"

Asher laughed again. "Of course."

"Then why the fuck didn't we?"

But then it dawned on Harry why Asher had done that.

It was to keep an advantage over him. Push the pain limit on his ankle to keep Harry the weaker of the two. "I should just fucking shoot you right now."

Of course Asher laughed at that. "It wasn't all about you. Where we left the truck was the drop off point. It was just unfortunate the room is in the high end of the Casbah, but that room was chosen for good reason. No windows, no elevated post positions close by for a sniper to perch on." He gestured to the cluster of run-down and neglected buildings behind them. "And no one would think to look for us here.

And it was all arranged without us having to do a damn thing."

Harry hated that he made sense.

An old taxi came over the hill and Asher flagged him down. He opened the back door for Harry and waited. "Get in. I'm hungry, and you know what happens when I'm hungry?"

"You get more annoying."

Asher's smile turned into a sneer. "I should have shot you in Madrid. Get in the fucking car."

Harry returned the favour by grinning right at him as he slid into the backseat. Asher slammed the door closed and climbed into the front passenger seat and had a lovely conversation with the driver as he drove down the hill.

Harry's Arabic wasn't great, but Asher seemed to be able to switch between languages like he was just swapping accents and not whole complex dialects.

Harry made out the words market, *mahjouba*, and *makrout*. Food, Harry deduced, and the driver laughed at something Asher had said.

He could charm the leg off a chair.

He really was insufferable.

Asher paid the fare, adding some extra for the recommendations, and when the taxi drove away, Asher pointed to one of the narrow walkways into the lower Casbah. "This way for the best mahjouba in the city."

Harry wasn't even sure what mahjouba was, but it wasn't long before his nose and stomach found the source. Asher ordered, Harry gave him the cash, and with a bag full of food and some drinks, Asher nodded to the town square that buffered the Casbah from the road and marina.

They found a bench seat amidst the crowd and sat to eat. Harry was on his third pancake, Asher on his second, when Harry decided he needed some answers.

"How many times have you been here, to Algiers?"

Asher kept his gaze out toward the sea. "Many times."

Harry had assumed as much. "You seem at home here."

Asher was quiet for a long second and still wouldn't look at Harry. "I have no home."

"Do you have an apartment anywhere? A house?"

"No."

"So everything you own is in your duffle bag," Harry noted.

"Everything." He looked at Harry then, his eyes hard. "Makes it easier to walk away, yes?"

Harry conceded half a shrug. "I guess."

"Your apartments held no personal effects," Asher said. "You rent them furnished, I assume, so what difference does it make?"

Now it was Harry who looked out to sea. Asher's words stung, but the truth always did. "No difference."

Asher finished his pastry and took some kind of cookie out of the bag. He handed it to Harry. "It's makrout. Try it."

He took one out for himself and bit into it, groaning as he did. It was obscene, and Harry almost forgot he was holding anything. He also had to tell himself to close his mouth.

Asher laughed. "Eat it, or I will."

Harry bit into it, and yeah, it was as good as the groan warranted. Harry couldn't remember the last time he'd eaten something purely for the enjoyment of it.

And yet, there was Asher sampling every country's culture that he visited. In between sniping people, that was. Harry was having a little trouble reconciling the two personas: touristy Asher, the guy who loved the food and the people, and the Asher who could pop a target from a mile away with a twenty-knot side wind.

Harry thought of himself as more of a 'what you see is what you get' kind of guy. Sure, he could kill people too, but he looked like he killed people.

Asher looked like a guy on vacation.

"How many languages do you speak?" Harry asked when he'd finished his lunch. He sipped his bottle of water and waited for Asher to answer.

"Fluently? Eight. Understand enough to get by? Maybe another five."

"Jesus. Did they feed you dictionaries as a kid?"

Asher cracked a smile, though it wasn't particularly a happy one. "Language was something I picked up so easily. Some tiny child can sit at a piano and play Mozart. I could do that with languages."

"A prodigy."

Asher made a thoughtful face. "Maybe that's why they didn't kill me, huh?"

Harry's eyes cut to his. This was his first personal insight into the real Asher Garin.

No one knew anything about Asher Garin.

No past, no history, no country.

Only rumours.

"You grow up in an orphanage?" Harry asked, maybe a little too bluntly. Asher shot him a scathing look, and that killer-Asher that Harry had trouble placing just a few minutes ago was right there. Harry tried for nonchalance. "I think I heard that you did."

Asher said nothing.

"You know everything there is to know about me, apparently," Harry added. He didn't mean to sound like a dick.

Asher's smile was cold. "Let's just say I had a very different childhood to yours."

"Do you know what kind of childhood I had? Was that in your file about me?"

"I know enough."

Harry sighed, past the point of caring. "I'm tired. We should go." It felt like they'd left Mr Sadik's home and crossed the border a week ago. They'd been awake going on thirty-six hours. They needed to sleep.

Asher pointed to the public restrooms. "I might suggest using a bathroom. In case you didn't realise, our room only has a basin."

Thankfully Asher had hailed a cab for the trip back up to their room. Harry hadn't even brought it up, but Asher had grumbled something about them needing to walk tomorrow when they met with this woman, their contact.

Their room was just as they'd left it, and Asher was quick to retrieve their bags from the hole in the ceiling. There were no jokes or innuendos now. Asher's smile was gone. Obviously the memories about his childhood hadn't been particularly pleasant, but none of their lives had been pleasant. Death and fucking misery lurked in every corner, in every memory.

The room felt too small. Not just with them both in it, but also with what was left unsaid. Tension and frustration took up most of the space between them. Two loners, with a penchant for killing people, forced to be together in a tiny apartment was asking for trouble. Especially when they were both exhausted.

Harry washed up the best he could in the small basin, scrubbing his face and brushing his teeth, to feel half human, at least. He pulled the small table in front of the door before he laid his tired and sore body down on the hard floor, pulled his backpack under his head, and closed his eyes.

"You can share the bed," Asher said.

Harry was almost too tired to answer. "You take it tonight. I'll take it tomorrow night. Or I'll take the floor again. I don't care. And if someone tries to come through the front door, I can just shoot them from here."

There was silence for a long moment, and before Harry drifted off, he remembered to ask, "What time are we meeting this woman?"

"Midday."

GIBSON KEPT his face to the wind as the ferry cut across the strait. The sea air was cool despite the sun. He pressed the phone to his ear, waiting for Parrish to answer. He picked up on the fifth ring. "Yes."

"We're crossing to Morocco. The black Jaguar spotted

leaving Madrid is now in the possession of a fisherman, who was kind enough to identify Harrigan in a photo. He made a special trip to Tangiers five nights ago, two men. Harrigan was one of them."

"And the other?"

"Can't say for certain but I'd bet money he's travelling with Garin."

Parrish made a growl of disgust. "Fuck."

Gibson gave him a few long seconds to regroup and reconsider their plans, waited for him to elaborate further instructions. None were forthcoming. "Boss?"

"I'll be in touch."

"We'll start in Tangiers," Gibson added, though Parrish's only response was a dial tone.

EIGHT

ASHER WOKE WITH A START, his heart racing. He sat
up, the taste of blood in his mouth. Had he bitten his tongue?

It's just a memory. Just a memory.

"You good?"

Harry's voice made Asher jump and reach for a weapon
that he didn't have. His heart was now in his throat. Asher
glared at Harry, who was sitting at the table, until his heart
rate calmed down.

"Bad dream?"

Asher didn't answer. He checked his watch. It was nine
o'clock. God, had he really slept that long? All while Harry
sat, very much awake, just metres away. Asher was lucky to
have woken up at all. Harry could have killed him, taken his
belongings, and been hours-gone.

Yet, there he sat.

"I'm hungry," Harry said.

Asher scrubbed his hand over his face and nodded. Thirty
minutes later they were eating *baghrir* with figs, cherries and
peaches, washing it all down with Turkish coffee.

Asher felt more human with every bite, though he was
amazed by just how much food Harry could eat. He could
easily put away twice what Asher ate, which shouldn't have
been surprising given he was twice his size.

He pushed his half-eaten plate toward Harry, a silent offer. He preferred the coffee anyway. Harry pinged his phone again, this time to look like it was located just outside of Paris. Asher wasn't sure what good it would do, if any at all. Would it confuse those tracking them? Would they find nothing in Morocco and go back to Europe?

Asher wasn't hopeful.

The small café they were in was old and dingy, tucked away in a narrow lane of the lower Casbah. There were three young men standing outside, and Asher noticed one of them trying to scope them out.

He sighed, not even bothering to put his coffee cup down. "We have some friends. Three, male, just kids, really."

Harry froze, his back to the door.

"Relax," Asher whispered calmly. "They're street thugs; possibly eighteen years old. After some quick cash, maybe a watch or a phone. They must think we're tourists."

Harry wiped his mouth with a napkin, swung his legs around on the small stool, and slowly stood to his full height.

One of the guys saw Harry get up, his eyes comically taking in the size of him, his expression making the other two turn around. The three of them gawped. Harry took one step in their direction and they scrambled to run off.

Asher laughed and sipped his coffee.

Harry grumbled. "Fucking punks."

Asher threw some money on the table. "Let's go."

They walked back toward the square through an open market, and passing a clothing stall, Asher decided new shirts were in order. "We should try and look half-decent today," he said, taking a white button-down shirt off a rack. He held it up against himself, and it would fit just fine.

Finding one for Harry, on the other hand . . .

The salesman came over, smiling. Asher greeted him in Arabic, asking for a shirt that might fit his friend. The salesman looked at Harry and grimaced, but he went to one rack in particular and pulled out a pull-on linen shirt, pale blue, with a round collar.

Asher held the shirt against Harry's broad chest. It should fit.

Harry smiled and mumbled, his lips barely moving. "What the hell is this?"

Asher grinned. "It's perfect. Now pay the good man."

Harry's nostrils flared, and Asher was certain he'd have thundered some obscenity if it wasn't for the older gent waiting expectantly for his money. But money paid, they made their way back to the room.

They needed to freshen up the best they could and get changed for their meeting. They couldn't very well turn up looking like they'd been on the run for five days.

Harry re-strapped his ankle on the bed while Asher pulled his shirt off and washed in the basin the best he could. He even shaved.

Had Harry been watching him? Asher felt eyes on him, but when he turned, Harry looked away.

Asher turned facing him as he buttoned up his new shirt, giving him all the view he wanted, while he gave Harry some room at the sink.

He too pulled his shirt off and bent over the basin to scrub his face, and Asher leaned against the table to enjoy the view. Harry had barely an ounce of body fat, his wide shoulders and muscular back tapered down to his waist. His lats and serratus anterior muscles defined and so damned sexy, Asher wanted to reach out and touch them.

He didn't.

He'd thought the other day that Harry didn't have any scars on his back, but there was one. A very faint line ran along the back of a rib, only visible under certain light and given Asher was barely two feet away and studying every inch of skin.

Harry was every bit his type.

And he didn't mind playing flirty games with Harry. He was easy to rankle, and it excited Asher to have Harry glare at him the way he did. He could just imagine Harry stalking toward him, furious and demanding . . .

Asher had to wonder just how far he had to push Harry to make that happen. He was thinking it wasn't far at all.

Then Harry turned around and Asher admired the front of him. Ripped in all the right places, decorated in scars and ink, and his huge arms that Asher could just imagine holding him down.

Damn.

He drew his gaze up to Harry's face to find him glaring at him. "Are you fucking done?" Harry asked.

Asher shook his head. "To, čo by som ti dovolila, aby si mi urobil."

Harry fumed. "I don't even know what fucking language that was, let alone what you said."

Asher grinned. "Want me to translate?"

"No."

"I can."

"I want you to shut the fuck up."

Asher looked directly at Harry's crotch, at the very proportionate bulge there. *Damn.* It made him ache for it. "Have anything to shut me up with?"

Now, Asher expected some angry retort, maybe the threat of violence, but when he finally drew his gaze up to Harry's, he saw something else there.

Well, there was anger, yes. But there was also something dark.

It was want.

Well now, that was interesting.

"Hand me the stupid fucking shirt."

Asher held it, and when Harry took it, Asher didn't let go. He was leaning back, just a little, his legs spread, so if Harry wanted to stand between them, he could.

Harry growled. His nostrils flared. "Don't try me, Asher."

Asher let go of the shirt with a smirk. "If we had more time, I absolutely would try you. Thank you for the invitation."

"It was not an invitation."

"Pretty sure it was."

Harry closed his eyes and sighed. Asher was almost certain he was counting to ten . . . or praying for patience. Mumbling something Asher couldn't hear, Harry pulled the shirt over his head, and fed his arms through the sleeves.

It was a tight fit.

It was a glorious fit.

"It's too small," Harry complained, pulling the hem down.

"Oh no, it's perfect." Asher fixed the rounded band collar, pulled at the fabric a little at the shoulder, and smiled up at him. "The colour matches your eyes."

He lasered his eyes into Asher, a hard, fierce glare, and Asher didn't know whether to take a step back or a step closer.

They were already close enough . . .

"We need to leave," Harry murmured. He sprayed on some deodorant, then knocked back two pain pills.

"I thought you said your ankle was fine."

"It is. I took those so I can put up with you."

Asher laughed. "Perfect."

They packed their bags back into the ceiling, locked up the room, and after a quick walk to the street, hailed a cab. Harry climbed into the back, Asher took the front, and he smiled at the driver.

"Algiers University, please."

———

THE SECOND ASHER laid eyes on Professor Kadira Amara, he knew she was an astute woman. She dressed sharp, she was incredibly smart, no nonsense. "Thank you for meeting with us," Asher said in Arabic. "We do appreciate your time."

She let them into her office: a small room with a large desk and more books than seemed possible. Professor Amara gestured to the two seats across from hers, and she sat with a sigh. She took one look at Harry, then spoke to Asher. "Arabic or English?"

"English, for my colleague, would be greatly appreciated."

Harry gave her an awkward smile. "My apologies. My Arabic is rusty."

Her gaze narrowed at him. "Your accent?"

Shit.

"Australian," Harry answered.

She turned her attention to Asher. "Which agency did you say you were with?"

"No agency."

She raised her eyebrow. "Newspaper?"

Asher put his hand up, palm forward. "No, no. We're conducting a private investigation into the death of Ikram Taleb."

"He was a professor," she said quietly. "Professor Ikram Taleb."

"His work here," Asher began. "What did he specialise in?"

"Nuclear fusion and engineering physics."

"What is that, exactly?"

She made a face. "The process of turning physics into engineering is complicated to summarise. Basically alternative energy resources to hydrocarbon fundamentals."

Asher nodded. "Did he teach or do research?"

"Research, mostly. He had many ongoing studies."

"In which areas?"

"The economics of energy production, radiological engineering. But hydrocarbon economy was his main focus."

"A subject list any government might show interest in," Asher hinted.

She rolled her eyes. "Most governments care only for money."

"Was Professor Taleb working on anything that may have been a conflict of interest or controversial? Anything that may have upset the wrong people?"

"Not that I know of."

"Had he been acting suspiciously at all, as though someone might have been threatening him?"

Professor Amara stared at Asher. "Not that I'm aware. Do you think that's why he was killed? The police said it was a misfire. Accidental."

"Professor," Harry said. "I can tell you it was no accident. He was killed via a targeted contract from a foreign government."

Jesus fucking Christ, Harry.

She sat back in her seat, pale. "Oh, I, uh . . ."

"Do you have access to his email?" Asher asked.

She shook her head. "No."

"Do you know what he was doing in Ghardaïa?" Harry pressed.

Professor Amara blinked, shaking her head as if to clear it. "Uh, he, um, he has family there. A home, a wife and three children."

Asher could feel Harry shrink back at that news. That a man he killed had a family.

Asher inhaled deeply and gave the professor a nod. "Thank you for your time. You've been most helpful. We'll leave you now. I understand you're incredibly busy."

Before Asher could stand, she asked, "Who killed him?"

Christ.

Asher was quick to answer before Harry could. "It's not the person who pulled the trigger we're after. It's whomever ordered the shot."

So she rephrased her question. "Which government had him killed?"

"Mine," Harry replied. "We're trying to find out why. And who his contact was."

Asher made a mental note to never bring Harry along to any kind of questioning ever again.

She cocked her head, confused. "Yours? What for? We don't export gas to Australia. The pipelines run to Spain and Portugal, Italy, Sardinia, and Slovenia." Then realisation crossed her features. Her eyes went to Asher's. "Those pipelines that supply Europe run from the Hassi R'Mel gas fields."

"Hassi R'Mel," Harry said, looking at Asher. "Just miles from Ghardaïa."

Professor Amara gave a grim nod. "And oil fields to the east. It may be prudent to check which companies export oil to your country," she said to Harry. "What they would want Professor Taleb dead for, I cannot begin to imagine. But the answers you seek may be there."

"Thank you, professor," Asher said with a nod. This time he stood. "We've taken enough of your time."

She stood also, though made no offer to walk them out, and Asher didn't blame her. They made their way out of the main building, down the steps, and quickly crossed the street, walking at pace.

"That has to be a connection, right?" Harry asked. "That he lived a few miles outside of Algeria's biggest gas and oil fields."

"Hm," Asher agreed. His phone vibrated in his pocket at that moment and he pulled it out, reading the message on the screen.

He stopped walking.

Harry pulled him into the shadows of an alley. "What is it?"

Asher looked up at Harry. "The fisherman who took us from Gibraltar to Tangiers was found dead. They have the car, footage from a highway camera, and you and I are wanted for his murder by the police in Gibraltar."

Harry stared at him, disbelieving. Because Asher knew that Harry knew that meant one thing: murderers crossing international borders—and not just any murderers, but one Australian government mercenary and one nomadic assassin —now put them on a different kind of radar.

"Interpol?"

Asher nodded. "At the request of the Royal Gibraltar Police."

"Fuck."

WAITING until it was dark to leave made sense. *There is very little option*, Asher told himself. He was quite content to sit on the bed patiently and wait.

Harry, on the other hand, paced like a caged tiger.

"Sit down," Asher said. "You're only hurting your ankle more with all that stomping and turning."

"I'm not stomping," Harry said. "And my ankle's fine."

Asher sighed. Whatever. "Being on Interpol's radar makes no difference."

"Except now we have to avoid the police everywhere we go."

"Did we not avoid them before?"

Harry growled at him. "They weren't actively looking for us before. This is just one more fucking hassle."

Asher kept his voice calm. "I sent everything we found out at our meeting to my informant."

Harry stopped pacing to stare at him. "Do we even keep chasing that information? Now that we're on Interpol's shitlist, hasn't the game changed?"

"The game hasn't changed at all. We keep focused. We head to Ghardaïa and hopefully—"

"The only thing we'll find in Ghardaïa is a dead man's wife and three kids and the pool of dried blood outside their family home."

Asher stood up from the bed so he could look Harry in the eye. "You did nothing wrong."

Harry snorted out a laugh. "I shot him in the head."

"You carried out an order from your government. You're a soldier they placed on the other side of the planet to use like a remote-control gun. A kite whose strings would be cut as soon as you became an inconvenience. Gone with the wind and no ties to your country."

Harry's jaw clenched, his eyes turned to blue steel. "Stop calling me that word."

Asher raised his chin. Now was probably not the time to goad Harry, to push that limit he'd wondered about earlier.

But Asher had never done things the easy way, and they did have hours to kill . . .

"What word is that?" Asher whispered. "Kite?"

Harry seethed. "Don't."

"What will you do to me if I say it again?"

"Asher," he growled.

"Mm, I like how you say my name like that, like it starts at about here," Asher murmured, putting his hand to Harry's sternum.

Harry batted his hand away. He inched closer, taller. "Shut the fuck up."

"If you want to put something in my mouth to keep me quiet," Asher said teasingly. He licked his lips and drew his eyes down to Harry's crotch and back up again. "Or you could bend me over the table."

Harry closed his eyes and let out a measured breath through his nose. He said nothing.

"How long has it been for you?" Asher asked, keeping his tone light. Harry was close to snapping. He could feel it. "I'm gonna guess it's been a while."

Harry opened his eyes, his gaze fierce and dark. "You gotta death wish?"

Asher smiled. *So close.* "Depends on exactly how you plan on sending me. On my knees? Or bent over the table? I like it rough, just so you know."

Harry took a step back and raised both hands. "You need. To stop. Fucking talking."

One step more . . .

"How about you make me?" He slowly ran his hand down his stomach to his crotch and gave himself a squeeze. "God, all this foreplay turns me on so much."

Harry fumed. His hands were fists at his sides. "Asher."

Asher smirked, his tongue at the corner of his mouth, and ever so slowly, he dropped to his knees. He looked up at Harry licking his lips properly and opened his mouth. "Wanna shut me up, Harry?"

With a snarl, Harry took one large step toward him. Asher

thought for a brief second Harry was going to follow through with a knee to Asher's face, but no. He yanked down the fly of his pants, pulled his cock out with one hand, fisted Asher's hair in his other, and fed his cock into Asher's mouth.

It happened so quickly, Asher didn't even have time to inspect and admire Harry's dick before it was rammed down his throat. He gagged at first, but Harry never stopped. He face fucked him, tightly gripping his hair and driving him home.

Harry was big. Asher had to open wide for him. He relaxed his throat and took him in as far as he could manage.

HARRY DIDN'T MEAN to hurt Asher. He didn't mean to just fuck his mouth without consideration or comfort.

The way Asher had prodded and prodded him, to get the reaction he'd wanted. The way he'd gone to his knees and licked his lips.

Harry was thrusting into Asher's mouth before he'd even realised what he was doing.

My God. The way he'd closed his eyes and hummed, taking Harry into his throat. Warm, wet. Sucking him, tonguing him.

He loosened his grip on Asher's head, guiding instead, but Asher had groaned in disappointment.

Christ. *He said he liked it rough.*

Harry wasn't going to last long anyway. It was too good, too hot, too tight, and it had been far too long . . .

He feels so good. So damn good.

Harry looked down at him. The sight almost brought him undone. Asher on his knees, his eyes glazed with bliss through dark eyelashes, his pink lips around Harry's cock. *Fuck.* "You want it?"

Asher smiled around the shaft, sliding his lips down to the base. Harry was in his throat . . . then Asher's hands snaked around the back of Harry's thighs and pulled him in closer.

And Harry surged, pleasure exploding in his core. He gripped Asher's head in both hands, thrusting in, and came down his throat. He fed him every drop, pulsing again and again, and Asher fucking hummed as he took it.

The room spun, Harry's bones went to jelly, and Asher released him. "Fucking hell," he mumbled.

Asher stood up, pulled a chair over and sat Harry in it. He went willingly, his vision swam, his head pounded. Asher gently tapped his face. "You okay?"

God, he hadn't felt that good in years. "Mm, yeah."

"Good," Asher said. He swung a leg over Harry's lap, aligning his crotch with Harry's face, and he unzipped his pants and pulled out his erection. He pulled back his foreskin, swiped his precome with his thumb, and gripped Harry's chin so he could swipe his thumb across Harry's bottom lip. "Open wide."

Harry wasn't used to being told what to do. Not in life, certainly not when it came to sex. But when Harry didn't open wide, Asher slipped his thumb into Harry's mouth and pulled his jaw down. Then he cupped his cheek, none too gently, and tapped his cockhead on Harry's tongue before thrusting in.

Harry hadn't given head in a long time. A *really* long time. He thought he might have forgotten how . . . but he closed his lips around Asher's shaft, and instinct and memory took over.

The heat, the hardness, the tang; he'd missed this.

Asher pushed his hips forward, standing right up to Harry now, his thighs against his shoulders and his hand on the back of Harry's head. "Fuck, yeah," Asher groaned. He flexed his hips, not even thrusting. Just in all the way and trying to go deeper still.

So Harry gripped his ass and squeezed, his fingers right up near his asshole, rubbing and teasing through his jeans. Asher trembled, swelling in Harry's mouth, and with a stilted cry, he shot his load down Harry's throat.

Asher's hands held Harry's head, rubbing gently at his

scalp, his neck and shoulders. Caressing and intimate, something Harry wasn't really familiar with. Then, before he pulled out, he ran his hand up, cupping Harry's throat, and he looked down.

"Now, that's fucking beautiful," he said, his voice low and gravelly.

He pulled out slowly, enjoying the view, but he didn't step back too far. He kept Harry's chin raised and he wiped his lips with his thumb, groaning as he did. His eyes were heavy lidded, glazed over. "You feel better now?" he asked, his voice sexy as fuck. "Not so stressed?"

Harry really wasn't in the mood for Asher to be a prick about what they'd done. After all, he was still standing, straddling Harry, with his dick hanging half-hard out of his pants. He made no attempt to tuck himself away.

Asher smirked. "Just so you know, next time you tell me to shut the fuck up, you best be prepared to shove your cock in my mouth. Got it?"

"I don't take orders from you."

Asher just laughed and ran his hand over his own chest and stomach, finally down to his dick. "That was so hot, I could almost go again."

Harry's dick twitched at that thought and he had to fix his fly.

Of course, Asher chuckled, low and throaty. "Now I'm sleepy. Considering we'll be on the move tonight, we should get some rest." Asher swung his leg over and walked to the bed and threw himself onto it. "I'm only offering once," he said, patting the mattress beside him. "Or you can sleep on the floor."

Harry looked at the floor, knowing all too well how uncomfortable it was and how little he'd slept the night before. But the idea of sharing a bed with Asher? It was absurd.

Even after what they'd just done.

He'd had Asher fucking Garin's dick in his mouth. He'd just had his dick in Asher's mouth. Harry realised in that moment they hadn't just exchanged body fluids, but a whole amount of trust too.

A few hours' sleep on a bed sounded pretty damn good.

Harry stood up and fixed his pants, then walked to the bed. "Doesn't mean anything."

Asher snorted. "Of course not."

Harry sat on the bed first, and Asher tried to scoot over to the wall as far as he could, but when Harry lay down, there really wasn't enough room for two. Asher had his back to the wall and his face resting on Harry's shoulder.

"You take up the entire bed," Asher mumbled, already half asleep.

Harry lay there, staring at the ceiling, wondering how on earth he got to be sharing a bed with Asher. With anyone would have been insane enough, but Asher Garin?

Did he still think Asher might kill him in his sleep?

Well, it was still a possibility.

But did he think he actually would?

No. He didn't.

Had what they'd just done compromised their objectives in anyway?

Harry didn't know for sure. His head was telling him not to be stupid, but his heart was . . . well, his heart was now beginning to make decisions, and that scared the shit outta him.

He risked a look at Asher, his face pressed against Harry's shoulder. His olive skin, his dark lashes, his pink lips . . . God, Asher's mouth was nothing but trouble. Beautiful, talented trouble.

As he watched Asher sleep, Harry could feel something under his ribs, something he'd never felt before. A need, an ember to begin with but beginning to burn a little warmer.

The need to protect him.

Which was ridiculous, given their professions and the life Harry lived. Never saw the same person twice, no friends, no dating, no family.

And now this guy, who had intended to kill him, who infuriated him like no one else ever had, was under his skin.

Like a fucking tick.

Harry rolled over onto his side, pissed at himself for allowing this to happen. Only the dip in the bed made Asher roll inward and burrow against his back.

Goddammit.

But then Asher slid an arm around Harry's waist, and it felt so good. So amazing, like everything he'd been missing in his life.

And it also felt a little bit wrong.

Grumbling to himself, a string of curses because, goddammit all to fucking hell, Harry wiggled and turned himself over so he now faced Asher. Stirring from sleep, Asher pulled back, alarmed. "What the . . . ?"

It was a good opportunity for Harry to lay his arm out, then he pulled Asher against him so Asher could use his arm as a pillow. "There's more room this way," Harry grumbled.

Asher sleepily chuckled into Harry's chest.

"Shut the fuck up."

NINE

HARRY SLEPT SOUNDLY for about two hours. He woke up with a start, disturbed by just how deeply he'd slept.

He'd not heard a thing.

Harry had slept with one eye open for a decade. But not now. Not with a warm body pressed against him, snuggled into him. Harry's arms had been wrapped around Asher. His sleeping-body had betrayed his mind.

And Asher hadn't moved. Not a muscle. Unless wriggling closer counted.

Harry had slept as though he'd been drugged. Albeit only for two hours, but still . . . someone could have picked the lock and crept into their room and shot them both, and he'd have not heard a thing.

At least you would have shielded Asher . . .

Christ.

That was the type of complication he didn't need.

He looked so peaceful asleep in Harry's arms. He fit so perfectly. God, it had been so long since Harry had had any kind of intimacy with a man.

It felt so unbelievably good. And so much more right with Asher than it should have been.

He peeled his arm out from under Asher and sat on the

edge of the bed. He scrubbed his hand over his face, trying to get his head in the game.

"What time is it?" Asher's voice croaked.

"Almost four. We've got three hours until it starts getting dark. Maybe we should look at some maps and begin working out a plan."

"I can think of something I'd much rather be doing for three hours." Asher stretched and ran his hand down to his dick. "Want me to roll onto my stomach, pull my jeans down?"

Harry stood up and stepped into the next room. He put his hands on the edge of the sink and said nothing.

Asher seemed far too pleased with this. "I've seen how big your cock is. Don't think I'll stop until you give it to me properly."

Harry hung his head. His patience—and self-control—were getting mighty thin. He ran the water and splashed his face.

"I can be persistent."

Harry peeled his too-tight linen shirt off and wiped his face with it. He wasn't fond of it anyway.

Asher moaned. "Are you teasing me? Look at your fucking body."

"You're not persistent. You're a pain in my ass." Harry threw his shirt at Asher's face. "And I'm not teasing you."

Asher laughed with a sigh. "You know, I thought if we took the edge off, if I had a taste of you, I wouldn't want you anymore. But now I just want more."

"Asher, we need to focus. We need a plan. Several plans, contingencies, back-ups, rendezvous points if we get separated, that kind of shit."

Asher sat up on the bed. "Rendezvous? So if we got split up, you'd miss me?"

Harry sighed. "Shut. The fuck. Up."

Asher got up off the bed, fluidly, smoothly. Like his bones didn't hurt like Harry's did. Like he wasn't feeling every ounce of tired. He washed his face too and dried it with the linen shirt. "I have a plan," he said casually.

"You do?"

"Of course I do. And you don't?"

"Well, yeah. For starters, we go to Ghardaïa, speak to the wife."

"Widow."

Harry stopped, sighed, and kept talking. "Speak to the widow. There's an airport not far from there. It's what the oil and gas bosses use, the tycoons and shit. We can fly out of there for the right price."

Asher smiled up at him. "You're not just a pretty face."

"What's your plan?"

"What you said."

"That's my plan, not yours."

"Mine is the same."

"It was not."

"Was too. Except mine was better."

Harry sighed. "You know what? I don't care. Your plan is great. Let's go with that."

Asher grinned. "Really? So do you want me bent over the table or on the bed?"

"That's not . . . That wasn't the plan."

"It was my *first* plan. Remember?"

Harry inhaled slow and deep, trying for patience, when a quick rap on the door shot them both into action.

Asher ripped open his duffle bag, took out a pistol, and threw it to Harry. It was a 9mm SR-2 Udav. "Where the fuck did you get this?" Harry hissed at him.

"Off the Russian who tried to kill you."

Then, out of the duffle bag, Asher lifted out a freaking rifle . . . no, a semi-automatic . . . no . . . Harry squinted at him. "What the fuck is that?"

"It's a Covert," he whispered, walking toward the door. Then he spoke in Arabic. "Who is it?"

The man replied something that Harry didn't quite catch

—he spoke in a rushed whisper—then Asher replied something else.

"Open the door," Asher murmured, then held his fingers about an inch apart. He stood behind the door, back a little, so he could see through the crack.

Harry opened the door a little but there was no way he was standing in front of it. He stood next to Asher, his boot jamming the door from opening any further. He pointed the pistol, ready to take the head off anything that tried to come through.

"It's the man who showed us to the room," Asher murmured. "He's alone. Let him in."

Harry let the door creak open, and Asher, holding his rifle down by his thigh, stepped around him to greet the man. "Come in."

Harry stood there with his pistol, ready.

The older man stepped in warily, doing a double take when he saw Harry. Then another when he noticed they were both armed. He put his palms up instinctively to show he meant no harm.

"What news do you bring?" Asher asked, this time in English. Harry assumed for his benefit.

"Three officers come," he said. "From special police. GIN officers. Asking about two foreigners."

Asher glanced at Harry. "GIN is combat police. Like SWAT."

Harry had gathered that much.

The man reached into his pocket and Harry regripped his pistol. The man noticed, of course, and shied away a little. He very carefully lifted a key from his pocket and handed it to Asher. "Five streets across, two up. Blue car. You need to leave. Now."

Asher stared at him. "Who sent you?"

"The same man who had me meet you, show you this room." He shrugged. "No name. Never a name. Just the number four."

Asher smiled and took the key.

The number four . . .

Who the hell was the number four?

"Thank you," Asher said in English, then again in Arabic. "We didn't mean to cause trouble. We'll leave tonight."

"No, now. He said you leave *now*." The man looked at his watch. "Prayer in five minutes. You leave then."

Asher's eyes flickered to Harry's before he turned back to the kind man and gave a nod. "Understood. Thank you."

The man backed out of the small room, sparing Harry only a brief glance before he was gone.

And Asher was already repacking his duffle bag. "We leave now."

Harry frowned. "So this . . . four person says we leave, and we just do whatever he says?"

Asher slid a pistol into the back of his jeans. "Yes. Exactly like that."

"Who is Four?"

Asher pulled up the zip on his duffle. "Pack your shit, Harry. Or I leave without you. When he says I move, I fucking move. It's how I stay alive. Now move."

Harry tucked Asher's pistol into his waistband and pulled his coat on to conceal it. He grabbed his backpack, slung it over his shoulder, and met Asher's hard glare with his own. It took all of three seconds. "Done."

Asher kept an eye on his watch and, when it was time, put one hand on the door. "Don't shoot unless we're shot at first."

"Do you think I'm an idiot?"

Asher raised one eyebrow.

The fuck?

Harry would have been pissed if that hadn't stung. And why did it sting? What the fuck was that emotion?

It's called indignation and pride, Harry. Because you care what he thinks about you.

Before Harry could reply, to Asher or to himself, Asher huffed and shook his head. "No. I don't. I think you're an idiot for turning me down, for not fucking me like I wanted. For that, you're an idiot. But not anything else."

If only Asher knew how thin Harry's self-control was.

Asher made a thoughtful face. "Actually, the dick sucking was pretty good."

Harry tapped his watch. "Shut the fuck up and get out the door."

Five streets over, two streets up was the instructions given, and in this rabbit warren of winding, narrow alleys it was so easy to get turned around and lost. Harry was beginning to think they'd taken a wrong turn, wondering how long it should take, wondering if they were running into a trap.

Wondering if this would be his last day.

Wondering if being on the run with Asher was how he wanted it all to end.

It really pissed Harry off that he enjoyed Asher's company. As much as he annoyed him, as much as Asher infuriated him, Harry absolutely hated that he liked him.

The sound of laughter somewhere close by startled Harry. The silence of afternoon prayer was over, and it was perfect timing too. They came to a street that cars could actually drive on, not just cobblestone walkways, and in the lines of cars parked along one side, sure enough, there was a blue sedan.

Asher pressed the key fob, the car beeped and unlocked. Asher put his bag in the backseat, Harry kept his by his feet in the passenger side, and in no time at all they were driving.

Could it have been that easy?

It wouldn't have been if Asher's informant hadn't sent the man with the keys to a car.

"I have a lot of questions," Harry said.

Asher patted down his pockets as he drove. "Like how I could be out of mints? We're going to have to stop."

"We're not going to stop for fucking mints."

"They keep me calm," Asher said.

"How do you not have diabetes? Or rotten teeth?"

"What is it that you say to me all the time?" Asher pretended to have to think about it. "Oh, that's right. Shut the fuck up."

Harry ignored that. "First question. Who is Four?"

"My informant."

"What is the number? Is it like some lame James Bond shit? 007? Or is it some identifier he was given instead of a name in some brutal cyborg factory?"

Asher shot him a wild glance. "You are never choosing which movies we watch. Those are terrible guesses."

"Watch your speed."

"Do not tell me how to drive."

"So are the mints a replacement for cigarettes? Because you're a little grumpy."

Asher's grip on the steering wheel tightened. "I never smoked." Then he nodded pointedly at Harry's pocket. "Can you please look on a map and tell me where I'm supposed to be going?"

Harry took out his phone. "You need to get on the N1. Follow the signs to the N1."

Traffic was beginning to bank up but still moved, thankfully. Just then, a swarm of police cars went screaming past, sirens wailing. Harry held his breath, Asher kept his eyes on the road until they'd gone past, and then he watched them in the rear-vision mirror. Harry turned to see, and thankfully, they kept going.

"Do you think they're looking for us?" Harry asked. Those cops were racing toward the Casbah, after all.

"Hard to tell." Asher put the radio on. It was in Arabic, naturally, so not understanding much, Harry kind of tuned it out.

He was just happy to keep putting miles between them. They made it to the N1 and, in a consistent line of traffic, made their way south and out of the city. The traffic thinned, the city became green farmland, and they weren't being followed. For a good long while, Harry watched the scenery pass by, beautiful green mountains in the fading daylight . . . Until he realised he was admiring the fucking scenery like he'd admired the architecture . . .

Christ.

That was Asher's fault. One hundred percent. Harry shot him a scathing look when he realised Asher had been quiet for a long time.

Harry assumed Asher was listening to the radio, just thankful that it kept him quiet. But maybe it was something else. It was the longest Asher had gone without speaking . . .

Was something wrong?

"You okay?" Harry asked.

Asher nodded.

"Well, that's not convincing."

He was quiet for a few more miles. "I need to speak to my informant."

"So call him."

He shook his head.

Harry clucked his tongue. "Oh, not in front of me. I see how it is."

"It's not my rule. It's his."

"Number Four."

Asher almost smiled. "Yes."

"How does he know everything?" Harry asked. "He's one step ahead. You said he's well connected, but he has no country. So who does he work for?"

"Himself."

"So he's like some secret independent agency that knows everyone's business, has eyes everywhere, contacts everywhere. Got us across every border so far, had vehicles when we needed. People on the ground to give us a room, a car. To warn us."

Asher considered this. "Yes. That's correct."

"Why didn't he call you to warn us? Why send the man to the door?"

"For the key to this car. If we'd have stolen something, we risk alerting the police and having them be on the lookout for the vehicle."

"Do you think those cops we passed were looking for us? Is that why your friend told us to leave straight away."

Asher gave Harry a look that said yes, that was exactly what he thought.

"So he has contacts in local police everywhere? Or just Algiers?"

"Not *contacts*," Asher said. "This isn't the '90s."

Harry glared at him. "So he has access to information," Harry deduced. "Christ. He's a hacker."

Asher laughed. "Something like that."

Harry kept staring at him until he explained more. No more information was forthcoming.

"Then why can't he just hack into Interpol and delete our files?"

Asher snorted. "Oh, Harry. You're cute."

"Don't be an ass. You make it sound like he's some almighty tech guru that can do shit like that. And he does have contacts, like the old guy with the room for us, and the guys who took us across the border. The fisherman."

Asher sighed. "Okay, some contacts."

"Like it's the '90s."

Asher shook his head and laughed. "You're insufferable."

They were quiet for a few more miles.

"So . . ." Harry tried to sound casual. "How long have you known him?"

Asher flinched a little. "A long time."

"How did you meet him?"

"Why are you so curious about him?"

"Because we're taking orders from him, and I want to know something about the man who seems to know a lot about me."

"He's saved our asses enough times this week to earn a little trust, yes?"

Asher was so defensive of him, and it just made Harry's curiosity worse. "So, is he—"

"Oh my God, you are jealous! I was only joking when I said it before, but it's true. You *are* jealous."

"I am not."

"Clearly you are."

"I'm curious," Harry bit out. "I've not worked with anyone for ten years. This is all very new to me. Being with you . . . Christ, I've not spent this much time with the same person since . . . well, a long time."

"Since when?" Asher asked, his gaze going from the road to Harry's. "Was there a special someone you spent time with?"

Harry rolled his eyes. "How could I have ever had anyone in my life like that?" Then he thought about Asher asking . . . "Wait? Did you?"

Asher laughed. "Not exactly a life for a boyfriend, no?"

Boyfriend.

The word rattled around in Harry's brain.

"Was there someone in your army days?" Asher asked.

"No. I was never in any place long enough."

"So. Men or women? Both?"

Harry considered telling him to fuck off, but in the end, he settled on a sigh and the truth. "Men."

His smile plucked at Harry's heart. "Isn't that a coincidence?" Asher said. "I happen to be a man who also is attracted to men. And here we are. Just us two."

God, they were back at this again. Asher was persistent, Harry had to admit.

"Yes, what a coincidence."

"In all the intel I had on you," Asher said, "nothing was ever mentioned about you being gay."

"You certainly won't find anything in my military record," Harry said flatly. "Or on any surveillance . . . Wait, so not even your special friend Four had that info?"

Asher shook his head. "No. I must tell him he was missing some very key details. He's getting complacent. Or you've just not had any kind of sex in a really, really long time."

There was no way Harry was admitting the latter was probably closer to the truth.

"I'm very disappointed about there being no surveillance," Asher said, almost wistfully. "Imagine that footage. With full audio."

"How much longer do I need to suffer being in this car with you?" Harry asked. "Is there a petrol station or a motel? A bridge, perhaps, that I could throw myself off."

Asher laughed. "We'll need fuel, but we should stop the night in some backwater motel. You'll have to throw yourself off a bridge some other day."

Harry sighed, disappointed, which, of course, made Asher grin at him.

———

WHEN THEY STOPPED FOR FUEL, Asher walked off with his phone to call Four—whoever the hell *he* was—and Harry filled up the car. He watched as others came and went, the customers, the vehicles.

He also noted the closest buildings, estimated distances, the angles for best long shots, the exits.

The pistol tucked into the back of his jeans was a comforting weight.

It was colder here than Harry had realised. The last time he was here, it had been hot. Now, the desert winter evening air had some bite.

Harry could see Asher, no more than a shadow in shadows, and Harry had no doubt that Asher was watching him too. Sure, he trusted Asher. Somewhat.

But not *that* much.

He went inside to pay and to see what they had in the way of food. It was a small station off the highway—the kind less likely to have recording cameras—so he didn't have high hopes, but he found some seasoned chickpeas, which he liked, and those soy crisps Asher had eaten in Tangiers. There were some questionable fruit packs that he left alone, but the flatbreads looked good and the tubs of hummus seemed to be homemade so he took two. He grabbed some bottles of water and made his way to the counter.

And there, at the checkout, were packs of those damn mints Asher liked.

Harry grumbled, and lord, how he hated himself, but he grabbed three . . . no, four packs and added them to his purchases. Now he was buying things for Asher? The crisps he liked and those damn mints that were going to rot his teeth . . .

Before the clerk had put the sale through, Harry swapped the mints out for the sugar-free ones. Asher was going to be pissed.

Harry hated himself a little less.

Asher was in the passenger seat when Harry walked back out, and Harry tossed the bag at him a bit too cheerfully. He started the car and drove back toward the highway. "I bought you a surprise."

"You did?" Asher's expression was so genuinely happy, for one split second Harry regretted not buying him the real thing. He rifled through the bag and was like an excited child pulling out the mints . . . until he read the label. His brow furrowed and he aimed his glare at Harry. "These are sugar free."

"You're welcome."

"I didn't say thank you."

"They're your favourite."

"These are sugar free. My favourite are not sugar free." He held up the small tin of mints like it offended him. "You did this on purpose?"

"Your dentist will thank me."

"I hate you."

"No you don't."

He shook the mints. "I haaaate you."

"I bought you those soy crisp things you like as well."

Whatever tirade he was about to unload faded slowly. He closed his mouth and pouted for a bit. "I still hate you."

Harry smiled. "You're welcome."

"I did not say thank you."

"Did you get ahold of your informant? The mysterious Number Four?"

"I'm not sure I can tell you."

"Why not? If I'm following his goddamned orders—"

"Because you got me the sugar-free mints. If you got me the real ones, I'd tell you everything."

"You absolutely would not."

"Now we will never know."

Harry laughed. "I'm actually surprised at how well we get along."

"I hate you."

TEN

HARRY, as Asher had instructed, had stayed in the car while he went in to speak to the motel office about a room.

The motel was rough, but it was off the highway, at the back of a small town an hour out of Ghardaïa.

There were two other cars in the lot, no cameras, no street-lights. Certainly no room service or hot spa.

Asher had said it would be better if he went in for the room because he spoke Arabic, but also because Harry, being a six-foot-three white man was someone who would be remembered in these parts. Asher could be boring and blend in. Harry, not so much.

Asher came out of the office with a key and walked to the end room. He unlocked the door and Harry followed him in with their two bags.

"There's only one bed," Harry grumbled.

"You complain about the bed and not the smell?"

The bed, the smell, the stained walls, it was all bad. God, the floor . . . "You got the bed last time, so tonight you take the floor."

Asher looked at the floor and grimaced. "Or we could share the bed."

"I thought you hated me."

"I do."

"But you expect me to share a bed with you?"

"Would it be the first time you ever fucked someone that didn't like you?"

Harry raised a brow at him. "We went from sharing a bed to fucking. That was quick."

Asher began to smile. "But you agree now?"

"I never said I agreed."

"You never said you didn't."

Harry put the bags down, made sure the door was locked, and Asher cocked his head, hopeful.

"I'm taking a shower," Harry said. "You're not invited." He heard Asher sigh as he closed the bathroom door.

The showerhead resembled an outside garden tap and the water ran brown for a good minute before it became clear, but it was warm and wet, the soap washing away the last few days of grime and sweat.

He'd definitely had worse.

He pulled his jeans back on and picked up his socks and boots, his shirt. He found Asher eating some bread and hummus. He stopped, mid-chew, and stared. "You're like a cruel butcher."

Harry blinked. "A what?"

"A cruel butcher shop." Asher waved his hand up and down at Harry's whole body. "You have the best goods on display but don't let me purchase."

God.

"Shut up and eat your bread."

"This hummus is good, by the way. Homemade."

Harry smiled and pulled on his socks. "It's colder here. The shower's not great, but better than nothing. We'll need to keep some bottled water to brush our teeth, so don't drink it all."

Asher stood up, his eyes still very much on Harry's naked torso. "Keep the shirt off. It's not that cold." He walked closer to Harry than he had to on his way to the bathroom. "And don't eat all the bread."

For one very long moment, Harry considered leaving his shirt off.

Then he came to his senses and sat down to eat his dinner with his shirt very much on. Asher came back out a few minutes later, wearing only his jeans, and he took one look at Harry and sighed. "I ask you for one thing."

Harry laughed and took another bite. "Tell me what your friend Four said."

"About what?"

"Whatever you asked him."

Asher glanced his way but didn't reply for a while. He sat on the floor, pulled his duffle bag over, took out the Compact Rifle he'd pulled out in Algiers earlier today, and he began to clean it.

Harry sat on the bed, leaning against the wall, his legs outstretched, and he watched Asher do his thing. First that gun, then the next, then the next.

He handled those weapons like a well-versed lover.

It was hot.

"See something you like?"

Harry must have been watching a little too intently. He shrugged without shame. "You're good with your hands."

Asher chuckled, surprised. "You know I am. When I held your head and fucked your mouth."

"Wasn't really your hands I was concentrating on."

"Want a repeat?"

Harry acted like he was considering it. "I'm undecided."

Asher kept cleaning his rifle. This was a MAC 50, a nice weapon. "That wasn't a no."

Harry nodded to the gun. "Is that one your favourite? What did you call it before? Your friend?"

"It is, yes. Never let me down yet. There are few people in this world we can say that about, yes?"

Harry wasn't expecting that as an answer, but he nodded. "True." Harry had no one. He'd thought he had his handler, his boss, his only connection to home.

Now he wasn't sure he had any of that.

Actually, he was certain he didn't.

Which meant the number of people in the world that hadn't let him down was . . . one.

Asher.

Well, he hadn't let him down yet. But would he?

Harry wasn't sure. He hoped not. Harry hadn't spent this much time with someone in a long time and he was beginning to like Asher—as much as he annoyed him—and the idea of Asher letting him down hurt way more than he was prepared for.

Emotions and feelings always compromised his objectives. Not to mention the liability and the risk.

"I don't have anyone," Harry added. "By design. It's how we were made, right?"

Asher's gaze cut to Harry, his hands pausing as he reassembled the rifle, and he gave a nod.

"But you have your friend Four," Harry added.

"I do."

Harry waited for him to continue, but instead, he finished with his rifle and said nothing.

So yes, he had Four. He had a friend, someone in the world who had never let him down.

Unease settled over Harry, greasy and slick in his belly, and he shivered.

"You cold?" Asher asked. "You should get under the blanket."

Harry looked at him, sitting on the floor. "Where will you sleep?"

"I'm good with the floor," Asher answered. "Slept in worse, right?"

Harry nodded and he warred with wanting to offer to share the bed, and not wanting Asher to think Harry was going soft. He pulled back the bedcover and sat there, feeling awkward. "Will you get cold? You can use my coat."

"I'll be fine."

"Did . . . uh, did you eat enough?"

Asher smiled, then he grinned. Then he laughed.

Harry lay down and pulled the covers up. "Shut the fuck up."

About two hours later, a shivering and very cold Asher climbed into the bed, getting under the covers. "C-c-cold."

Harry could have grumbled and kicked him out, but instead, he shuffled over a little and opened his arms. Asher snuggled in, Harry rubbed his back, and his shivering evened out with his breathing.

Harry's heart knocked against his ribs, right where Asher's face was pressed. He was surprised he couldn't feel it.

Had Harry shared a bed with a man in how long? Ever?

Not like this.

But holy hell, it felt good.

To hell with the complications or the compromises, the risk. If he could just have this, for even one night, he'd take it.

"THE TRAIL'S GONE COLD," Gibson said into the phone.

"There has to be something," Parrish muttered. "Are you sure they were there?"

"They were here all right." Gibson eyed the three men who had said they'd seen them. One very big white man, very angry, they'd said. Probably because they'd intended to mug them until the white guy had stood up and they'd crapped themselves. *Idiots.*

Hull had shown them a photograph. All three men nodded. It was definitely Harrigan. "But no one knows where they are now."

"The Interpol notice will slow them down," Parrish said. "They'll be taking back roads to God knows where trying to stay hidden."

"The Interpol notice sent them underground," Gibson muttered. "Now they're hiding. Asher Garin is a ghost. The man's a freaking enigma. He's gotta be the brains behind this—"

"Don't underestimate Harrigan," Parrish warned. "He's been on the ground over there for a decade. On his own."

"He's not on his own anymore."

Parrish was quiet for a few beats. "I've got surveillance on it," he said quietly. "For an operation that doesn't exist, so it could take some time."

"There is no surveillance in the Casbah," Gibson said, looking up and down the narrow and dilapidated alleyway of sloping stairs and cracked tiles. "And the people who live here won't talk to the police. It's why Garin and Harrigan chose this place. They are two steps ahead. They have to have someone helping them. Someone with intel."

"Harrigan's phone is dark. No calls in, no calls out. He pinged another location but—"

"Forget the locations on his phone." Gibson shook his head. This was pointless. And it really wasn't his place to question Parrish, but they were at a dead end. "We need to rethink. Why didn't Garin kill Harrigan when he had the chance?"

Another beat of silence. "Because he's more useful to him alive."

"I'm not buying that. These men work better alone. Harrigan must have something that Garin needs."

Parrish seemed to consider this for a long moment. "Hm."

"Where do we go now?" Gibson asked. "Want us to lie low? At least until we figure out why they came to Algeria, of all places."

Parrish was quiet again though Gibson could hear fingers on a keyboard. "Six months ago, Harrigan had an assignment there."

"Here, in Algiers?"

"No. In Algeria. I will send the information through to you now."

"Why would he come back?"

"I don't know."

Gibson tried to rein in his temper. "Did you not think we should have known that before? That he was here six months ago?"

"You know what you *need* to know," Parrish bellowed. "And Gibson, there isn't a country over there he hasn't been assigned to. Wherever you go, he's been there before you. That's what you need to know. That's why he's two steps ahead. You want to find him, you need to start thinking like him."

Gibson ended the call, too pissed off to speak. Hull was watching him. "What did he say?"

"We might have a location."

A few moments later, his phone beeped. He read the details Parrish sent through, then looked up at Hull. "We're gonna need some wheels."

DESIRE COURSED through Harry's blood. Want, need, hot and heady. He wanted this . . . needed it. He wanted to sink into the pleasure and give himself over to it. Drown in it. He wanted it to never end. They writhed together, moved as one.

Asher groaned.

And Harry woke up.

He froze, and Asher ground his ass against Harry's erection. "Don't stop now."

Oh God.

Harry put his hand on Asher's hip, not to guide him, but to stop him.

Asher pushed back against him. "I said don't stop."

Harry growled. "Asher."

"You want it. Your body does not lie. You're rock hard."

Harry almost gave in. He could have, so easily. *And he did want it.*

Then Harry noticed Asher's arm moving in long, sure strokes.

Christ.

"I'm close," he murmured.

Harry shot off the bed, stepping away in the small room, keeping his back to Asher. If he saw what he was doing . . . his resolve was hanging by a single thread as it was.

"You're just gonna stop?" Asher said, his voice rough.

"Asher, I'm sorry. We shouldn't . . . I shouldn't have . . . I was dreaming. Sorry."

"Fuck you."

The anger with which Asher spat those words almost made Harry turn around.

He cursed at him again, this time in Croatian, maybe Slovakian. Maybe both.

"You won't even look at me," Asher yelled, this time in English, before he shoved Harry in the back.

Harry hadn't expected the rage. He hadn't expected Asher to push him. He spun, instinct kicking in, and grabbed Asher's arm. "The fuck?"

Asher tried to pull his arm away, but Harry wasn't letting him go. So Asher came at him again, trying to push Harry against the wall. He fisted his shirt. Anger and something else flashed in his eyes. Harry couldn't quite make out the emotion in the dark.

Asher let out a string of curses through clenched teeth, pressing his forearm against Harry's chest. He clawed at him, trying to grab him, grapple him. "You shouldn't promise me," Asher hissed.

Promise him?

"I never promised you anything," Harry said, wrestling him, trying to hold him. Asher was no match for him, not physically, and Harry didn't want to hurt him. "Calm down."

Asher was mad, yes, but the fight in him was wrong. This wasn't a fight for dominance. Harry could easily throw him off. One good hit and Asher would be finished. Harry had fought close combat many times. He could kill with his bare hands.

Something in this fight was wrong.

"Asher, what the fuck are you doing?"

In their wrestle, Asher's blunt nails scraped over Harry's skin. He wasn't trying to get away; he was trying to get closer.

Christ.

Harry understood then what this was.

It wasn't a fight for domination.

It was a fight to be dominated.

Asher struggled harder, twisting his arm out of Harry's hold, and he gripped Harry's cock. His eyes met Harry's, fierce and defiant. Daring him. "You want it. Why won't you give it to me?"

Jesus Christ.

Harry was stunned and confused. Until Asher swung his fist at Harry's jaw, connecting, hard, but not enough to rattle him.

Just enough to piss him the fuck off.

He came in for another swing and Harry deflected the punch, grabbing Asher's fist and twisting him around, pulling him against him, Asher's back to Harry's front.

Asher froze, taking one second to breathe, before he began to struggle again. Harry held him tight, his arm across Asher's chest. Asher tried to mule kick him, thrashing, and Harry had to hold him tight.

So tight.

Asher pushed back against Harry, his ass against Harry's crotch. "You're still hard," Asher breathed. "You want it as much as me."

Harry growled, holding him rough enough to bruise. "You don't want it like this."

Asher fought to get his hands free. Not to fight against Harry . . . but to undo the button on his jeans. Then he kicked again, elbowed, and struggled. And fought. In their tussle, Harry caught an elbow to the face and heel to the thigh, and his own rage took over.

He twisted Asher's arm up behind his back and walked him, almost lifting him, and shoved him over the edge of the bed. Harry held him down, pressed his weight on him, his forearm across Asher's back. His erection pressed against Asher's ass.

Goddammit.

"Do it," Asher bit out. He managed to pull his jeans down with his free hand. "Do it."

"You should be careful what you wish for," Harry mumbled as he undid his fly and pulled out his cock. Asher smiled into the bedding and Harry rammed into him. No preparation, no lube. No mercy. Rough and hard, unforgiving.

Asher gripped the sheets and cried out, his back arching underneath Harry. He gasped, his breathing stuttering, his eyes wide. Harry reached around and gripped Asher's jaw, whispering in his ear, "Is this what you wanted?"

Asher groaned, long and loud. "Yes. God, yes."

Harry gave in.

He gave in to Asher's demands. He gave in to the pleasure, to the ecstasy. He chased that feeling, the rush, the high. He buried himself deep, over and over, holding him down and fucking him. Pure desire and animal-need drove him forward, closer and closer, with every thrust until he fell, free-falling, over the edge.

His orgasm exploded, detonating and obliterating everything else but this moment. This ecstasy. He came deep inside him, his cock impossibly hard and swollen, filling him with his come.

Harry cried out, shuddering as his orgasm rocketed through him. He'd never known pleasure like this. So intense, so powerful.

Asher blinked in surprise, then smiling into the mattress, he laughed.

ELEVEN

ASHER FELT GOOD.

Actually, Asher hadn't felt this good in a very long time.

He didn't want Harry to pull out. He wanted to feel that good forever. His exhausted weight on top of him was heaven, and he knew Harry would probably have . . . issues . . . with what had just transpired.

Harry lifted his weight off first, then slowly pulled out his spent cock. Asher didn't want to move. He already missed the feel of Harry inside of him.

Even though he still carried part of him.

God, it feels so good.

"I uh, I'm sorry," Harry stammered weakly. "God, I . . ."

Asher chuckled and rolled over, revealing his own spent cock and pool of come on the bed. "Sorry for what? That was so hot."

Harry stood there, his half-hard cock hanging heavy out of his jeans. He seemed confused. "Are you . . . did you . . . ?"

"Oh, I am, and I did." Asher preened, happy as a cat lazing in the sun. "You did me so good."

Harry tucked his dick back in his pants. "Asher, I . . ."

"Don't put it away. Tell me you want to do it again. Pump me full of your—"

Harry scrubbed his hand over his face. "Jesus. Please don't."

Asher laughed and pulled his jeans up, for no other reason than comfort. He left the fly wide open though. "So, while I still have your semen inside me," Asher said, and Harry winced. "We should discuss sex health, though there's a saying in English about the horse already bolting—"

"My sexual health is fine. All clear. I'm sorry. I was rough and didn't use any lubrication, and I didn't care for you like I should. And I shouldn't have finished inside you."

"Care for me?" Asher grinned as he got to his feet. "You took the best care of me. Gave it to me just how I like it." He tapped Harry's cheek. "And you can finish inside me again, as many times as you want. And just so you know, now I know how good you can give it, I will want it *all* the time."

Harry shook his head and pulled at his short hair, flummoxed. "Are you gonna try and belt the shit outta me again first?"

Asher grinned. "You mean foreplay?"

Harry sighed and let his head loll back. "No, that was not . . . you know what, it doesn't matter. There won't be a next time."

"Yes, there will be."

"No, there won't be."

"Oh yes, there will be. You know there will be, because you want it." Asher patted his belly. "I'm going to shower. But now that we're both up, we can find some breakfast. I'm hungry."

ASHER HAD a spring in his step. He couldn't help it. He also had a sore ass, but in the very best of ways.

"Can you stop smiling?" Harry asked. He was driving, casting odd looks at Asher every so often. "It's starting to scare me."

Asher grinned at him. "I've had a good morning."

Harry shook his head again and mumbled under his breath. He tightened his grip on the steering wheel.

Asher was certain Harry was about to apologise again, like he'd done at the motel and again over breakfast. Asher didn't want to hear it. "Now when we meet this woman, I will do the speaking. The conversation will more than likely not be in English, so if you have any questions you wish asked, tell me now."

"I want to know who Professor Taleb worked for. Not the university. Who *else* did he work for? What research did he do, and who for? What work he'd done at the gas or fuel sites. Did he work on site or fully remote? Names of anyone she can give us." Harry sighed, as if his own questions annoyed him. "I don't know if any of it matters now."

"Why doesn't it matter?"

"Because the man is dead. Why cause his widow more pain?"

"She might know something. It might seem small to her, insignificant."

"Like what?"

"I don't know yet."

Harry scowled for a mile before he shook his head. "Why can't your informant, agent Four, or whatever his name is, find whatever it is we're after? If he has the connections and intel that you claim he does, why do we need to do this? Why can't he find it?"

"Because not everything is electronic. Some things are physical. Sometimes you have to see it in their eyes."

Harry chewed on the inside of his lip for another mile. "If your number Four believes my handler has been neutralising innocent civilians for financial gain, then he has to have proof, right?"

"He has . . . some."

Harry shook his head. "Bullshit. He would have all the electronic proof he needs." He shot Asher a direct stare. "What aren't you telling me?"

"He needs physical proof."

"Like what?" Harry asked. "Files? Video? Recorded conversation?" Then he froze, like a penny had dropped from a great height. He pulled the car over to an abrupt stop on the side of the road, just on the outskirts of Ghardaïa. "Me. He needs me."

Asher didn't exactly understand why the truth soured in his belly like curdled milk.

"You need to tell me what the fuck is going on?" Harry said. "Right now. What do you want with me?"

"Harry."

"You didn't pull me out of Madrid because we'd stand more of a chance at surviving together. That was bullshit then. It's bullshit now. You pulled me out, you didn't kill me when you had the chance, because you need me."

"Yes. Of course. You cannot be surprised. It's what we do, Harry."

"You lied to me."

"Where was the lie? What did I tell you that was a lie?"

"You should have told me. When I asked you what the plan was, in the very beginning. You should have told me the truth. You need me because I'm the only one who can bring down my fucking government."

"Yes. And if I told you, you wouldn't have come with me."

"For good fucking reason!" He thumped the steering wheel. "For fuck's sake, Asher."

Asher pointed his finger at him. "You should be mad. You should be fucking enraged. But not at me. Your handler, your government, put a hit on you. And me. They sold you out, put a price on your head. And me! They want me dead too, remember?"

"You've done work for them too? Contracts, assignments, hits for my country?"

"Yes. Many countries."

Harry blinked and sat back in his seat, as though Asher's words had physically hit him.

"We're a liability, a loose end they need tied up and gone

because we can expose them. You can expose them. You need to see this through," Asher added quietly. "We need to see this through because it is our only chance at walking away."

Harry looked out the windscreen, shaking his head as though his thoughts ran wild and regrouped. After a long few seconds, he looked back to Asher. "And what do you get out of this?"

"I just told you."

"Your chance to walk away?" Harry squinted at him. "You can walk away anytime you like."

Asher laughed because, if only that was true. "We need to see this through to the end, Harry. We need to put a stop to your handler—"

Harry barked out a laugh, incredulous. "Stop? Do you know how high up the chain that is?"

"That's why we need proof."

"Christ, Asher. What's the end game here? You're going to blow a hole in the Australian government? Blackmail them? Or just kill them?"

Asher made a face, implying he'd settle for any or either.

"And then what?" Harry pressed. "We just walk away?"

Asher met his eyes, serious, honest. "Yes."

"Walk into what? A normal life? Be a law-abiding, tax-paying citizen?"

The way Harry said that, dripping with sarcasm and contempt, stung. Asher sat back in his seat, looking out to the desert town before them. It took him a moment to find his voice. "Yes."

Harry was stunned, clearly. And at a loss for words. He opened his mouth—

"Just shut the fuck up," Asher said. "I was in a really good mood this morning, and you're ruining it, Harry."

Harry rubbed his thumb and fingers in his eyes, then scrubbed his hand over his face. He mumbled something under his breath, then shot a fierce gaze at Asher. "When we're done here with the professor's wife, you're going to tell me everything."

Asher said nothing.

"You're going to tell me everything," Harry bit out through clenched teeth. "I'm not asking."

Asher held his gaze. "Hmm. Sounds like foreplay conversation to me."

Harry seethed, nostrils flared. He raised a finger, opened his mouth, and failed to speak. In the end, he growled, swore, started the car, and drove.

PROFESSOR TALEB'S house was exactly as Harry remembered. The front, anyway. That was all he'd seen. The street, too. Though the blood stain, from where Harry had shot the man, had been removed.

It was hard to get blood out of dirt, Harry knew from experience. He wondered what they'd used as Asher knocked on the door. "I will do the talking," Asher said as the door opened. He spoke briefly with an older woman dressed in black who, after looking at Harry like he was shit on her shoe, opened the door and let them in.

The house was nice: terracotta floor, washed walls with white and blue tiles. The curtains were drawn, the living room was dark. A woman, mid-thirties, sat on a sofa. She was younger than Harry imagined she'd be, wore all black, sat straight-backed, her eyes were sharp and profoundly sad.

Asher talked, softly, like a melody. Charming and warm. Sympathetic and strong. Harry didn't even know what Asher had told her, why they were there, or who they represented. The plan was to say they worked for the gas export company, but if Asher had actually told her that, Harry had no clue.

Harry was probably better off not knowing, considering he was the one who had killed her husband.

It was wrong for him to be here.

A small boy, maybe eight years old, came out from a room. It was the same boy who had chased the ball in the street the day Harry had shot Taleb. Harry had waited for the boy to go inside. Though he had no doubt the young boy had seen the end result.

The boy went to his mother and she drew him into her arms, holding him. She murmured something and gently touched his face, and the boy went to the older woman.

Harry wasn't expecting to see Taleb's children.

He should have stayed in the car.

It was then Harry realised all eyes were on him. Asher gave him a discreet nudge but his eyes weren't so guarded. "Everything okay?"

"Yes, I'm fine. I apologise. Please continue."

As soon as Harry spoke, Mrs Taleb stared at him. "You are Australian," she murmured before her gaze cut to Asher's. Harry didn't need to understand the words she said to him next. He understood the tone well enough.

"Mrs Taleb," Harry said. He was clearly not the first Australian she'd met. "If you have a name of any other Australian—"

"Harry," Asher hissed at him.

Harry ignored him and spoke directly to Mrs Taleb. "We may have reason to believe the man who gave the order to kill your husband was Australian. If you have a name, any name, of anyone your husband may have dealt with or spoken to, I promise you we will find them."

She stared at him, her chest rising and falling, her eyes defiant. "And you will make them pay?"

Harry nodded. "You have my word."

Then she told them all she knew.

Asher schooled his expression, his reaction, and very politely thanked her again for her time, and they walked out. He was even calm as he drove a block or two, and Harry was reluctant to admit it was unnerving.

"She—"

"Ce dracu'!" he yelled. He thumped the steering wheel. "Ce nu ai înțeles?" Then he thumped his own head. "Ești prost?"

Harry wasn't sure what language that was. Maybe Slovakian? Possibly Turkish.

"Are you fucking stupid?"

That one was in English.

"I got us an answer!"

"I told you to let me do the talking!" Asher mumbled something else, cursed again, and huffed out a sigh. "Who taught you your interview techniques? A wrecking ball?"

Harry wasn't one bit sorry. "I got us an answer. I got us a whole lot of answers. As soon as she heard my accent, she reacted. You saw it. I know you did."

"I was getting the information from her."

"I got it a whole lot quicker. And I got physical proof." He held up a USB.

Asher growled and literally gnashed his teeth. "I want to shoot you so bad right now. Right in the fucking head."

Harry really wasn't sure why Asher was so pissed. Harry did get them exactly what they'd needed. But, he had to admit, it was fun having Asher be the pissed off one for a change. "Is this your idea of foreplay? Because I'm a little confused. Are we starting early?"

Asher glared at him, hard. But then he had to look out the window because the fucker smiled. "I really hate you right now."

Harry chuckled. "You are flirting. My God. If you want to find us a motel, I can fix you right up."

Asher shot him a look before concentrating on driving. "I told you not to tease me."

"And I told you to be careful what you wish for."

Asher chewed on his tongue, his knuckles were white on the steering wheel, and he levelled a glare at Harry. It was both heated and daring.

He really was getting off on this.

The truth was, Harry was enjoying it too. They'd had two sexual encounters in a few days and Harry couldn't remember the last time he'd been so lucky. And if he was being honest with himself, Harry would love some more. The idea of finding some dank motel, bending Asher over the bed, and burying himself inside him, again and again, was *very* appealing.

Harry's dick was extremely interested.

He shook his head and ignored the ache in his balls. "We need to find out what's on the USB, and everything we can about Solaris Global."

It wasn't the name of a *man* Mrs Taleb knew. It was a company name.

A company that her husband had worked with, written reports for, and in the end, fought with. A company that had been skimming product and profit from its clients for years.

Harry then realised they were driving out of town. "Where are we going?"

"To Hassi R'Mel gas and oil fields."

Now it was Harry's turn to stare. "I wasn't aware this was a suicide mission. Do you think we can just drive through the gates like it's a tourist destination?"

Asher rolled his eyes. "Give me one reason why I shouldn't shoot you right now?"

"It's not that you shouldn't. It's that you couldn't. You physically couldn't shoot me right now because you suck at close combat." Harry wasn't kidding. "You try pulling a gun on me right now and I will fuck you up."

Asher glared. He looked so mad he could just about spit. But there was something else in his eyes. Two different kinds of fire. "Is this your idea of foreplay, Harry?" he said gruffly. "You keep threatening me like that, I just might think you're starting to like me."

Harry grinned at him, and Asher laughed.

Harry wasn't sure if this was fun or insane.

Maybe a little of both.

It was also turning him on. The push and pull, the challenge. The physicality. The way Asher smirked, the way he seethed. The way fighting turned Asher on. It was all hot.

So yeah, it was definitely both. Fun *and* insane.

THEY PARKED the car well off the road two miles out from the first entrance gate to the gas field. The entire area was an ocean of desert and waves of sand. They were hidden well enough, except from planes or drones.

"We should come back at night," Harry suggested. He had Asher's binoculars aimed at the gates to the gas field. The binoculars were state of the art, high-tech, a very nice piece. They gave distance, range, crystal clear. It was no wonder Asher could shoot a target from this distance.

Asher was too busy typing on his phone. "Just shut up and tell me what you see."

"One road in," Harry said. "Perimeter is a chain-link fence, eight-foot high, razor wire on top. Six security cameras I can see: infrared by the look of them. The gate has two security men, one inside the booth, one out. Armed with a G36."

Asher looked up from his phone. "I respect that."

Harry resisted the urge to sigh. He also resisted the urge to crack Asher across the head with his own binoculars. "The Heckler & Koch G36 is standard issue rifle of the Algerian special forces."

Asher nodded. "I know." He went back to his phone.

Of course he knew.

Were these guards actual military trained soldiers? Harry would have to assume yes.

Asher didn't seem surprised or worried. "What else do you see?"

"Wait. We have a utility truck entering the premises."

"Is it marked? Company name?"

"No . . . Jesus Christ. That huge-ass metal frame vehicles go through isn't just a gate. It's a freaking X-ray machine. Military-grade cargo inspection system. The kind they use at seaports and border crossings, only a helluva lot more high-tech. There would be another three heavily armed guards, at least, in that office module next to the gate."

"Hm." Asher, again, didn't seem surprised. "These gas

and oil fields are a multibillion-dollar industry, Harry, that makes up a ridiculous percentage of the country's GDP. What did you think they'd have?"

Harry felt a little foolish when he spelled it out like that. "I don't know. I've never had to think about it before."

"Never had to scope out a place for a job, Harry? Never had to break in so you could kill someone?"

Harry thought back over the years, over the jobs he'd done. "No. I either intercepted them travelling or as they were arriving or leaving somewhere. Home, usually. Or work. Easier that way." Harry just realised what Asher had said. He stared at him. "We are *not* breaking into this facility. Absolutely fucking not."

Asher laughed. "I am many things, Harry. Stupid is not one of them."

"Then what are we doing here?"

"Seeing what kind of security clearance the good professor had. Or what vehicles come and go, how often. How many guards and what kind of tech we'd be up against if we did actually decide to break in."

"Correction. How many *you'd* be up against. There is no we in that mess of a scenario."

"You would let me go in by myself?" Asher almost sounded offended.

"Solo. You'd be more solo than Han and the lemon drink combined."

"You would not let me go alone," Asher scoffed.

"Shut the fuck up," Harry said. Asher began to say something else, but Harry beat him to it. "No, I mean it. Be quiet. We have another incoming. A van, white. Logo on the side . . . Solaris. Single driver—"

Harry's words died in his throat.

"What is it?" Asher whispered.

Harry felt sick. He hadn't known what to expect, but he certainly hadn't expected this. He handed him the binoculars.

Asher held them to his eyes and expertly adjusted the

settings as he looked at the van and its driver. "You know him," he said calmly.

"His name is Trevor Whitmore. Second lieutenant in the SRG."

Asher lowered the binoculars and looked at Harry. "He was in your unit?"

"Not mine, but the one under it. We ran some training ops with that unit." Harry started the engine and turned back for the town of Ghardaïa.

"I take it we're done watching them?" Asher said sarcastically.

Harry's shock was starting to give way to anger. "I've seen enough."

TWELVE

THE SECOND MOTEL was worse than the first. Harry thought it was more of a seedy boarding house than motel, but it was well-hidden. And with their car parked around the back, it was highly unlikely anyone would come looking for them here.

Harry wondered if he cared anymore.

If anyone came looking for them, it would give Harry a good excuse to beat the piss out of someone.

He was really fucking pissed off.

There were too many coincidences.

Trevor Whitmore worked for Solaris. The same energy company that Professor Taleb was working for. The same company, more than likely, that had him killed. Trevor Whitmore was ex-Australian special forces. Hell, maybe he was still enlisted.

It wasn't uncommon for ex-military to work private security.

But Whitmore knew Harry's handler. Harry's handler, who'd had Professor Taleb killed. Harry's handler, who had put a price on Harry's head.

Was seeing Whitmore irrefutable proof?

No. Just a whole lot of coincidences.

Harry didn't believe in coincidences.

Especially with everything Asher had said. Which admittedly wasn't much, but it was enough.

Harry was sure now, if he wasn't already, that what Asher was telling him was the truth.

Harry put his bag down, looked around the godawful dark and dirty room, and took out his phone. Did he risk calling his handler? Did he call him now and ask what the fuck was going on? Did he call him and act like he knew nothing?

He was staring at his phone when he heard a buzz. Not Harry's phone. It was Asher's. His phone had never rung before. Harry's eyes went to Asher's, and Asher smiled as he answered, the call on speaker. "Hello, darling," a smooth male voice said.

Asher laughed. "You're on speaker, and the very handsome and well-hung Harry is with me. Please tell me you found something already."

Harry's mouth fell open.

Four didn't even miss a beat. "Solaris is one of many subsidiary shell companies under an umbrella corporation registered in Switzerland. Each one registered as a subsidiary of the next."

"Let me guess," Asher said dryly. "Untraceable."

"My darling, have you no faith in me?"

Asher smiled, staring directly at Harry. "You know I do."

Harry glared at him. *My darling.* For fuck's sake.

"The company Solaris shows activity," the voice on the phone said. There was an accent but Harry couldn't place it. "But it's a front. It has to be. Financials are too neat and tidy. The information is very helpful though, thank you."

Asher was still smiling at Harry. "I'm glad we could help."

"We're going to need that USB, though."

"Of course."

The man hummed. "And how is that handsome and well-hung Harry treating you?"

Harry raised an eyebrow. Asher laughed. "Dreadfully."

Jesus Christ.

He sounded amused. "Oh, my darling. That sounds terrible for you."

Asher looked Harry up and down. "So terrible."

Harry cleared his throat. "I can hear this conversation. I'm standing right here."

Still grinning, Asher took the phone off speaker and pressed it to his ear. Whatever the man said to him made him laugh. "Yes, please do. … Oh, you know I will." He chuckled again. "Yes. Soon."

He ended the call, and Harry glared at him. "Well hung?"

Asher shrugged. "I'm not going to lie to him."

Harry resisted the urge to growl. "Yes, soon, what?"

"What?"

"You just said 'yes, soon.' What does that mean?" He tried not to yell. "What are you doing soon?"

Asher stared at him. He wasn't smiling now. That look of fire and daring was back. "Soon," he said with a sneer. "I will see him soon. It's how we end all conversations and have done for many years." He raised his chin, his smile smug. "Jealous?"

"No."

He took a step closer. "Are you jealous, Harry?"

"No. And we're not doing that fight-sex thing again, so back off."

"Fight-sex is my favourite."

"That's messed up."

Asher laughed. "You can't tell me you didn't like it. I have your come in me to prove—"

"Jesus, Asher. Do you have to talk like that?"

Asher grinned like this was all part of the game. He undid the button on his jeans. "We have a few hours to fill in, Harry. I can't think of anything else for us to do, can you?"

"A hundred different things."

He undid his fly. "But nothing like this."

Christ.

"You're pissed off," Asher continued. "You're angry that you saw your old army friend at the security gate. You're pissed off that your government sold you out. You have pent up energy. Anger." He held his hands out like claws. "You want someone to pay. You want to put your hands around their necks—"

"Someone, yes. The assholes who sold me out, yes. Not you."

"Not even if I ask nicely?"

"No."

Asher sighed petulantly and sat on the bed. "You ruined the mood."

"There was no mood." Harry pulled over one of the chairs at the small table and sat on it. "And considering what I did to you this morning, you should be thanking me for saying no."

Asher wiggled his ass and smiled. "I'm just fine, thanks. You let me worry about my ass."

Harry raised an eyebrow at him. He needed to change the subject. "What's the plan from here? Where do we go?"

"The plan was more fucking, but you said no."

God. "I meant with everything else."

Asher scooted up the bed to lean against the wall. His fly was still undone. Harry deliberately didn't look at it. "We wait."

"For what?"

Asher shrugged. "For information on where we go next."

"From your friend with the mysterious accent. Who calls you his darling."

Asher grinned. "You *are* jealous."

Yes, you are. Admit it. As much as you loathe this man, you like him too.

Harry ignored the voice in his head that mocked him. "I am not."

Asher chuckled. "But I think you are."

Harry growled at him, and for a long, drawn out few minutes, neither of them spoke. Until it got the best of Harry. "How do you know him? What's his name? I don't even know what to call him. I can't keep calling him Four."

"You can. He would be so amused."

"His name."

"His name is not your concern," Asher said coolly.

Harry growled at him again.

"You shouldn't snarl at me like that," he replied with a smirk. "It turns me on."

Harry sighed and rolled his eyes, all out of patience. "I need some answers, Asher. So you either start talking or I'm gone. And no bullshit. I want the truth."

Asher stared at him, like he was trying to decide if this was Harry's tipping point. But he stared too long, he stayed silent too long. Harry stood and snatched up his backpack.

"Sit down," Asher said. "Give me a minute. It's not easy for me to talk of this. I've never spoken of this. To anyone."

Now it was Harry who had to size up Asher's sincerity.

He was nervous, pained even. He frowned, his eyebrows furrowing. "I've known him a long time," Asher said. "Ten years. He's been the most constant thing in my life. The only constant person in my life. Ever. I have no one. No family, no country to call home. I have . . . only him."

Harry sat back down.

"He was a target," Asher said. "An assignment. He was on the run from his own country. He had accessed information he wasn't supposed to have seen, and they put a price on his head."

"Sounds familiar."

Asher nodded, though his smile wasn't a happy one. "I found him and I watched him, and I put together a plan." He sighed. "See, I was young, and I had nothing. No one. All the jobs I got came through *bad* people. The wrong people. Unsanctioned, mercenary. They didn't just kill people. They trafficked whatever they could: money, drugs, weapons. People." He had a distant look in his eyes, as if his memories had taken him somewhere dark. He shook his head and met Harry's gaze. "I can kill bad people. I have no problem with that. It's what we do, and I'm very good at it. But I can't be part of the shipment of women." He looked down at his lap and whispered, "And children."

Harry could tell that whatever Asher had seen, been witness to, been part of, was not good.

"So you put together a plan," Harry murmured, trying to move Asher out of the places his memories had taken him. "Made a deal with him that was beneficial to you both."

Asher nodded. "Yes. He's very good at what he does. There is nothing he can't do with a computer. He's a genius. Literally. At mathematics, codes, numbers. He has a brain like a machine. His government had him accessing information on other countries, allies, enemies; security, financial, nuclear, you name it. He found operations he was not supposed to find, and someone decided he'd seen too much."

"And you were supposed to kill him."

"It was an easy job. He was out of the country, which was rare. His people had lined it up that way, so they could use his death on foreign soil for trade leverage."

"Nice."

Asher smiled sardonically. "His was not a nice government."

"So you captured him instead of killing him and told him you'd both be better off working together," Harry deduced. "That sounds very familiar too. Is that how you begin all working relationships?" He motioned between them.

Asher almost smiled. "You were easier to convince than him."

"You held a gun to my head. Literally."

"And you had one pointed at mine."

"I'm still unsure if not pulling the trigger was the right thing to do." Harry wanted to lighten the mood to keep him talking. "We've managed okay so far. Without being killed. Or killing each other. Though we are on Interpol's Red Notice list, which is great. It's a first for me."

Asher sighed, his smile fading slowly. "He's working on having that revoked. I don't know how. I didn't ask. I never ask how he does what he does."

"You trust him implicitly? Whatever he says, what he tells you to do."

"Yes." Asher's gaze, his reply, was so certain. "I saved his life. I reported the job complete. I found some drug dealer, made him dress in my friend's uniform before I shot him. A shotgun blast to the face. Took most of the head off. I sent in photos as proof, but the local police found his blood-splattered ID and passport, and the uniform, and called it in officially. His own country never even asked for the body." Asher shrugged. "I got us out of the country we were in. He was a free man, I got paid, and we set him up in a place where no one would find him."

"Just like that?"

"Just like that."

"What was the trade-off?"

"He's like my handler. He works his computer magic, manoeuvres me as needed. I find him information on the ground that he needs."

"Information he needs for what?"

Asher shrugged. "To get rid of bad guys."

Harry stared, having to blink a few times. "Vigilantism, extortion, blackmail. Pretty sure that makes you the bad guys."

Asher laughed. "We're all bad guys, Harry. You and me, *we* are the bad guys." He shook his head, amused. "You kill for your government. I kill for anyone's government. They might call it service or honourable duty, but it's all murder."

Harry chewed on those words for a long moment, bitter and sour. True.

Except . . .

"You kill for anyone's government, but then you said that Four manoeuvres you, helps you."

"He does. It's freelance work. You might be surprised by how many governments prefer someone"—he put his hands to his chest—"without allegiance to any flag."

"I wished it surprised me." Harry sighed, heavy with the weight of that fact. "What does Four get out of it?"

"He looks into the targets and who wants them dead. More often than not there's money laundering, terrorists financing, fraud, bribery, the list goes on."

"Corruption."

"To the core, in most cases."

"And what does Four do with that information? Sell it to another government?"

Asher laughed again. "Oh no. He takes it."

Harry blinked, joining the dots. "He steals money from corrupt governments? Because, fuck, that's gonna end well."

"He intercepts it, redirects it. Data networks cover almost every corner of the globe. Satellites, relay stations, encryptions. There's nothing he doesn't have access to. And the money? It's just numbers, zeroes and decimal points. And it's completely untraceable."

"Someone will catch up with him."

"You can't catch someone who doesn't exist."

Harry didn't quite believe it. "But he's a real person. Everyone is trackable, traceable. Findable."

Asher smiled, almost serenely. He slowly shook his head. "No, they're not. But now you understand why I will never say his name."

Harry stared at him, and Asher stared right back.

"So, when or if your number Four calls again," Harry said, "we just do everything he says?"

"Yes. That's exactly what we do."

Harry scrubbed a hand over his hair and sighed. "So what are we supposed to do in the meantime?"

A slow smile spread across Asher's face and he gave a suggestive nod down to his crotch, at his unbuttoned fly. "I can think of something you could be doing with that mouth instead of all this talking. Come over here and suck this." He rubbed himself, giving himself a good squeeze.

Harry glared at him.

But then he looked at the bulge in Asher's jeans, then up to the smug smirk on that asshole's face.

Asher laughed, because he totally knew Harry was going to do it.

Harry stood up and pressed one knee on the mattress, then none too gently, dragged Asher down the bed by his ankle. "Shut the fuck up. You want your dick sucked or not?"

Some hours later, Four called again. Asher listened to the five second call, then pocketed his phone. "Get your bag, we're leaving. Now."

Harry was already on his feet. "Where are we going?"

"Airport."

ASHER HAD EXPECTED Hassi R'Mel airport to be no more than some huge hangars and a landing strip in the middle of the Saharan desert, but he was surprised by the modern terminal. A few miles from the gas and oil fields, and while it was a public airport, its primary purpose was to cater to the private planes and jets of the extremely wealthy owners of said gas or oil fields, which probably explained the funding. In the fading daylight, as the sun set over the desert, Asher might even say it was pretty.

"I don't want to point out the obvious," Harry said as they drove into the lot. "Even if we're not recognised as wanted persons, how the fuck are we going to get through security? I have four passports, two pistols, and a whole stack of cash, and you have enough weapons to start your own war."

Asher smiled at that and slowly drove through an entrance to the right of the main terminal. "Private flights are separate to public, and you'd be surprised at the discretion money can buy."

"Private?" Harry sighed. "How much . . . you know what? Never mind."

Asher drove past a large hangar, and upon seeing other cars parked in a lot alongside the fence, he parked with them.

They could see two men, aviation mechanics, Asher would deduce by their coveralls. Then another was loading something into a plane, and a man in a suit who appeared to be supervising.

"I don't like this," Harry whispered.

Truth be told, Asher wasn't too comfortable either, but he'd never been let down yet. "Just relax. We need to look the part. Confident. And pleasant, if you could try smiling."

Harry rolled his eyes. "This is gonna get us both killed." Then he took one of his pistols, lifted his jeans leg and shoved the gun in his boot, then pulled his jeans back down. Then he shot Asher a glare. "What?"

Asher shrugged, indifferent. "Hope the safety is on. Though I do have to say, the irony of you shooting yourself in the foot would be beautiful."

"I hate you."

"No you don't. Come on, let's go."

They took their bags and walked back to the hangar. They were to meet a man called Bashar, and as it turned out, Bashar was the man in the suit. He met them, expectant, it would seem, with his clipboard in hand. Asher did all the talking, and apart from Bashar giving Harry the once-over, they never spoke.

Which was probably a good thing.

"The aircraft is being readied," Bashar said, walking them over to the second plane in the hangar. "Please wait here. The pilot will be with you in five or ten minutes."

Then they were left alone.

Harry was stoic, with his back to the plane, taking in every detail of the hangar. "I don't like this," he whispered.

Other people walked about: the two mechanics, a radio somewhere, a man driving one of the taxiing trucks. No one pinged Asher's radar, but he understood why Harry didn't like being exposed in the open like this, waiting.

"Relax," Asher said. "Being nervous makes you look suspicious."

"Why is it taking so long?"

"It's not."

"What if someone asks too many questions?"

"Stick to the story. We are an Australian and French national, civil engineers for one of the gas companies out of Saudi."

"That's the stupidest shit I've ever heard." He counted on his fingers. "One, I'm pretty sure anyone sent by a Saudi gas company would be wearing Armani suits and not look like they've been on the run for a week. Two, we look nothing like civil engineers. We look like fugitive hitmen. And three, I can speak French. Why can't I be the French guy?"

"We don't need to look like anything. It's purely for the manifest, records on paper, nothing else. *If* they ask, which they have not. It's not likely they will. They are paid for their discretion. God only knows what they've seen in and out of this hangar. And yes, you can *speak* French. It's rather admirable and a bit cute, but you bludgeon the accent to death."

Harry let out a long, slow breath. It wasn't a sigh, Asher could tell. It was a measure to stay his temper. "If we make it out of this alive, I'm gonna kill you myself."

Asher laughed. "I shall look forward to you trying." He took out his tin of breath mints and popped one in his mouth. "Mint?"

Harry glared at him for a long second, then took one. "I thought you didn't like the sugar-free ones?"

"You know," Asher admitted. "They're not bad."

A door closed at the back of the hangar and two men walked out, talking, laughing.

Harry did a double take and turned his back to them. "Fuck."

"Who is it?" Asher asked, his voice neutral.

"The guy on the left. He's from the same team as the guy on the security gate. Ex-special forces."

Which meant he'd recognise Harry . . .

"Keep calm," Asher whispered. "I don't see a weapon. But they are walking this way."

Harry let his backpack slide off his shoulder a little, ready, if he needed it. Asher hoped it wouldn't come to that . . . They needed to get on the plane.

The two men walked closer and their conversation stopped as they neared. Asher thought they might be going to the first plane, and they were . . . until the man on the left saw Harry. He looked twice and stopped.

"Harrigan?" he asked. He was early thirties, blond, smiling. "Is that you?"

Harry turned, and quickly reading the man's surprise and smile, he reacted the same. "Fitz?"

The man grinned wider. "Holy shit. It is you!" He held out his hand, which Harry shook. "You're working here now?"

"Private sector. I go where I'm needed," Harry replied.

"Nice. Just got back fifteen minutes ago from vacation in Malta. Beaches, brewskies, and babes for two weeks."

Harry cleared his throat and not so subtly nodded toward Asher, as if he shouldn't say such things in front of him. Then he gestured to Fitz's shirt with Solaris embroidered on the left breast. "So, you're working here, right?"

"Yeah, there's a few of us now," he said. "From the old squad."

Then the man he was with spoke, his Arabic English stilted. "Oh, two more Aussies came this afternoon also." He held up two fingers. "Fly in here and drove out straight away."

"Really?" Fritz said. "Two more of us? We'll be taking over soon," he joked. Clearly his vacation time had kept him out of the loop. "Didn't catch any names?" he asked his friend.

The man shrugged. "No. Sorry."

It was fine . . . Asher didn't need names. He had a pretty good idea who those two men were. The same two Australian men who had been chasing them for days. Harry met Asher's gaze, ever so briefly, and Asher knew Harry thought the same.

They needed to move. Now.

Asher tapped his watch and, with a very fake French accent, asked, "How long must we wait?"

Bashar and a man in a pilot's uniform appeared with the two mechanics, and Harry side-stepped in front of Asher. In a split second, on instinct, he put himself between Asher and any threat.

Bashar put his hand up. "Apologies. I didn't mean to startle you."

Fitz laughed. "Believe me, that's not something you wanna do to this guy. I've seen him . . ." His words trailed off and his smile faded as he watched what was happening.

One mechanic took the wheel chock out, the other opened the plane door and lowered the step. The pilot climbed in, and Bashar ushered Harry and Asher to the stairs on the plane. "We have just heard," he whispered in French. "The police are on their way. You need to leave."

Fuck.

They were all but pushed onto the plane. The door was closed and the plane moving before they'd even taken their seats. The waiting to take off was excruciating. What was only moments felt like hours. But soon they were hurtling down the runway and Asher only exhaled when the plane lifted off the ground.

Harry sagged with relief.

"Look," Asher said, pointing out his window.

Harry stood up and leaned over him to see. Down below, getting smaller and further way, was a line of blue and red flashing lights on their way to the hangar.

"That was far too close," he mumbled and fell back in his seat.

"And your friend?" Asher asked. "Now *that* was close."

"In a Solaris shirt, for fuck's sake. What are the odds of seeing two ex-military guys here? From my division. They've gotta be working for my handler, right? The same guy who had the professor killed. It's the same company. Solaris is *his* company."

Asher shook his head. "And the two Australian men who flew in today."

"It's gotta be Gibson and Hull. How the hell did they know we were here?"

"I don't know. But I'd bet good money that it's them who turned up with the entire police force."

"Why, though?" Harry asked. "Why not just come back alone and try to shoot us without all the cops around?"

"Public airport," Asher suggested. "They can't open fire in a public airport without it being a whole international incident. If they got caught, not even their government could get them out of that."

"But the police can," Harry finished. "Open fire in an airport."

"Exactly. They'd have known if the police swarmed in on you and me, it'd be a blood bath and we'd be flown out in body bags."

"They'd have completed their mission."

"Yes, but now," Asher added, "they'll know where we're headed, and they won't be far behind us. We'll have to hit the ground running, so we might want to use this flying time to rest, maybe get some sleep."

He doubted Harry would be resting much. The way his jaw was clenched, his eyes narrowed out the window.

Asher sighed and settled into his seat. The plane was older and by no means large inside, but it was still one of the nicest planes Asher had been on. There were just two seats across, one either side of the narrow aisle, but each seat was like a leather recliner and, considering where they'd spent the last few days, it was the most comfortable chair he could remember ever sitting in.

"How does your handler organise all this?" Harry asked.

Asher's eyelids were heavy and he had to blink himself awake. "I told you. He has access to everything. Satellites, computers, people. And an absurd amount of money."

Harry squinted as if he were trying to work out a difficult math equation in his head. "If he has so much money, why do you still work? Why don't you just live in some chateau in France or Italy with a new identity?"

Asher smiled. "Because it's his money. He does his thing. I do mine."

"But you work with him. You're the information on the ground; you do the footwork. He does the cyber shit. You can't tell me he wouldn't buy you a life somewhere to set you up. Look at what he's done for you this week alone."

"He has offered me that many times."

"Why didn't you take it?"

Asher sighed and answered with a shrug. "Because he has his life, and this is what I do. It's what I've done since I was young. Being on the go, the challenge of it all. The thrill of it. It's all I've ever known."

Harry considered this for a few long seconds. "But now? You said before you want a normal life. So what changed?"

Asher studied Harry's face, noting the creases at the corners of his eyes, the few flecks of silver in his blond hair. He was gorgeous, and Asher had to wonder just how beautiful he must have been before he started this life.

"Time," Asher finally replied. "I'm not as fast as I was, and I know it."

"You're plenty fast enough."

Asher found himself smiling at Harry. "My body hurts more now than it did when I was twenty. I used to be able to sleep on the floor, or in a foxhole, or not sleep at all, but now not so much. I know it, and the people who want me dead know it too." He met his gaze. "You have to feel the same."

Harry frowned and conceded a shrug. "Maybe."

"It's tough on the body, worse on the mind," Asher said quietly. "I want to retire on my terms, not on theirs. When I was younger, I never expected to reach the age I am now. I never expected to make twenty or twenty-five, then thirty. Now thirty-five is coming a little too fast, and . . ." He felt a little foolish for saying this, for admitting it to him. "And I want to make forty, or even fifty. I want to know what normal is."

"Would you not get bored with a normal life?"

Asher laughed. "Probably."

Harry was quiet, pensive for a few minutes. "Do you think guys like us will ever be allowed to live a normal life? Do we even deserve it?"

"What we deserve is up to our makers. It's not for us to decide. Anyway, who is responsible for the puppet's behaviour? The puppet or those who work the strings?"

"We're the ones who pull the trigger."

"If we didn't, someone else would. Always. This game we play has been played for thousands of years. Only the field changes, that's all. It's political and dirty." Asher sighed. "And there are rarely any winners."

Harry was quiet after that, though he had his thinking face on. The way his eyebrows furrowed and his eyes focused on something only he could see.

"Can I ask you something?" Asher asked.

Harry glanced his way. "Mm."

"When we were standing at the plane and Bashar and the pilot appeared, you stood in front of me."

"No I didn't."

Asher smiled. "You protected me."

"No I didn't."

"Yes, you did."

"It was part of the cover. In front of Fitz. I told him I was private sector and made it out like I was your security. Nothing else."

"Mm hmm."

"Shut the fuck up. It wasn't anything more."

"I've never had anyone do that for me. Ever."

"Don't go reading into anything. It didn't mean anything."

Asher put his hand to his heart, half joking, half not. "It meant something to me. So you shut the fuck up. I knew you liked me."

Harry glared and huffed out his nose like a bull, though he didn't argue. And were the tips of his ears turning red?

Holy shit.

Was Asher actually right? Harry did like him! Probably equal parts hated him too, but that reaction . . . Harry *liked* him.

Asher couldn't help but smile, despite the odd squeezing of his heart. "For what it's worth, I like you too," Asher admitted. "But I also *don't* like you for a good portion of every day."

"Gee, thanks."

"I happen to like you a whole lot more when you have my dick in your mouth or when your dick is in my ass. That's my favourite."

Harry scoffed. "Do you have any shame?"

"None. I like what I like, and I have no problem in asking for it."

"I've noticed."

Asher glanced back toward the bathroom. "I would be all for joining the mile-high club, but I'm rather tired. And how comfortable are these seats?"

Harry chuckled, but he ran his hand along the arm rest. "They're pretty comfortable." Then he rubbed his stomach. "Bit hungry though. We should have eaten this afternoon."

"Check the supplies," Asher said, nodding to the cabinets behind the cockpit. "They're usually stocked. I doubt it'd be stocked as though we had an attendant to serve us wine and cheese, but there should be something in there."

Harry raised a suspicious eyebrow. "Travel on private jets often?"

"Not for a while."

"With Four?"

God, the way he says that name. He really was jealous. "Not with him. He sends a plane for me."

"Must be nice," Harry mumbled. He got out of his seat and walked to the storage unit, head lowered so he cleared the ceiling. "Oh, hell yes," he said, pulling out a cannister of Pringles. "Can we eat whatever?"

Asher laughed. "I'm sure we can." His eyelids were getting heavy again.

Harry had a few things tucked under his arm. "Oh, for fuck's sake," he grumbled. "You gotta be kidding me."

Asher looked up then, concerned.

Harry held up a packet of Asher's favourite mints. "Did Four request these be stocked just for you?"

Asher laughed at that. "Highly unlikely."

Harry handed them to him as he went back to his seat. "They're not sugar free, so you're welcome."

Smiling, Asher tucked them into his top pocket, reclined his seat, and closed his eyes.

ASHER WOKE up some hours later. The cabin was dark, dimly lit. Harry was asleep, breathing soundly, the cockpit door was slightly ajar. Asher didn't like the fact that they'd been asleep, vulnerable, in the company of a stranger.

It was likely the pilot had only needed to use the bathroom. But still, it made Asher uneasy.

Asher turned the overhead light on, then proceeded to use the bathroom. When he was done, he took a bottle of water and knocked on the cockpit door. The pilot startled, and Asher smiled, offering him the water.

The pilot pulled his headphones off one ear and took the bottle. "Oh, thank you."

He was clearly nervous, and Asher had to wonder if that was because he wasn't used to people approaching the cockpit or if he knew who Asher and Harry were.

"How much longer?" Asher asked with a smile. He wasn't at all familiar with a cockpit, and he wouldn't begin to know if something was or wasn't out of place, but it was still good to see it.

"Should have wheels down in an hour."

"Good. Thank you."

Asher was going to shut the door but thought better of it.

Maybe he wanted to hear any radio conversations. Maybe he should have been listening the whole time. So, leaving the door open, Asher went back to his seat and stared at the back of the pilot's head for a good hour. There was no radio communication in that time, not that Asher heard, but still, Asher had a bad feeling.

It got the better of him, so he took his duffle bag out of the storage compartment and stashed it between his feet.

"Everything okay?" Harry asked, his voice low and sleepy.

Asher doubted the pilot could hear them, but he spoke in a whisper all the same. "Not sure." He unzipped the duffle bag, took out his handgun, and stashed it beside his thigh and the armrest on the seat.

Harry was more awake now. He sat up, scrubbed his hand over his face, keeping his eyes on the cockpit door. "Do I need to sort anyone out?"

"How about we let him land the plane first."

Harry smirked. "Probably a good idea."

"We're about an hour out."

He nodded. "Okay."

"When I woke up, the cockpit door was open," Asher said. "I don't like the idea of anyone being around while we sleep."

"Maybe he needed to piss."

"Which meant he walked by both of us, and we had no idea."

Harry looked back at the cockpit. "I should have stayed awake, sorry."

"Or I should have," Asher said. But the comfortable seats and the vibration of the plane had put him out like a light. It didn't help that he'd hardly slept a wink the last week.

"Okay, so from now on, we sleep in shifts," Harry said. Then he stood up and made his way to the bathroom. "Speaking of needing to piss . . ."

Nice.

Everything aside, Asher liked how they were starting to

think as a team. How long it would last, he had no idea. How long he wanted it to last was another matter altogether.

He liked Harry.

Sure, he was grumpy and his sense of humour could use some work, but he was also thoughtful and protective. And Asher knew, without a doubt, that Harry would have his back if and when it came down to it.

They were so used to being by themselves, this had been a big adjustment for both of them. But there was camaraderie in their solitude. They lived similar lives, shared similar experiences—not many of them pleasant—and they understood each other.

Mostly.

Sometimes they just wanted to punch the living shit out of each other, but that was normal, given the circumstances.

These weren't normal circumstances.

Thinking back to how Harry had protected him outside the plane earlier, Asher had to wonder if he'd do the same. Would he use his own body to protect Harry?

He honestly didn't know.

The side of him that kept himself alive all these years would like to think no, that his own self-preservation was more important. But there was that creeping feeling, that heart-squeezing feeling, that part of Asher was sure he would. His instinct would be to protect Harry, at all costs.

No matter the price.

Somewhere in the last few days—between arguing and laughing, seeing how the man's mind worked, sharing a bed with him, and the incredible sex—he'd grown feelings for Harry. Something akin to a weed had lodged itself in his chest and was beginning to sprout.

Asher had never had feelings for anyone before.

Not ever.

Much to his utter dismay, he liked Harry. He would protect him. He would fight for him.

For the first time in his life, Asher would now consider the thoughts and actions of someone else other than himself.

It was confusing, daunting, frightening.

It actually pissed Asher off.

Harry came back to his seat. "What time did we leave?"

"It was just on 6:00 pm, Algerian time."

"And how long did they say the flight would take?"

"They didn't, but I googled it. Six hours. Why?"

Harry held up his wrist, showing Asher his watch. "It's after one in the morning, Algerian time. We've been flying for seven already. How much fuel does a plane this size have?"

Asher took out his phone and double checked the time. Harry was right. He stood up, tucked his pistol into the back of his jeans, and went to the cockpit door, this time standing a little further in. The pilot looked up at him, startled. Asher wasn't smiling now. "Where are we landing?"

"Uh, an airstrip outside of Jeddah, as instructed."

Saudi Arabia.

Why didn't Asher believe him?

"Why is it taking so long?" Asher asked. The pilot hesitated to answer, so this time Asher asked again in Arabic.

"It's not," he said quickly. "Headwinds, perhaps? We have just enough fuel to get us to Saudi. We're on time."

"Hm."

Asher went back to his seat. "I don't believe him," he said quietly to Harry. "Can you land a plane?"

Harry's eyes went wide. "Uh, no. Why?"

"Because I'd very much like to shoot him."

Harry smirked. "Let him get us on the ground first." But without prompting, he took his other pistol from his backpack and tucked it in the back of his jeans.

The descent was normal. Asher heard the pilot talking about landing, which he assumed was all good and well. They had to speak to ground control, right?

The landing was fine. Bumpy, but fine. Outside was pitch black. It was the middle of the night in Saudi Arabia, after all. Asher could see faint runway lights, along with two sets of headlights, which he hoped was friendly. They would need a car, after all. The plane came to a slow stop, the lights in the cabin came on, and the pilot rushed out. He opened the door, lowered the steps, then, stepping out of their way, he gestured for them to disembark.

Asher wasn't stupid. He looked to the pilot. "You first."

The pilot nodded quickly, nervously, but began down the steps. Asher didn't know if the man's natural state of being was anxious, but he wasn't taking the risk.

Harry went next, Asher close behind. There were four men waiting for them, and by the time Asher took the last step down, each had guns drawn and pointed at them.

"You've gotta be fucking kidding me," Harry said.

It was very dark, so it was hard to tell, but they appeared to be holding Uzis.

Uzis?

Then one of them spoke to the other, smiling. It was an Arabic dialect Asher wasn't overly familiar with.

Where the hell are we?

"Put your bags down slowly," one man said in stilted English.

These men were not organised. They were excited and nervous. Hardly professionals. But there was an air of desperation that Asher wasn't about to write off. He threw his duffle bag down with a sigh and Harry let his backpack drop near his feet.

"They haven't killed us yet," Asher said to Harry. "So they must want us alive. Let me guess." Asher stared at the man who had spoken. "You think Interpol will pay?"

"Double fee," he said with a smile that showed off his missing teeth. "My brother is paid for flying you out of Algeria. We will be paid for handing you over. If not Interpol, someone will pay."

"Brother," Asher mumbled, staring at the pilot. He took a step to hide behind his brother.

"Oh, someone will pay all right," Harry said. Then, in the blink of an eye, he took his gun from the back of his jeans and shot all four men in the head. They fell down like crumpled dolls, and the pilot fell back onto his ass, scrambling backwards in shock and fear.

"Those were some beautiful shots," Asher said to Harry. And they were. Four rounds, four headshots, in less than two seconds. "I'm impressed."

Harry smiled at him. "Thanks." Then he turned to the pilot, who was still scrambling backwards, all legs and arms, going nowhere fast. "You!"

The pilot shook his head, frantic, pale. "No, no. My brother," he cried, looking at the man on the ground with a bullet hole above his left eye. "Nooo."

"You called him," Asher deduced calmly. "While we were asleep. You told him who we are, that we could be worth something. Whoever owns this plane is going to be so pissed."

He shook his head *no*, mouthed the word a few times, but no sound came out. Tears streamed down his face.

Harry sighed. "Yeah, fuck you too," he said, then shot the pilot square between the eyes.

"Goddammit, Harry," Asher said.

"He sold us out!"

"I was going to ask him where we are."

"Oh." He looked around. "Are we not in Saudi Arabia?"

Asher shook his head. "Don't think so. I couldn't make out the dialect." He took one of the Uzis from the closest dead man. "These are twenty years old. Corroded, haven't seen a decent oil in years, probably doesn't even fire."

"They were amateurs," Harry said.

Asher dropped the gun near the dead man and picked up his bag. "We need to leave. Now."

Harry grabbed his bag and hurried alongside Asher to the cars waiting by the landing strip. They were older style Toyota Cruisers. One didn't look any better than the other but only one had keys in the ignition.

"You drive," Asher said, putting his duffle bag on the floor in the back.

Harry reversed the car, headlights on. There was no sealed

road, just a sandy path through the desert. Their only guide was tyre tracks.

Asher had his phone out, and he called Four's number. He picked up on the second ring. "Asher, my darling. How was your flight?"

"Change of plans," Asher said quickly. "I need a location check. Can you track me?"

Four's tone changed immediately, suddenly very serious, and there was a faint clicking of fingers on a keyboard. "What the hell happened?"

"Pilot sold us out."

"Fuck!" More keyboard clicking. "I'm zeroing in on your location . . . Oh Jesus . . ."

"What?"

"Tell me you're driving, that you have a vehicle of some kind."

"Yes. Harry's driving. But I don't know where we are. It was Arabic, but the dialect was not familiar to me. Their guns were old. There isn't exactly a road—"

"You need to drive east. Right now. And as fast as you can."

"Bit hard to know where east is when it's pitch black," Asher replied.

"Okay, okay," Four said, fingers tapping on the keyboard. "Hang on, I can see you're moving. You're going in the right direction. Keep driving. Don't stop for anything. You've got about twenty miles to go."

This didn't sound good. Asher rarely heard him speak with such urgency. He looked at Harry. "Twenty miles until what?"

"Till you cross the border into Oman."

Asher baulked. "Oman?!"

"I hope you shot that fucking pilot," Four said. "He flew you into Yemen, Asher. He dropped you off in a war zone."

THIRTEEN

"THERE ARE ONLY two border crossings into Oman,"
Four explained. "But you're not near either of them. You're
too far north. You're in the freaking Empty Quarter, Asher."

The Empty Quarter. Great.

"We're on some kind of road," Asher said. "Except it's not
a road. It's sand. I think we're in an old ravine; there are walls
either side of us. They could be big fucking dunes. I can't tell.
We're in the middle of the fucking desert. And it's pitch
black."

"Keep driving. Do not stop. I don't know if you'll come to
a fence of some kind or if it will be manned. But if you have
headlights on, they'll know you're coming."

Fuck.

"You couldn't be in a worse part of a worse country," Four
murmured, panicked, urgent. "There are roadblocks, checkpoints, that are not military. That entire region is run by
rebels. And they will not mess around, Asher. You need to get
across that border."

"Yeah, thanks."

"How much cash do you have?"

Asher looked to Harry. "How much cash do we have?"

"About 50K. Give or take. Mostly euros and American
dollars." He was glaring out the windscreen, into the dark,

his knuckles white on the steering wheel, concentrating. "We gonna buy our way through?"

Asher shrugged. He tucked the phone between his ear and shoulder so he could use his hands and he emptied Harry's backpack. He stuffed everything under his seat; bundles of cash, his toiletry bag, passports, and Harry's other pistol, ammunition. "Maybe. Better than shooting. It's not an official crossing point. I don't know if there'll even be a point of entry. Or if there'll be one guard or a whole rebel squadron."

Asher could hear Four typing away frantically. "I'm seeing what I can find out," he mumbled. "Okay, I can't see any kind of road on the Yemen side, but there's an unsealed road on the Oman side of the border. You're heading toward it. I can't see any kind of compound or fence. Satellite imagery of Yemen is non-existent."

Harry glanced up to the rear-view mirror. "Ah, fuck. We got company on our six. Coming fast. One set of headlights. Looks high, a four-wheel drive, maybe."

"I have to go," Asher said into the phone.

"You better call me back in ten minutes, Asher Garin, or so help me God."

Asher disconnected the call and turned in his seat. He reached through to the back and unzipped his duffle bag and pulled out his MP7. "Hello, pretty baby," he said.

"Christ," Harry mumbled. "You always talk to your guns like that?" He was driving fast, but the vehicle behind them was coming faster. Then he saw what kind of gun Asher had. "What the fuck is that?"

"Just you worry about driving and not running us off some embankment." He clipped in the mag and loaded one round into the chamber. Then he rolled down his window, hung backwards out it, bracing himself against the door frame with his foot on the backrest of his seat.

Asher saw the muzzle flash behind them before he heard the thud and metal ting of a bullet hitting their car. And then another. Harry ducked instinctively. "Asher," he yelled. "Jesus. Get in the fucking car."

Asher lined up the sight. The cool press of metal against his skin was always a familiar comfort. Even when he was perched backwards out of a moving car being shot at. He fired three rounds. "Tyre. Tyre. Engine block."

The vehicle behind them veered off the road into a sand-bank and an abrupt stop.

Asher righted himself back into his seat, grinning at Harry. He was buzzing! "That was fun!"

Harry shook his head. "You're insane." But after a few seconds, a smile won out. "That was some pretty good shooting."

"Not as good as your four clean headshots," Asher allowed.

"It was five. And you took out a car."

"Because it was a bigger target," Asher said. "Moving at eighty kilometres an hour, in the desert, at night. While hanging out of the window. Backwards. And if I shot the shooter or the driver, they could still keep coming. Take out the car, they're not going anywhere for a while. So, you're welcome."

Harry rolled his eyes. "Might wanna put your *pretty baby* away. There's something up ahead." He squinted out the windshield, slowing the car down.

"More reason to keep it out."

What Harry had seen up ahead turned out to be one burned-out truck on its side, then another and another, placed in such a way any vehicle wishing to pass had to slow right down to zigzag through.

From fifty kilometres an hour down to five.

They were sitting ducks.

Three shadowy figures stepped out from the dark, heavily armed with AK-47s and grim faces blocking their path through the weave of burned-out vehicles. These guys weren't amateurs like the fools back at the plane.

"Let me do the talking," Asher murmured. "And don't fire unless they do. To my left at ten o'clock there's secondary men on the ridge with launchers or some shit. I saw a flash of metal."

Harry's face was neutral, blank. Asher wasn't sure if it was his game face or if he was scared.

He was going with the latter.

One of the men stood by Harry's window, his gun pointed at Harry's head. Harry kept both hands on the wheel. Another stood in front of the car, rifle aimed at them. The third went to Asher's side.

Asher put one hand up and wound the window down with the other. He spoke Arabic, hoping these men did too. "My name is Michael. I'm a fixer guide for this man. He—"

The man opened Asher's door. "Get out."

Asher got out slowly, hands up. "I am a fixer, a guide, for this man. He is Australian. We need to get to Oman so he can fly home. I have a bag with his papers on my seat."

The man standing in the front of their car now pointed his rifle at Asher while the man closest to Asher went to the seat. He took the backpack and walked to the front of the hood so he could look inside it.

The other two men never took their eyes, or their guns, off Harry and Asher. Not for one second.

The man opened the bag, looked inside, then glanced over at Asher. He'd no doubt seen the four remaining bundles of cash, Asher assumed. Then he took out the passport and looked over it, though it may as well have been a scrap of garbage for all the interest he showed.

"It's all he has," Asher said quietly.

The man stared at him for a long few seconds. For too long. Asher was sure this was it. This was where it all ended. And for some stupid heart-stopping second, he regretted bringing Harry into this.

They weren't supposed to die like this.

Asher didn't breathe. Time didn't exist. All that remained was regret.

Then the man took the passport and held it out for Asher to take. That was all he offered. He kept the backpack and took a few steps backward. The other men stepped back as well.

Holy fucking shit.

Not a word was said, but Asher understood. He nodded, almost bowing his head, and couldn't get in the car fast enough. "Drive," he whispered. "Drive!"

Harry drove slowly and accelerated faster as they cleared the last burned-out truck. And he kept driving. Neither of them spoke—neither of them even freaking breathed—until they'd gone a few kilometres. Asher waited for gunfire or the rocket launcher . . . but it never came.

The valley with ridge lines, or dunes, or whatever the fuck they were in flattened out, from what Asher could see. The road became more of an actual road, and Asher let out an unsteady breath. "Fuck. You okay?"

Harry nodded. "You?"

Asher nodded in return. "Yeah. I've been through all kinds of tense situations, but that's in my top five, for sure."

"I'm thinking it's number one for me," Harry said.

Asher laughed out of relief. "I thought we were dead for sure." He decided not to tell Harry that he'd thought of him in that moment . . . It was something Asher would have to unpack later, if at all.

"What was in the backpack?"

"About forty thousand."

"No wonder he took it and asked no more questions."

Asher nodded, his heart now back to its normal rate. He took out his phone and called Four. "It's me—"

"Tell me you're okay?"

"We're okay."

He let rip in his native tongue, a whole rant that Asher didn't quite catch. He got the gist though. Four was relieved but pissed off about the pilot and helpless that he couldn't do more.

"I said we're fine," Asher said again. "Forty thousand dollars lighter, but alive. And we still have our guns, so there's that. May need a change of underwear though."

He half laughed, half sighed. "Thank God you're okay."

"Whatever we were going to Saudi Arabia for will have to wait."

"Don't worry about that. Do you still have the USB?"

"Yes." Asher could feel it in his sock. "Can you still see our location?"

"Yes. You're in Oman. In about fifty kilometres, you'll come to an intersection. Turn left. There will be a town on your right. Get fuel if you have to, but I want you to keep moving. Get to Muscat and I'll arrange transport from there. You should be safe in Oman . . . well, safer. They *do* have an extradition treaty with Gibraltar, but it's not likely to be enforced; they don't exactly have much faith in Interpol. Just try not to break any Omani laws and you should be okay. You still may need to lie low for a few days because I don't know who I know in Oman. Let me see what I can arrange."

"Thank you."

Four was quiet for a long moment. "I'm glad you're okay."

Asher smiled, but then he remembered . . . "Oh. When we left the airport in Algeria, our two Australian tracker friends were on our tail. Just minutes behind us."

"Christ."

"Find out where they are now."

"I will. You be safe."

"Talk soon."

Asher ended the call, took out his sugar-free mints, and popped one in his mouth. He handed one to Harry, who took it without a snide or sarcastic comment. "Thanks."

And they drove for what felt like hours, until the sun was up and neither of them could keep their eyes open. They made it to Muscat, not a huge city, but large enough to afford them some anonymity, and Asher found them a motel.

This one was nicer than any of the other motels they'd stayed in. Well, there were no stains on the floor, which was nice. The shadier places tended to not have cameras or ask questions or demand ID, and they appreciated the cash payment, just like Asher appreciated the bed and the hot shower. There was even a TV.

He dumped his duffle bag at the foot of the bed and sighed, scrubbing his hand over his face. "I'm too tired to argue about the bed. It's a double. We'll both fit. If you lie on your side, maybe."

Harry took Asher's arm and turned him around. He had an odd expression, much like the scared look he'd worn when they faced the rebels. Then he slid his other hand up to Asher's jaw, his gaze a penetrating blue.

"What are you doing?" Asher whispered.

Harry's hand at Asher's jaw tilted his face upwards, and he held him there. Harry moved in, leaned closer . . .

Asher realised, far too late, that Harry was about to kiss him. His heart was hammering and he thought he might pass out, or puke, or die. "Harry," he whispered. He was so close, their noses almost touching. Asher's blood was electric, he felt warm all over, and his head was spinning.

Then Harry closed the final inch and kissed him.

"WHAT DO you mean they never landed in Saudi Arabia?" Parrish barked down the phone. "Where the fuck did they go?"

"We're waiting on the flight logs," Gibson said. "The plane they were in can only get so far without a refuel—seven hours, maybe."

"Hm."

"Oh, and get this. Brett Fitzgerald spoke to Harrigan when they were waiting on the pilot. Had no idea he was wanted by the cops. Just got back from two weeks' vacation and had no idea about anything, apparently. Said Harrigan told him he was in the private sector nowadays and was with a French guy. We showed Fitz the photo of Asher Garin and he said it was him. Without a doubt."

"Christ."

"We were a few minutes behind them. So freaking close. Now we've lost all that time. They're hours ahead of us again. If we hadn't gone for the cops to make it all look legit, we would have had them for sure. Now we don't even know where they are."

Parrish huffed out a sigh. "They were heading to Saudi, for Chrissake. From Algeria to Saudi Arabia. Like they're looking for information. Information I don't want them to find."

"What do you want us to do?"

"Find out what the hell they were doing in and around those oil fields. Who they spoke to, what they found. And if they left on a private jet, find out who the hell paid for that."

"Yes, sir."

"And next time, don't wait. To hell with making it look legit. When you get close again, you do whatever it is you have to do to take Harrigan down."

"Yes, sir."

"Whatever it takes."

"Understood."

FOURTEEN

HARRY HADN'T ACTUALLY PLANNED to kiss Asher. Sure, he'd thought about it. A lot. But he never set out to actually kiss him. Asher wasn't the kissing kind. He liked sex rough and hard . . .

But Harry needed . . . something. He needed human touch, gentle and reassuring, safe and all man.

As soon as they were inside their motel room, Harry was flooded with relief. As if stepping inside the small room and locking the door, they'd closed off the outside world, the stress, the fear.

Harry was exhausted from carrying the weight of it all, and now he felt bare without it.

He needed something.

He needed Asher.

Harry could count on one hand the times he truly thought he was about to die, and today had been one of them. In all the other situations, Harry had had some level of control, be it a gun in his hand, room to overpower his opponent, even just the fact he was bigger, better.

But in that valley with those rebels, he was outgunned, unarmed, and vulnerable. He was completely at their mercy and utterly disposable. No one would even look for him, let alone miss him.

Is that what his victims felt in their final moments?

Harry didn't want to think about it.

He needed to feel alive. He needed to feel wanted. He wanted to feel good, he wanted pleasure, both given and taken.

He really just needed a moment of something nice.

So he pulled Asher close, surprising him. He cupped Asher's jaw. The feel of stubble sent a shiver through him. Asher was stunned, his eyes widening, his lips parting. "What are you doing?"

If Harry spoke, he'd lose his nerve.

He waited for Asher to pull away, to rebuke him, push him off and scoff at him for being weird. But he didn't. Instead, he whispered Harry's name.

So Harry kissed him. Lips soft and warm, with a gentleness that made Harry's heart feel two sizes too big. Stubble against his palm that made Harry's spine tingle.

Until Asher shot back, anger and confusion on his face, breathing hard. Harry expected Asher to shove him then, or mock him, or even punch him for attempting such an intimate thing as kissing.

Asher shook his head and tried to say something, but there were no words. The look on his face said enough.

This is not what we are.

This is not what this is.

Harry wanted to apologise, the excitement in his belly souring with the sting of rejection. But then Asher's eyes went to Harry's mouth and he sucked back a breath, his hands went to Harry's face, pulling him in and crushing his mouth to his.

Not exactly gentle. Desperate. Wanting and needing this as much as Harry wanted, needed. But Harry didn't want this to be another rough and rushed fuck. He wanted to revel in the feel of it.

So Harry slowed the kiss, tilted Asher's face up a little more, pulled him flush against him, and kissed him again. Slower this time with open lips, wanting and inviting. He tilted his head, kissing him a little deeper, and after a second, as if he were dazed, Asher responded.

His eyelids slowly closed as if he felt what Harry felt. Open mouths, warm tongues, and hands exploring, pulling each other closer, holding on tight. Harry deepened the kiss and Asher let him, gave in, surrendered.

Harry walked him backwards to the bed, holding the back of his head as he laid him down, never breaking eye contact. He kissed him again, teasing him with his tongue, sucking on his bottom lip, staring into his beautiful hazel eyes. "I'm gonna fuck you slow," Harry murmured.

Asher's breath caught, his eyes wide, imploring. Honest and vulnerable.

Harry slid his hand along Asher's jaw. "Yes?"

He nodded quickly. "Yes, yes. Please."

Harry kissed him, grunting as he pressed his bodyweight onto Asher's, feeling his arousal, hot and hard. It ignited the desire already smouldering in Harry's belly.

He wanted nothing more than to be inside Asher, buried to the hilt. He just wished they had lube. He didn't want to hurt Asher. Not this time.

Not anymore.

Then he realised something . . . they might not have had lube. But they had the next best thing.

Harry pulled back to rest on his knees between Asher's legs, and he picked up one of Asher's feet. "I need your boots off." He began undoing the laces, and Asher made short work of his other boot, and when they were done he rid Asher of his jeans and briefs as well, and finally his shirt.

Asher was completely naked before him. He was thin but strong, lithe and perfect. He had dark chest hair and a happy trail, which Harry found insanely attractive. His uncut cock lay thick and heavy across his hip.

"Holy fuck," Harry whispered.

"See something you like?"

"All of it. All of you."

Smiling, Asher took his dick in his hand and gave himself a few languid strokes. "Take off your shirt."

Harry did as he was told, tossing it onto the floor. Then he popped the button on his jeans. Asher's dark eyes trailed down to Harry's crotch and he licked his lips.

Harry couldn't help it. He needed to taste his kiss again, and he wanted Asher's tongue in his mouth. He leaned over and claimed his mouth in a bruising kiss and sucked on Asher's tongue.

Asher groaned and let himself be kissed like that, the hand on his cock forgotten. So Harry took over. "I need you to come first," Harry said. "So I can use your come as lube."

Asher's cock twitched in Harry's hand and Asher moaned. "Oh fuck."

He really likes that.

He likes the filthy talk.

Harry kissed down Asher's jaw to his ear, where he sucked on the lobe and grunted, low and raspy. "I'm gonna fuck your own come back inside you," Harry murmured. "Then I'll fill you with mine."

Asher's cock swelled and surged, his back arched, and he came in spurts onto his belly.

Not giving him a moment to recover, Harry lifted Asher's legs up to rest on his chest. Harry pulled his cock out, ready, swiped up Asher's release, and spread it across Asher's hole, pushing his finger inside him.

Asher cried out and tried to pull away, still sensitive from his orgasm. But Harry held him steady and kept stretching him, adding spit and smearing his own precome as well.

Asher was mumbling incoherently and tweaking his own nipples when Harry couldn't wait another second. He positioned himself, leaned forward on Asher's legs, folding him in half, and sunk his cock inside him.

Asher's eyes went wide before they rolled back in his head, his mouth open, as Harry pushed all the way in. He wanted to take this slow, he wanted to feel this connection with Asher, to share something good, but Harry wasn't sure how long he'd last.

Asher was tight and welcoming, taking every inch Harry could give him. When he was buried to the hilt, he rocked forward so he could kiss Asher again, filling him at both ends.

Asher groaned, sounds of pleasure Harry had never heard from him before. He thrust slow, rocking, gliding in and out, in and out. His cock, his tongue.

It felt so good.

Every cell in his body was a live wire, every synapse was firing, urging him to go faster, deeper. But he held steady. He'd said he'd fuck him slow and that was what he was going to do.

But then Asher's hands dragged down Harry's back, holding, gripping, rocking his hips, trying to increase the pace. "Slow," Harry whispered.

Asher's lips were wet, red and kiss-swollen, his gaze locked on Harry's. "I need . . . I need . . . please." Then his fingers dug into Harry sides, his back, desperate for purchase.

So desperate.

Harry took both Asher's wrists and pinned them to the mattress above his head, causing him to thrust a little harder, changing the angle.

Asher gasped, a look of surprised pleasure on his face, and he whined as Harry pushed Asher's hips upward and he drove deeper into him. And that was it. Any hope of trying to go slowly, to drag this out, was over.

The pleasure was too much. It felt too damn good, and Harry's orgasm barrelled into him like a tidal wave. He thrust in deep, one last time—his cock was so impossibly hard—and he came.

Asher moaned. "Oh God, yes." And when Harry collapsed on top of him, still inside him, Asher wrapped his arms around him and kissed Harry's neck, his shoulder. He even rolled his hips, clearly trying to coax more movement out of Harry, and when Harry began to pull out, Asher wrapped his legs around him. "Stay inside me."

Harry never wanted to leave.

Then Asher ran his hand down to Harry's ass, giving it a good squeeze, until he reached down further and touched fabric. "You're still wearing jeans?"

"And boots." Harry's chuckle became a groan as his senses came back to him. He kissed Asher's neck, his jaw, his mouth. They kissed, slow and languid. There was no urgency now. Just tenderness and emotions Harry wasn't ready to name.

When he slipped out of him, he rolled them onto their sides, still holding Asher in his arms. Asher nestled his head on Harry's arm, burrowing into his chest, and he inhaled. "God, we need to shower."

Harry laughed, rubbing circles on Asher's back. "Or we could sleep first."

Asher hummed contentedly. "I don't want to inflate your ego, and I fear that this will, but that was maybe the best sex I've ever had."

Harry tightened his hold on him, preening at the compliment. "Consider my ego inflated."

"All credit should go to your dick, not you."

Harry snorted. "Consider my ego deflated."

He sighed out a contented sound, his words mumbled. "I'm tired."

Harry hadn't opened his eyes yet. "Same. We could just rest a while."

"Thought we were going to take it in shifts to sleep," he mumbled.

"I'll keep one eye open," Harry lied. Both eyes were very much shut. But he had Asher in his arms, they were safe—for the moment, at least. They had shared something just now, an intimacy Harry had never felt before. It was more than just human touch, or physical release.

It was something else. Something that made his heart thump, something that began to bloom under his ribs and settle in his bones.

Harry wasn't giving this up for anyone.

HARRY HADN'T MEANT to fall asleep. He figured maybe he'd doze a little, but both he and Asher slept like the dead for hours. It was his stomach that woke him up.

And the body heat of another man who happened to be plastered to him. Asher was still pressed in tight, his arm heavy across Harry's ribs, and he was sound asleep.

His dark lashes, his closed eyelids, his high cheekbones, parted lips.

Asher was so attractive when he slept. Well, he was attractive when he was awake too, unless he was driving Harry crazy. But asleep? He was peaceful and so beautiful.

He was also completely naked.

Harry could have lain there and watched him forever, but that wasn't a luxury they had.

He peeled his arm out from under Asher's head. He fussed and mumbled his grievance, but Harry needed to get up.

"What are you doing?" Asher mumbled, his eyes barely open but a decent scowl of disapproval on his face.

"I need a piss, and I need food." He began unlacing his boots. "And a shower."

"Hmm." Asher scrubbed a hand over his face. "When you go into the bathroom, tell me if the shower is big enough for two."

Harry smiled, looking over his shoulder to get a full-body look at a very naked Asher. *Christ, he was so perfect.* "Don't tempt me."

Asher chuckled and rolled onto his side, pulling a pillow under his head, and he wiggled his ass. "Well, I'm still very well lubricated, considering I have my come *and* yours in me."

Harry cringed. "God, do you have to say it like that?"

Asher opened his eyes to stare at Harry. "Need I remind you of what you said to me when you were fucking me?"

Harry pulled his boot off. "No, thanks. I'm fine. And that's different. That's in the heat of the moment, not in conversation."

Asher laughed. "I cannot believe you are a prude. Harry Harrigan is a blushing prude."

"No I'm not. I just don't—"

"You have a filthy mouth when you say it to me but then get all embarrassed when I say it back to you." He sighed with a smile. "It's actually kinda cute."

Oh, for fuck's sake.

Harry started on his other boot, a bit gentler with his still sore ankle. "We need food, and we need a plan. We need to figure out how long we're here for, and where we go next?"

"Our plan," he said, "is to wait for Four to let us know how and when we're leaving. He said it could be a few days. So we sit tight. Maybe find a store for some new clothes and a laundromat."

Harry slowly pulled his boot off, then his socks. He stood up and walked to the bathroom. "Food first. I'm starving."

"No, first you need to tell me if the shower is big enough for two. Or am I staying right here?" Then he shivered. "Actually, too bad if it's small. I'm cold now you're not here."

Asher followed Harry into the bathroom. The shower wasn't exactly big enough for both of them, but that didn't stop them.

AS THEY WALKED DOWN to the esplanade where they'd found a grocery store, Harry didn't know what to expect from Muscat. He'd never thought about the place before now, certainly never been there, but what he didn't expect was an azure-coloured bay, palm trees, wide streets, and a whole tourist destination.

Again, he found himself looking at the architecture, at the white buildings that reflected the heat, the tiles, the marble, the pointed arches. Arabian and Portuguese influence, and a few thousand years of history.

Then he realised what he was doing, and he grumbled. "For fuck's sake."

"What's the matter?" Asher looked around, taking in their surroundings with laser focus.

"No, nothing like that." Harry shook his head. He actually felt safe here. The sun, the warm ocean breeze. Then he realised that he just noticed *that*, then got even more annoyed at himself. "You know what? I blame you. I just noticed the architecture. Appreciated it, even. And the breeze. And the azure water. I'm not even fucking kidding. *Azure*. In my head, I called it azure. I have never said that word in my life."

Asher laughed. "And this is my fault?"

"One hundred percent." Harry bit into his apple and spoke around his mouthful. "You made me look at the architecture in Algiers. Now it's something I notice."

Asher was clearly delighted by this. "Then you're welcome. Which do you prefer?"

"They're both different. You can't compare them. Each has its own history."

"Oh, and now you're an expert on history."

"Shut the fuck up. You started this."

Asher laughed again, and they continued their walk back to the motel, bickering and laughing the whole way.

Harry had forgotten what it was like to have actual conversations with people. He'd forgotten what it was like to enjoy someone's company. He'd spent the last ten years of his life alone, either keeping his head down or looking over his shoulder for so long, he'd forgotten what it was like to look up.

He'd scoffed at Asher's admission that he wanted a 'normal life' and now Harry was thinking maybe, just maybe, he might like that too.

However unlikely it was. Hell, it was unlikely they'd even survive the mess they were in, let alone have any chance at normalcy afterwards.

And then it occurred to Harry that he'd just included Asher in his plans for *afterwards*.

Would Asher even be in his life after all this shit? Or would he just walk away? Would they go their separate ways? Should they?

Probably.

"Uh-oh," Asher said, as he put the bag of groceries on the table in their room. "You've got your thinking face on."

"The fuck is my thinking face?"

"The face you make when you're thinking about bad things or something you don't like."

"I do not make a face."

"You absolutely do."

He groaned. "Whatever."

"What were you thinking about?"

"Nothing."

"My God, you cannot lie. For someone in our line of work, that's a skill you should have mastered by now."

"I can lie just fine." Then Harry reconsidered. "Just not to you, apparently. Which, again, is your fucking fault."

Grinning, Asher threw a breakfast bar to Harry. "Aww, that's so sweet."

"Can you lie to me?" As soon as he'd asked that question, Harry regretted it. "You know what? Don't answer that. I don't want to know."

Asher sat on the bed, leaning his back against the headboard, his legs outstretched, crossed at the ankles. He studied Harry for a long few moments, apparently amused. He bit into his breakfast bar. "I probably could. But I haven't."

"Well, that's a lie, so yes you can."

He shook his head. "Okay, so maybe in the beginning. When I didn't give a fuck if you lived or died. Back then, I could have. Sure. But not anymore."

"Since when?" Harry asked. "What changed?"

Asher shrugged and chewed thoughtfully, and he took so long to answer, Harry was beginning to think he wouldn't. "Morocco. About day four."

Morocco?

"What happened on day four?"

"Nothing. I don't know. You'd hurt your ankle, even though you pretended you hadn't, and you were grumpy. Always grumbling about something. But I knew you were really a nice guy under the scowl and the glare. And all the scars."

"Nice guy?"

"Yep." He shrugged. "And I saw the size of your dick. That sealed the deal."

Harry rolled his eyes and sighed. He wasn't going to dignify that with a response, but in the end, it got the better of him. "You think I'm nice?"

Asher nodded. "I do." He ate more of his breakfast bar, and then he added, "You're nice to me. You've even been a little protective of me, once or twice, and no one's ever done that for me before."

Harry stared at him, unsure of how to take that.

Asher was being honest with him now. He was looking at his legs, picking at a thread at his knee, a slight blush on his cheek. There was no faking that.

"And you found more of my favourite mints," Asher said, looking at him now. "Sugar free, but still. It's the thought that counts."

Harry couldn't help but smile, but his mind went back to his original thoughts. "What's the plan, Asher?"

"I told you. We need to dump the car. We can drive to a shopping mall and leave the car in the parking lot. We need to buy new clothes. Shirts, at least. People might notice us too much if we look like hitmen on the run."

"No, I mean, after all this ends. However it ends, if it ever ends. If we don't die, that is," Harry said, his voice low. "Where do we go? Where *can* we go? Or where are you going, I should probably ask. I don't mean to assume we're going anywhere together. I just hate not knowing . . ." He felt so foolish. "I'm used to having a clear-cut plan. Sorry."

Asher studied him again, an unreadable look on his face. "Are you saying you want us to stick together? When all this is over?" He smiled. "If we don't die, that is."

Harry wanted to tell him to shut the fuck up, but he'd already said enough.

The silence dragged on, and it was Asher who broke it. "I don't know, Harry, where we'll end up. I don't even know if we'll see tomorrow. I've already told you I want a shot at a normal life. I don't even know what that is, let alone where I could have one. I don't have a home, Harry. I don't have ties to anywhere. I was moved around from the age of five or six, never settling in any one place. Deliberately, so I wouldn't have loyalty to any flag or soil." He shook his head. "Where *can* I go?"

Harry met his gaze, unable to look away. "Sorry." He felt like shit for bringing it up. "Would you maybe go live with your darling number Four?"

He'd meant it as a joke, to lighten the mood, and at least Asher wasn't frowning anymore. "Oh my god, you're so jealous."

Harry didn't reply, just rolled his eyes and tried not to smile.

THEY DID GO SHOPPING LATER, though it was easier to find new clothes to fit Asher than it was Harry. They left their stolen car in the parking lot, keys in the ignition, so some car thief could get rid of it for them.

They even grabbed themselves some lunch. Harry wasn't stupid or naïve enough to think he was safe there. He was still wary of his surroundings, the people, the eyes that followed them, watching the shadows, knowing where the exits were at all times.

But Harry liked Muscat.

Okay, so maybe not the city itself, he realised. But being with Asher, free to shop and eat. They were outside the shopping mall, surrounded by civilians enjoying lunch in the shade. The sky was blue, birds flew overhead.

A normal life.

Asher finished his *shuwa* wrap, casually wiped his hands with a serviette while he chewed and swallowed. "I think we've been made," he said quietly. "On your seven o'clock. Don't turn around."

Reality hit Harry like a sledgehammer, though he was outwardly calm. He took a sip of water. "How many?"

"Just one that I can see. He's in the alley. I don't think he knows I've spotted him. Did you bring your gun?"

"Nope. You?"

Asher shook his head. "No."

"I'll take care of him," Harry said. "Stay here."

Asher grabbed his arm. "Wait. A car pulled up."

Harry turned then, to see a man getting into a black sedan. He was hurried, his gaze locking with Harry's before he climbed in, and the car sped away.

"Yep," Harry said. "We've been made."

"We need to leave," Asher said. They slipped into a crowd of people getting on a bus, climbed aboard, and took their seats. People filed on after them, and the waiting made Harry nervous.

"Why did he leave?" Harry wondered out loud. "He could have followed us."

"Would you approach us? If you knew who we are. You and me, together?" Asher shook his head. "I certainly wouldn't."

Harry grunted, because Asher was probably right.

Harry might be able to walk into an alley to face an unknown number of enemies, not knowing if they were armed or not—and he would have done exactly that two minutes ago—but not many people had the skills to back themselves.

"If he's in the game," Asher added quietly. "Then we can assume our location is no longer a secret."

Harry nodded. Fuck.

So much for a normal life.

Asher nudged him with his elbow. "Stop scowling. You're scaring the baby."

Harry hadn't even noticed the toddler peering at them from over his mother's shoulder in front of them. And while Harry was pissed enough to see the whole world burn, there was Asher, pulling funny faces in attempts to elicit a gummy smile from a baby in return.

FIFTEEN

HARRY WAS STILL PISSED off when they got back to their motel room. They had to walk a distance from the bus stop, which didn't help, taking back alleys and side streets.

As they got to their door, a woman two rooms up was just leaving. She had a small child, maybe two or three years old, clinging to her leg. Harry tried to smile at the kid, not wanting to scare them, but it only seemed to make things worse. The kid began to cry and the mother picked them up, but they stared in the way kids do, so Harry tried waving.

"The fuck are you doing?" Asher whispered, unlocking the door.

"Trying not to scare the kid." He went in and threw the bag of clothes on the bed.

"Christ. You'll give her nightmares."

"How come you can do it?"

"Because I'm not an angry man-mountain."

Harry growled at him. "Fuck you." He wasn't in the mood for stupid jokes now. They'd been spotted; their location was compromised and there would no doubt be a swarm of contract hitmen heading to Muscat this very second. "We need to leave."

"And go where?"

"Anywhere. We should have kept the car."

Asher stared with disbelief. "It was stolen. From four Yemeni wannabe extortionists that you shot dead. And then we crossed the border illegally. Remember?"

Harry glared at him. "So we just stay here? And wait?"

"Yes." Asher shook his head and took his phone out, thumbed into the contacts, and hit Call. Harry assumed he was calling Four. His precious fucking Four. "Please tell me you have something? We're going to be having some uninvited guests arriving soon. ... No, we were spotted less than an hour ago. We're back in our room but Harry's nervous . . ."

"I'm not nervous," Harry interjected. "We're sitting fucking ducks."

Asher stared at him. "Sitting fucking ducks. What does that even mean. Who is fucking ducks? What kind of fucked-up person does that?"

Harry sighed and stormed into the bathroom, slamming the door behind him. He needed to calm down . . .

Actually, he needed to do a lot of things, and the first was emotionally removing himself from this entire situation.

He was an idiot for allowing himself to feel anything for Asher. It served only to compromise him and put himself in danger. He'd survived the last decade just fine without him. Without anyone. And he was now, what? Wishing to have a 'normal life' with Asher? Playing house, watching TV, cooking dinners, being lovers . . .

Boyfriends?

For fuck's sake.

Harry had gone and lost his damn mind.

He opened the door, probably a little too forcefully, making Asher glance his way. He was still talking on the phone, but he eyed Harry from head to foot. "Okay," he said into the phone. "Tomorrow night. Got it. ... Oh, don't worry. I'm sure I can think of something we can do without leaving this motel room until then. Talk soon."

He clicked off the call and smirked at Harry. "You know, I do love it when you're angry. It turns me on."

"Don't start."

He smiled, his tongue wetting the corner of his mouth. "And we did buy lube this morning." He ran his hand down to cup his balls. "Even though I prefer it when you use mine."

Christ.

Harry took a deep breath, trying to calm himself. "Asher."

He got off the bed and went to the bag of grocery items on the table. "Four thinks he's got a way out for us tomorrow night." He rummaged through the bag and triumphantly produced a small bottle of personal lubricant. "Probably not great, but personally, I'm surprised they stocked it at all." He threw it on the bed. "And we have a lot of time to fill in." He unbuttoned his jeans, his dark gaze piercing Harry. "You still angry? Pissed off? Wanna pummel something, Harry? You know I like it when you're rough with me."

"Asher, don't," Harry whispered, trying again to maintain his composure.

He grinned, as if it was challenge accepted. He shoved his hand into his briefs and began stroking. "Wanna see how many times you can come inside me?"

And that was it.

Harry took one large step, spun Asher around, and pushed him to kneel on the bed. He ripped his jeans down, exposing Asher's ass, then took the lube, drizzling it down his crack. Asher moaned when Harry undid his fly, and he dropped his head down to the mattress as Harry swiped his erection through the lube.

"You want it rough," Harry grunted. "Then take it."

He pushed his blunt cockhead into Asher, hard and fast, plunging into him without preparation.

Asher groaned, his back arching, and tried to lean forward, but Harry gripped his hips and held him in place. "You said you wanted it," he bit out. The immediate wet, tight heat was almost too much to bear, but the pleasure drove him to start fucking.

He held onto Asher's hips and thrust into him, hard and fast, drilling him up to the hilt with every pass.

Asher gripped the bed covers, moaning too loudly. So

Harry pulled Asher up by his shoulder, impaling him with his cock, and covered his mouth with his hand. "Be quiet."

Asher was rocking, moaning and whining, muffled by Harry's hand. Asher gripped his own erection and began to pleasure himself until his whole body went rigid, then jerked and spasmed. His body vibrated, Harry's cock pushing further in, and Asher came.

He rode out his orgasm fully impaled on Harry's cock, and when he sagged heavily, Harry let him slump on the bed, gripped his hips, and kept fucking him. Asher cried out with each thrust, and Harry fucked him harder, deeper, chasing and climbing his pleasure to its peak, until he finally tumbled over the edge.

He came hard, and Asher groaned with each pulse, taking every drop.

Harry's head spun, all his senses absent except for pleasure. All he ever wanted was to know this feeling, this bliss, and nothing else.

He was still holding Asher's hips, rocking into him, wringing out every ounce. He knew he'd probably hurt him, even though Asher had orgasmed, Harry doubted it was without pain.

Harry pulled out slowly, his cock still heavy, still full, and let Asher slump onto the bed. Harry was about to ask him if he was okay, wondering how guilty he should feel for giving Asher exactly what he wanted, when Asher moaned out a laugh and held up one finger. "That's one."

So help me God.

Round two was after dinner. They'd watched two terrible movies and Asher hadn't moved from the bed. When he was bored with the television, he rolled onto his front and pulled his jeans down to reveal his ass cheeks.

Round three was before sunrise. They'd slept with big-spoon Harry's arms wrapped tight around little-spoon Asher. Asher wasn't wearing any clothes at all, and Harry didn't know how Asher could want any more sex, but he writhed and rubbed against Harry's morning wood. "I'm so full of your come I don't need lube," he mumbled, his voice thick with sleep and desire. "Just more of you."

So Harry gave him round number three.

A few hours later, both showered and fed, Harry was sitting at the table and Asher began looking at him again, sizing him up, daring.

Harry knew that look all too well and shook his head. "No. You'll be too sore."

"How about I decide what's good for my body and you just deliver the goods?"

Harry snorted out a laugh. "I've delivered enough goods. You're just bored."

Asher whined like a spoiled child, then cursed him out in a language Harry didn't know, so Harry crash-tackled him on the bed, both of them laughing. Harry held Asher tight until Asher stopped struggling, they kissed and bit at each other's necks and ears, but it never became anything more. Eventually Asher rested his head on Harry's chest, and they watched another movie. This one was actually okay.

Or maybe it had nothing to do with the movie and everything to do with getting to lay in bed, his arms around a man. And a man he felt something for. And he did feel something. Despite the seesaw of wanting to be with him and wanting to wring his bloody neck, Harry knew he was leaning more to the side of wanting to be with him.

He liked Asher, as much as that annoyed him. As much as it did his head in and would probably see them both killed . . .

Harry gave Asher a squeeze and kissed the top of his head before he realised what he'd done. It was a personal, intimate, and honest thing to do. *Shit.* He froze.

Asher just laughed. "How much do you hate yourself right now?"

"Shut the fuck up."

After a few beats of silence, Asher's fingers trailed along Harry's skin where his shirt had ridden up. Harry laughed and held Asher's hand still. "Are you ticklish?" Asher asked, as if it was the most absurd thing he'd ever heard.

"I wasn't before now."

Harry let go of Asher's hand, so of course Asher inched Harry's shirt up. When Harry didn't protest, Asher sat up and pulled Harry's shirt high up on his chest. "I want to look," Asher said. Harry took the hint and tugged it over his head. Asher ran his finger along the two-inch scar on his side. "What's this one from?"

"Knife. In Vienna, about eight years ago. When I didn't bleed to death, I sewed it up myself."

Asher frowned, lightly touching another inch-long scar that ran the line of his ribs. "And this one?"

"Same knife fight. Same guy gave me this one too." Harry pointed out another scar on his forearm.

"Did you kill him?"

"Yes."

"With his knife?"

"Yes."

"Good." Still frowning, Asher touched a faint silvered scar on his other side. "And this one? It's old."

"Emergency appendectomy when I was eight. No keyhole surgery for me."

Asher skimmed his fingers over the three indented scars just right of his sternum. "What did this?"

"Steel knuckles."

"Jesus Christ."

"Wasn't even a target. I was staying in a shithole pub in Minsk for a job. I'd been out for food late one night, and when I was heading up to my room, some local tough guy in the bar downstairs thought he could take me in a fight."

Asher chuckled. "And how did that work out for him?"

"Very poorly. But not before he struck me in the chest."

His smile faded as he touched the two round scars, one on Harry's right shoulder, the other on the side of his pec. "Bullets?"

Harry nodded. "Six years ago, in Budapest." He met Asher's eyes because he knew what question was coming next. "Yes, he died. I was taken to hospital by ambulance.

Doctors removed the bullets in the emergency room, saved my life. And I managed to walk out, albeit not very well, before the cops got there."

There were other nicks and dents, but Asher didn't ask about those. It was all just more violence and lucky escapes. "Which one hurt the most?"

"Bullets burn. Hurt like a bitch, but they missed any organs, so they were mostly muscle damage. But the steel knuckles hurt the most, probably. They'd cracked my sternum, which took months to heal."

Asher shook his head. "Have you considered taking people out from a mile away? It really is so much easier."

Harry snorted and traced his thumb down Asher's jaw. It was another tender, intimate gesture, but Harry was past caring. The way Asher's eyes drew up to his, hazel with flecks of gold and orange, so beautiful. And the faint blush on Asher's cheeks . . .

Yeah. Harry was way past caring. He was way past trying to deny he had feelings for Asher. The way his heart thumped against his ribs, how that warmth burned in his chest.

Then Asher ran his fingers to the Southern Cross tattoo over Harry's heart. "And this . . ."

Harry sighed. "I got that when I was still part of my active unit. It felt patriotic at the time, but now I'm not so sure."

"Not sure about what?"

"What being patriotic means," Harry murmured. "To a country that sold me out."

Asher shook his head. "Your country didn't sell you out. Your handler did."

"My handler," Harry said, "is a high-ranking military man. One of the highest there is. It's hard not to assume it's not on behalf of all of the Australian government."

Asher frowned. "We need to get that USB to Four. Maybe it'll clear our names."

"And maybe it won't."

His gaze met Harry's. "Maybe."

Harry didn't want to bring this up right now, but he didn't

really have a choice. "Is that why you didn't kill me when you had the chance? Back in Madrid? Why you wanted us to work together?"

Hurt flashed in Asher's eyes. "The hit on both of us came from your government. From your handler. If we want to know why or have it revoked, I needed your help. I told you this, Harry. I'm not lying."

"You said you did jobs for my government?" Harry didn't get it. "Was it gas or oil related? Is that what made you realise something was wrong?"

"Yes. Like I said, Four looks between the lines. He wants to know why someone is marked for death, and 99.9% of the time there's money involved. It's usually a whole lot of money."

"And you said you'd been following my work."

Asher nodded. They'd already talked about this; it wasn't a revelation. "Four noticed the patterns. He watches everything that goes on in the underbelly. The hits, the contracts, watchlists, blackmails, who's paying who, who wants who dead and why, that kind of thing. He follows the money, and your handler is in the business of money. Stealing it, skimming it, profiteering. Please don't be mad. I might not have told you everything in the beginning, but I didn't exactly lie to you."

"I'm not mad." The truth was, Harry had assumed as much. "It's nice to hear you say it though."

Asher met his gaze and sighed. "The rest is the truth. We are better off sticking together. That was true. Me wanting a normal life. That's true. You being not completely insufferable. Maybe that's true."

Harry snorted. "You're not completely insufferable either."

Asher's smile was both sad and sweet as he lay back down, his head on Harry's bare chest. He was quiet while Harry rubbed his arm and drew circles on his back. The TV was still on but Harry wasn't watching it. He was sure Asher wasn't either. They were both in their own heads, happy in each other's arms.

The world outside didn't exist. The people chasing them didn't exist. The brevity of whatever this was didn't exist. It was here and now, it was real, and it was the best thing Harry could remember having.

After a long silence, still with his head on Harry's chest, Asher spoke.

"I like your tattoo," he whispered. "You have that identity and I'm sorry if your handler makes you doubt being patriotic. Everything you've done has been for your country. Or so you were led to believe. Everything you've been through, every dark minute, every scar, every day you've been alone . . . Your country should honour you."

"I doubt they'll see it that way."

"Four will make it so."

There it was again. *Four*. "You trust him."

"With my life," he answered immediately. Then after a second, he added, "With yours."

Harry rubbed Asher's back.

"He's like a brother to me. Family. The only family I've ever known."

Harry leaned up and kissed the top of Asher's head. "Then I'm glad you have him."

"Do you have family?"

"No." Then he sighed and offered a part of himself that no one else knew. "My parent's disowned me. Kicked me out for being gay. I'd just turned eighteen and I knew they wouldn't take it well, but . . . my dad went nuclear and beat the shit out of me."

Asher looked up at Harry then, his eyes full of concern. "He hit you?"

"I refused to hit him back at the time. Which I regret, actually. I should have fucking belted him."

"I'm so sorry," Asher whispered.

Harry shrugged. "I'd been in the cadets for years, so joining the army felt right. Told them I had no family, which by then, I didn't. And the army became my family. For years. Until I went solo, and I've been on my own ever since."

"It's not an easy life."

"No, it's not."

Asher put his head back on Harry's chest and was quiet again. "You know that feeling," he said, eventually. "You know where you come from, where you belong, that identity you feel in your bones, in your core. That tattoo on your chest. No matter where you are, you know who you are, where you're from."

Harry gave him a squeeze and let him talk.

"I don't have that. I am . . . without a nationality. I have no home, no country. I am . . . blank. I have no sense of identity."

Harry wasn't sure what he could say to that. "They can trace your DNA now. It will tell you where your blood is from. Your heritage."

"Maybe, and I've thought of that. But it wouldn't matter because I don't feel it. It'd be like having someone else's arm sewn onto my body and calling it mine." He shook his head. "I spent my earliest years that I can remember in a Croatian orphanage. I arrived there when I was three or four, I think. And I was reminded every day that I did not belong. That I was stranac. A foreigner, someone who did not belong." He let out a long breath. "Until I was five, I thought stranac was my name."

Jesus. "Oh, Asher."

He looked up at Harry, sighed and collected his thoughts. "When I was about six, I was loaded into a truck with other boys and taken to a military training school outside of Belgrade in Serbia. By the time I was twelve, I'd lived in Kosovo, Bulgaria, Albania, Turkey, Italy, France. No papers. I never had any papers, any records. If they'd killed me, no one would have ever known." He smiled sadly. "But I was smart, and fast. I adapted and I learned. I was just a boy when I started running mule jobs, taking items or information to people. At the age of ten, I could shoot any target from four hundred metres, five hundred if the wind was right. I was fifteen when I shot my first human target. I was good at everything, so they kept me. Not many other boys made it . . ."

Harry cupped Asher's face and thumbed his cheek. There was such sadness in those beautiful eyes that Harry was lost for words. What on earth could he say?

"I still don't have any official certification. I think one of the matrons at the orphanage gave me the name Asher Garin when I first arrived. I've searched and Four has searched, but there is no record of me anywhere." He shrugged. "There were other children at the orphanage, and looking back, I can see that maybe we were displaced or stolen from the war. Some parents came and found their child, but no one ever claimed me."

Harry was stricken, heartbroken for that small boy all those years ago. He couldn't imagine the horrors he'd have seen. "The war?"

"There was once, only once, the mention of Sarajevo," Asher murmured. "At the orphanage, I overheard them talking. They said something about when the truck of children had arrived from Sarajevo. Trafficking is worse in war . . . women and children are sold. Maybe I was one of the lucky ones, I don't know."

Jesus fucking Christ.

"I'm so sorry," Harry whispered.

Asher simply shrugged. "No one ever came for me. It's very likely my parents were killed." He inhaled deeply, his eyes focused on a memory for a long moment. "I went back to Sarajevo, years later, to see if I could feel any kind of connection."

"And did you?"

He shook his head. "No. It actually felt strange. The opposite of a connection. It was uneasy, even. Like something was telling me I should leave."

Harry placed a gentle kiss on Asher's forehead. "I'm sorry that happened to you."

Asher was quiet again, reflective, sad. And all Harry could

do was hold him tight, hoping he would feel comfort and connection, even if just for that moment.

"Can I tell you something?" Asher whispered.

"Of course."

He was quiet for a few moments, obviously trying to get his thoughts and words in order. "I don't know if it's a memory or a dream. But there's a road. I can see it. I think it's a memory. It feels like a memory, but I think I was very young. I'm with my parents, I think. I don't know. I can't see them but I feel at peace, without a care. I feel safe and loved. I don't have much of a reference for either of those things so it's difficult to explain."

Harry rubbed his back. *This poor man.* "It sounds nice."

"It's a country road, I think. Maybe it's a long driveway, I don't know. There is a field on one side and trees on the other. I don't know if we're driving or walking. I can see it in my mind, and I have no clue where it is, but I think that was my home."

Harry tightened his arms around Asher, holding him close, and kissed the side of his head. He wanted Asher to hold onto that memory, that image. "What colour is the sky?"

Asher froze for the briefest moment. "Um . . . It's morning, I think. Or sunset. The sunlight is in the trees. Orange and yellow."

"Are there flowers in the field?"

He was quiet again, maybe trying to recall. "No, I don't think so. It's green. A farmer's field."

Harry breathed in deep and held Asher, nestling him into his strong arms. "It sounds lovely, and I'm glad you have that."

Asher swallowed hard, his voice barely a whisper. "Thank you, Harry."

A FEW HOURS LATER, Asher still hadn't said much. Bringing up his past mustn't have been easy. What he'd divulged to Harry was bad enough, but Harry could only imagine how bad the memories were that he didn't talk about.

They were due down at the seaport docks, to meet Four's organised transport at nine at night. It was a freighter, apparently. And would take them out of Oman, up the Persian Gulf, to their new destination, somewhere along the Saudi coastline.

"We'll need food," Asher said. "I think we can assume the ship we'll be on isn't a cruise liner with restaurants."

Harry checked his watch. It was going on six, so there was plenty of time. "We can get something on the way, but we'll have your bag full of guns, which probably isn't a great idea. Or I can go now to the small store we passed on the walk here. It's just the next block down. I'll be five minutes."

Asher considered this. "It would be better if we ate before we go. There's no saying when we'll eat again. Get some of those breakfast bars and bottled water." He got off the bed and walked into the bathroom where the duffle bag was stashed. He came out with Harry's favourite pistol and handed it to him. "And take this. Just in case."

"Okay." He checked the gun, then slid it into the back of his jeans and put his jacket on. Then, with just his finger, he lifted Asher's chin and kissed him softly. "I'm taking the room key. Keep the door locked. Pull the table across the door. It might not block it, but it can give you an extra second if someone kicks the door in."

Asher rolled his eyes. "You said you'd be five minutes. And you better not be any longer because I'm going to need you to fuck me again before we go. Probably twice."

Harry sighed, hating how his body liked the idea of that. Well, maybe he didn't hate it too much. He went to the door. "I won't be long."

The walk to the store was short and pleasant. The sun was setting, the sky was an array of orange and pinks and cloudless. He still kept hyperaware of his surroundings, though he found nothing out of the ordinary.

He bought some granola bars, some dried apricots, some water, and of course, he found Asher's favourite mints. This time, he smiled as he added two tins to his purchases. He paid in cash and headed back to the motel.

Harry realised, as he rounded the corner, that he was actually happy.

He was happy with Asher.

It was foolish and crazy, and probably stupid . . .

Most definitely stupid.

But Harry had a sneaking suspicion that the ember of warmth that beat in his chest, that seed which had taken root under his ribs, was love.

He was smiling to himself, like the idiot he was, when he got to the motel door and it pushed open.

Harry dropped his bag of groceries, took out his gun, and kicked the door in. The table was pushed askew, the bedding was half on the floor.

Asher was gone.

SIXTEEN

"ASHER!"

Nothing.

Harry was trying not to panic.

He checked the bathroom. The duffle bag was still there, all the guns and rifles still inside.

Asher would never leave without his babies.

Terror and fear clawed their way up Harry's throat. Cold dread ran icy fingers down his spine.

And then he saw a single mint on the floor under the bedding . . . not just one, but the tin was there too. Harry snatched them up . . . Asher would never spill his stupid fucking beloved mints on the floor. If he'd done a runner, he'd never leave them, or his guns, behind.

Something was wrong.

God, please no, no, no.

Harry jumped to his feet and ran out the door, hoping to find what, he had no idea. There were no cars, no people on the street. Nothing out of the ordinary.

Asher, where are you?

"Asher," he murmured, pulling at his hair.

As he spun around, he noticed from the corner of his eye the curtains move in the window from the room two doors up. The room where the woman with the baby was staying.

Harry ran over and knocked on her door. "Please. Did you see anything. Where he went?"

No reply.

He banged again, not caring how desperate he sounded. He *was* desperate. "Please. He is . . . he is everything to me. Please. Did you see anything?"

The door cracked open, and the woman peered at him through the opening. "Two men take him," she said quietly. "In white van."

Oh my fucking God.

Cold rushed from his scalp to his toes, his heart squeezed, his stomach rolled. He could barely speak. "Did you see anything else?"

She shook her head. "Nothing. Please, no trouble. I have small child."

He understood. "Thank you." He took a step back . . . to go to his room, to run the streets, he had no idea.

"They talk like you," the woman said.

He spun around. "What? Pardon?"

"I heard one speak. His accent is yours."

Harry's world tilted and spun the wrong way. He staggered back to their room, lost, and for the first time in his life, Harry was legitimately scared.

Two Australian men had to be Gibson and Hull. His ex-squad members. The same two pieces of shit who'd been tracking them across Europe and North Africa.

Those assholes had taken Asher, and Harry had no way to find him. He had no way of knowing where to look, where to even start.

One thing he did know was, when he caught up to Gibson and Hull, they would wish they'd never been born.

With no other option, he took out his phone and found his handler's number. Parrish. The man who Harry had once thought of as a father-figure, the same man Harry was now going to take exquisite pleasure in torturing.

He pressed Call.

There was no point in hiding; they clearly knew where he was.

It rang and rang, and Harry could picture the look on Parrish's face when he saw who was calling.

It answered just before cutting out. He sounded half asleep. "Harry."

"Where have they taken him?"

"Where have who taken who?"

"Don't play fucking games with me, Parrish. I know everything. You put a contract out on my head and you didn't think I'd find out? You're fucking stupider than you look. Now where have they taken him?"

"I don't know what—"

"Bullshit!" Harry screamed. He held his phone so tight, he thought it might crack. "You sent Gibson and Hull to chase us. They killed that fisherman in Gibraltar and you pinned it on us by sending information to Interpol. I know what you've done."

"You don't know anything," he said coldly.

"Where have they taken him?" Harry said again, his voice real fucking low. "So help me God, Parrish. After everything I've done for you. For the country you claim to love . . . you've been making gas and oil deals to line your own pockets for years, having people killed when they got in your way. You're going down for all of it."

Silence.

"Did you hear what I said?" Harry asked.

"You don't have proof."

Harry laughed, sounding a little crazy. "Yes we do. You're fucking finished. But don't worry. The punishment for what they will charge you with will be a walk in the park compared to what I'm gonna do to you."

There was more silence for a long time.

"Harry," he said, his tone more appeasing now. "I'm sure we can discuss this—"

"You tell me where he is, and you might wanna start praying they haven't harmed a hair on his head, or I will fucking kill everyone. You hear me? Every single person you ever loved."

Harry heard him swallow.

"I don't know where they are," he said quietly. "They were in Oman last I heard. You and Garin were spotted in Muscat. They were already in Saudi, so it wasn't far . . . I don't know where they are exactly. They haven't called it in yet."

"What instruction did you give them?" No, that wasn't the right question. "Did you give them a kill-order?"

Silence.

"I told them to bring you in," Parrish said.

Harry knew that wasn't the truth. "Liar."

"By any means necessary," he added. "You, Harry. Not Garin. They must think they can lure you out of hiding."

"Which might be the case if I knew where they fucking were!" Harry was so mad he was beginning to shake. "You find them. And you call me back. And you better pray to any fucking God who will listen that Asher's okay."

"Harry, I can't—"

"How's your family, Parrish?" Harry asked, his voice chillingly pleasant. "How is Linda? She keeping well? And your two kids, Andrew and Joanna? Gee, they might even have kids of their own by now? They all well, Parrish?"

"You don't threaten my family—"

"It's not a threat. It's a promise. You have ten minutes."

"It's the middle of the night—"

Harry disconnected the call. His heart was thundering, his blood pressure through the roof. He was so fucking mad. And scared. And helpless. He felt sick with worry, and his pulse pounded in his ears.

It took him a second to realise that muted buzzing noise wasn't inside his head.

It was a phone.

Harry dropped to his knees and pulled the bed covers up . . . and there was Asher's phone under the bed. *What the hell?*

Harry had to reach for it, but it stopped buzzing just as he got to see the screen. It was Four.

The screen went black, and of course Asher had his phone locked. It was a six number code that Harry had no hope of guessing. Knowing Asher, it'd be six presses of the number four.

Harry tried it.

It wasn't it. He couldn't risk locking the phone completely, so he didn't try again. Harry briefly wondered who he could find in Muscat to unlock it. Probably any fifteen-year-old could do it. He picked up his phone and began searching the internet. Surely there was a video on YouTube . . .

Asher's phone buzzed again with an incoming call from Four. Harry hit Answer.

"Where are you, Asher?" Four asked, his voice deep and clipped with worry. "You were a no show at the ship."

"It's Harry. They took him. The two Australian guys who were following us. They *took* him."

"What?" There was a beat of silence before Harry could hear a flurry of clicking on a keyboard. "Who? When?"

"I don't know. Ten minutes ago, maybe fifteen, twenty. The woman next door saw them. Said it was a white van. They had my accent. It's gotta be them." Harry was talking fast, panicking, but so relieved. He sat on the end of the bed. "I called Parrish. My handler. He told me he sent them. I told him I wanted a location. I gave him ten minutes, but I doubt he'll call. I need to find him. I don't think you understand. I'm going to find those motherfuckers, and if they've hurt him, I swear to god, I will—"

"You called Parrish?"

"Yes."

"Okay," Four said. "That's good. It means he would have called someone after. I can follow his call network—" There was more tapping.

"He left his guns behind," Harry said, "and the stupid mints that he likes. I knew something was wrong. His phone was under the bed. The screen is locked. I couldn't call you."

Harry subconsciously flipped the lid on the tin of mints. "Oh my god," he mumbled.

"What?" Four said, alarmed.

Harry could have laughed. He scrubbed his hand over his face. "The USB. It's in the tin of mints. He would have left it behind deliberately."

Four made a breathy sound, a bit like relief. "He's a smart man."

"I need to find him. Please." Harry didn't care if he sounded emotional. He *was* emotional.

"Okay, I'm running some triangulations. Parrish made a call after yours to a number in Sydney. It lasted twenty-two seconds. But then he called a different number, location . . . Oman."

Harry was on his feet. "Where?"

"It's coming, hang on . . . Whoever he called is still moving. We have to assume they have Asher, or they know who does. What I need you to do, Harry, is stay calm, think rationally. You need to do this right. I'm going to send you the location. You need to get your ass there, right now. Steal a car if you have to. You need to get him, bring him back."

"I will."

"And Harry?"

"Yes?"

"Make them pay. No one hurts him, ever," he whispered. "Don't just kill them. Make them beg for death."

Harry smiled. Maybe Four wasn't so bad after all. "Oh, I plan to."

THE UTILITY HARRY stole was very likely older than him. He found it with the windows down, cracked seats, corroded dashboard, dented and rusted exterior. Not too unlike himself, Harry thought, older than anything else on the market but an absolute tank.

He had the duffle bag of guns on the seat beside him, his

phone on his lap with a map on screen, a little red dot his destination.

Parrish never did call him back, not that Harry was surprised, but he would make Parrish pay for that.

For this whole damn fucking mess.

Harry's plan now consisted of two objectives. Get Asher back and take Parrish down.

Nothing else mattered.

He had to take Highway 17 south, out of Muscat and back into the desert mountains. It was dark now, and Harry couldn't see past the side of the highway, but he had Four on speaker. Yes, Harry had a map, but he couldn't read Arabic, which made signs a nightmare, but with Four guiding him via satellite—or whatever whiz-tech shit Asher had talked about—it was so much easier.

It also kept Harry calm, which was probably the reason Four had insisted Harry call him the minute he had some transport.

When Four had said Harry would come to a huge inter-section, he did. When he said Harry would go through a tunnel, he did. So when he said Harry would see a huge Shell petrol station and he would need to exit the highway, that's what Harry did.

It made driving incredibly easy.

The beacon or phone, or whatever it was Four was actually tracking for Asher's location, had stopped moving. Which meant they'd probably had Asher out of the van for about ten minutes already.

Harry tried not to think about what they could be doing to him. Harry had never really liked Gibson. He was all about the power-grab, thinking his rank gave him the right to treat other people like shit. Whereas Hull just did whatever he was told.

Could they do some serious damage to Asher? Absolutely.

Would they kill him? Not if their plan was to lure Harry. They wouldn't kill him yet, anyway.

At least Harry hoped so.

"There should be a road that goes behind the Shell," Four said. "It leads to the town about half a mile from the highway."

"Okay, I see lights. Houselights, streetlights."

"Good. Stay on the road you're on. The town is in between two mountains, so it's long and narrow. You'll pass a supermarket and a school."

He did.

"Now about two miles out of town you'll pass an old shooting range. About two hundred metres after that, on your right, there's a road. Or a track. Or it could just be tyre tracks in the sand, Harry. I can't see it clearly."

Harry began to slow down. "How far off the road are they?"

"About a kilometre." There was the faint clicking of fingers on a keyboard. "I think it's an old military training ground. Closed down in the '90s."

Just fucking great.

"The terrain looks rough, Harry," he added.

"No doubt." Harry saw the turn off ahead and came to a slow stop. It was an older road, claimed by the desert, but there were fresh tyre tracks on the sand. He killed his headlights. "Okay, I'm going in quiet. I'll see how far I can get before I go on foot. And thank you for getting me this far."

"Just get him back."

"That's the plan."

Four was quiet for a long few seconds. "Call me when you're done. Or better yet, have him call me."

"Will do."

Harry clicked off the call and edged the utility slowly along the same path the van had gone. Without headlights, he couldn't go fast anyway, but the night was clear, the moonlight in his favour, and given the lack of all light pollution out in the middle of the freaking desert, he could see quite well.

A few hundred metres in, where the van had gone down a ridgeline onto flatter ground, Harry drove up. Just far enough to get the utility out of view and hopefully give him an elevated viewpoint, and he turned off the engine.

The silence was so damn loud.

He took the duffle bag and trekked further along, crouching and fast, down into what looked like an old creek bed, and soon enough some weathered shack-like buildings came into view. One longer rectangular building, one smaller square one, maybe just over a hundred metres away. The white van was parked near the bigger shack, but also another four-wheel drive.

Which meant a possible four or five other people, not including how many were in the van with Asher.

Harry found a good spot to get a view from and took Asher's binoculars from the duffle bag. The smaller shack appeared empty. No lights, no activity. The larger building had black plastic over the glassless windows, but there was an orange glow from the edges. Three men stood outside, guarding each side Harry could see. He assumed there was a fourth man on the far side.

They wore dark fatigues with beanies, each man was armed with AK-47s, and the guy at the front had a walkie-talkie. Possibly some Omani special unit? About to be very dead.

Harry had to choose which gun to take them out with. One of Asher's babies, the MAC 50, probably, though it would take time to set up, and he had doubts on the Compact's accuracy over the distance. He really was better in close-contact.

Then he heard yelling from inside the shack, and he no longer cared about the guns.

He took both his pistols, one in each hand, both with suppressors, and crept out of the trench. He ran, low to the ground toward the shack, the uneven ground, rocks and sand, was unforgiving on his tender ankle.

He didn't care.

He heard more voices from inside the shack. Gibson was

yelling—Harry knew the voice—and muffled grunts like someone was being used as a punching bag.

Asher.

Running faster now, Harry raised the gun in his right hand and aimed it at the man with the walkie-talkie in front of the shack. He seemed surprised to see him until Harry shot him in the chest.

Harry kept running, now toward the right side of the shack.

The man turned just as Harry reached him and Harry shot him in the head. Not his prettiest shot, but effective, none-theless. Without stopping for even a second, Harry ran toward the back of the building and almost collided with another of the guards. He was so close that when Harry shot him point blank in the face, a fine red mist plumed upward from where the man fell backwards, sideways, absent the back of his head.

Harry stepped over him, slipping one gun into the waist-band of his jeans, and went in search of the fourth guard. He must have heard the thuds, surely.

Harry had to move fast.

He rounded the far end of the building, to what had been the left side when he'd watched with the binoculars. There was no guard. Harry ducked down low and ran the full side of the building, back around to the front. The first dead guard was there. But no one else.

Harry wanted to forget the fourth guy and just get inside as fast as he could, but he knew better than to leave a threat behind. So he backtracked to the rear of the building just as the guard was heading back the other way.

It really wasn't Harry's style to shoot someone in the back. "Psst."

The man spun around at the sound, and Harry shot him in the forehead. *Much more Harry's style.*

Now it was time for the main event.

Harry didn't know how many men were inside or how armed they were, but he did still have the element of surprise on his side. Harry could only guess no one could hear anything over the way Gibson was yelling.

Dumbass.

Harry was at the back of the shack, and there was a door. There was no handle, but the hinges creaked loudly when he pushed on it.

There's no hiding that.

"Go and see what that was," Gibson yelled.

Harry stepped into what was a smaller room. It was dark, the only light coming through another doorway. There, he was met by another guy dressed in black fatigues like the other guards. He made a startled sound before Harry shot him in the heart.

There was definitely no element of surprise now.

He strode into the main room, taking in every detail. How many? Who had weapons, who was the biggest threat? Another man dressed as a guard sat along the far wall. He was laughing until he saw Harry. He got to his feet just as Harry shot him in the head.

Hull stood to Harry's right, Gibson to his left, and Asher was tied to a chair, his head lolled forward.

Gibson wasn't armed. He had his shirt off like punching the shit out of a man that was tied to a chair while not wearing a shirt made him more manly.

Hull, on the other hand, *was* armed. He had a pistol in a shoulder holster. Which was fucking stupid. Harry should have shot him for that alone . . .

Actually, that's a good idea.

Harry shot Hull in the head.

He fell backwards with a dead weight thump and Gibson took a large step back. "Harry! What the . . . ?"

"You shut your fucking mouth," Harry said, pointing his gun at him. He put a hand on Asher's shoulder. "Asher, you okay?"

Asher moaned and a long strand of bloody drool fell from his face to his thigh.

While Harry was momentarily distracted, Gibson took a

step to the left. Harry shot him in the knee and he fell to the ground, screaming.

Harry lifted Asher's face so he could see him better. One eye was already swollen shut, the other not far from it. He had cuts on his cheeks, his lip. The side of his jaw was already swollen and bruised. *Jesus fucking Christ.*

Gibson was now clutching his leg and doing that hiss-breathing, complete with froth and spittle. "You fucking shot me!"

Harry stared at him. "And I'm going to do it again." He undid Asher's hands, seeing his knuckles and arms were bruised as well. Defensive marks? Harry was eerily calm, long past angry. There wasn't a name for the emotion he felt right then. Nuclear fucking rage didn't quite cut it.

He put another gentle hand on Asher's shoulder, unsure of where he might be injured. "You okay?"

Asher lifted his bruised and bloodied face and tried to smile, lips split and swollen. "Peachy."

Gibson was now trying to scoot backwards, Harry realised, to the wall where a bag was with his handgun on top. It was pitiful to watch. Soooo Harry shot him in the other knee. Gibson howled and his hands shook violently as he held his leg and tried to breathe through the pain.

"The first bullet was for killing that fisherman in Gibraltar," Harry said. "The second was for being on Parrish's side. How much money does he give you to betray your country? What was your price for treason?"

Gibson shook his head but he was indignant and arrogant to the end. He snarled, pale now, spittle on his lips as he spoke. "Fuck you."

Using his head like a soccer ball, Harry kicked him in the face, kicking hard enough that it broke most of his front teeth and probably his nose. It put him flat on his back anyway. He coughed and spat blood, groaning, rolling onto his side.

Harry leaned over him. "Christ, Gibson, you're so bad at this. The *elite* team you put together for whatever the fuck this was supposed to be was a joke. They're all very dead, and I'm going to make it look like you did it. Your government will disown you. They won't even claim your worthless fucking corpse."

Still crouching over Gibson, Harry pointed to Asher. "Look at him, what you did to my man. You had no beef with Asher. You wanted me but weren't good enough to take me on because you're a piece of shit fucking coward. So, your punishment for what you've done to him. Shall we get started? Remember those drills we'd run back in training, to see how much we could endure? You're going to want to compartmentalise the pain. Separate the mental from the physical."

Gibson groaned again and spat a bloody broken tooth at Harry. It was pathetic. Harry laughed and stood up. "You're not even fucking worth it." He aimed his gun at Gibson's mangled face and pulled the trigger.

"Harry?" Asher murmured.

"Yeah, I'm here," he said, going to him and kneeling.

"Can't see."

His eyes were so swollen, it made Harry want to shoot Gibson again. "It's over now. I'm getting you out of here," Harry said. "Just gimme one sec."

Harry put his own gun in Hull's hand, took Hull's stupid pistol from his stupid holster and fired a quick two rounds into Hull's head again. He gave it a quick wipe then put that gun in Gibson's hand. Would it be enough to confuse the cops or a medical examiner? Not if they looked too hard. Not when they tested Hull and Gibson's guns and found the weapon that killed the fisherman in Gibraltar. Harry hoped that'd be the end of how hard they looked.

"We need to leave," Harry said. "Can you walk?"

Asher was shaky getting to his bare feet, clutching his ribs with one hand, holding his other out to Harry.

Harry went to him, holding him up. "God, what did they do to you?"

Asher hissed, and there was no way he could sling his arm around Harry's shoulder, no way he could walk. "I'm going to carry you," Harry said, scooping him up bridal style.

Asher was listless, helpless. "Knew you'd find me."

The four-wheel drive was closest, so Harry went to it first. Keys were in the ignition. Harry would've normally grumbled about how these idiots made it all too easy, but this time he was grateful. He helped Asher into the front passenger side and drove them toward the old riverbed-trench and stopped, opening his door.

"Harry?" Asher mumbled, alarmed.

"Just getting the duffle bag," he replied.

He found it and was soon back behind the wheel.

"Harry? The USB . . ."

"I found it. I've got it."

Asher sagged, his breaths short and sharp.

Harry got them back out onto the road, took out his phone, and called Four. He answered on the first ring. "Tell me you have him?"

"I do."

"Oh, thank God." It sounded like Four might have cried with relief. He sucked back a shaky breath. "Let me speak to him."

"He's in pretty bad shape," Harry said, trying to keep an eye on the road and on Asher at the same time. He was still drooling blood, and God, his face . . . Harry spoke into the phone, more urgent this time. "I need you to get us out of Oman. Tonight. Now. I don't care how or where it takes us."

Asher moaned, his voice barely a murmur. "Harry?"

Harry shot him a look. "Yes, baby, I'm right here."

Asher held out his hand blindly. Harry took it, and Asher squeezed, holding tight, his hand shaking a little.

"Harry," Four said. "I want you to head toward the Muscat seaport. Follow the signs to Highway 1. I need to make some calls, and I will phone you back in ten minutes." There was a beat of silence. "And Harry?"

"Yeah?"

"Thank you."

SEVENTEEN

ASHER DIDN'T REMEMBER MUCH.

He remembered hearing an Australian accent mumble something outside their motel door no more than thirty seconds after Harry had left. Asher had assumed Harry had forgotten something, so he stupidly opened the door.

So stupid.

Harry had told him not to open the door for anyone. In fact, Harry had told him to push the table across to block the doorway. Asher hadn't done that either.

They'd spent the last few days in a bubble of sorts, after so many days of it just the two of them, and Asher got complacent. He got stupid.

And he got caught.

He should have been grateful he didn't get a bullet in his head right then and there.

He'd already put the USB in the tin of mints, but as the two men grabbed him, Asher knew he had to hide it from them; he managed to kick it under the bed in the struggle. He hadn't meant to drop his phone though. He worried then if Harry would be able to track him if Asher didn't have his phone . . . but it was too late. The bigger of the two men kneed Asher with an uppercut to the chin, and Asher's world went dark.

He came to sometime later and quickly realised he was in the back of a moving van. He was lying on his side, his hands were tied behind his back, and there were two different men in the back with him now. They wore dark army uniforms that Asher didn't recognise. They sneered at him and one of them kick-stomped Asher in the stomach.

Asher had laughed through the pain. "He's gonna find me," he said. "And he's gonna fuck you all up."

It probably wasn't smart to goad his captors, but he couldn't help himself. Because Asher knew, like he knew the sky was blue, that Harry would stop at nothing to find him.

And he thought, in that split second, that he was glad he'd left his phone behind because Harry would know then that he didn't leave of his own accord. Would Harry think that Asher skipped out on him if he didn't find the phone? Not to mention the duffle bag of guns . . . Would Harry doubt Asher's loyalty to him?

No. He wouldn't. Like Asher wouldn't doubt Harry's loyalty.

Harry would find a way to track him down.

Asher had to believe that.

The second man punched him in the side of the head, and through a swirl of pain and nausea, he fell back into darkness.

When they dragged him out of the van, Asher couldn't see much. It was dark, he had no shoes on and could feel sand under his feet. There was another vehicle there already, and Asher counted four other men. The two Australian men, who Harry had identified in the photographs as Gibson and Hull, dragged him inside and tied him onto an old wooden chair, and Gibson proceeded to hit him, taunt him, tell him they were just gonna play with him for a bit until they called Harry, maybe send him photos of how Asher was holding up.

Then Harry would come, like the predictable dog he was.

Asher looked Gibson right in the eyes. "He's gonna fuck you up the most."

He could remember the first several hits, but everything went dark after a blow to his temple.

Reality seeped back in and out in waves, blurred with pain, both dull and sharp, and it seemed to last for an age.

But dear God, when he heard Harry's voice, he could have cried. He tried to shake off the blur, the haze. His vision was all wrong, and he realised he could only see out of one eye, and even then, no more than a slit of blur.

He heard gunshots.

He worried for Harry, but then his large, warm, gentle hand on his shoulder grounded him. Saved him.

Harry.

Asher tried to stay conscious, to stay awake. He tried to fight off the darkness that kept lapping at the edges, but it was all too heavy. Everything hurt. His head felt as if it'd been run over with a steamroller. His ribs weren't much better. He couldn't see at all now, and not having vision was terrifying. He couldn't see any threat and he'd spent his entire life relying on his ability to read any situation.

But even not being able to see, Asher knew he was safe now.

Harry had come for him.

He knew he would, but it still filled him with something he wasn't familiar with. He grasped Harry's hand, held it as tight as he could, and never wanted to let him go.

He was safe with Harry, so he surrendered to the darkness where there was no pain.

———

ASHER WAS BEING CARRIED in big strong arms, a familiar scent with saltwater and the sound of seagulls.

Then he was on a boat, down in the belly with the sound of engines, of water churning. The smell of livestock cloyed in his throat, but there was a big warm body beside him, strong arm around him, measured breaths, and murmured words of reassurance.

Asher came to again when he was being moved. Harry was carrying him once more. He tried to open his eyes but couldn't. "Harry," he struggled. Everything hurt so damn much.

"I got you, baby," he replied. "Just going on a little ride in a truck. It's all okay."

And it was. He was with Harry. That was all he needed to know.

THE NEXT TIME Asher woke up, he still couldn't see. But he felt cold things on his face and he tried to remove them. A hand on his wrist stopped him. "Hey," Harry murmured. "It's to help with the swelling."

Asher tried to speak, but his mouth felt like the Arabian Desert. "Water?"

Harry put a straw to his lips. "Sip on this."

That water was the wettest, bestest water he'd ever had.

"Where are we?"

"Pakistan, near the Iranian border. We crossed the gulf to Gwadar, and we were taken to a small town near the border. Four organised it all. There's a lady here who's tending to your injuries. Are you hungry? You must be. Let me get you something soft. How's your jaw? Asher, I was so worried. Christ, when I found out it was them who took you—"

"Harry," Asher murmured.

"Yes."

Asher held up his hand. "Hold my hand."

"Okay." Harry's warm fingers wrapped around Asher's, and Asher felt an immediate sense of relief, of calm.

And he slept.

ASHER HAD LOST all sense of time. The only gauge he had of night or day was the temperature. Whatever was in those strips of fabric he often woke to find plastered on his face were working because he could open his eyes a little.

His ribs made any kind of movement painful, and it made sleeping fitful at best. He didn't need X-rays to tell him things were broken in there. How many ribs, he could only guess. It felt like all of them, on both sides, but his right side was worse. His jaw hurt, he'd lost one molar and another one was wobbly, and he couldn't open his mouth too wide, but he didn't think his jaw was broken.

His hands and arms were bruised and cut, though he had no recollection of how. Being grabbed and struggling, probably. He had some very suspicious bruises in the shape of fingers that made Harry seethe every time he saw them.

Harry.

Harry had been an absolute saviour. An angel. Soft whispers, gentle touches, and always willing to hold Asher's hand when he needed it.

And he did need it.

Maybe for the first time in his life, he needed someone. And now he had someone—also a first—who was by his side, willingly. Someone to care for him, look after him, tend to him. He gave him sips of water; he mashed up his food and fed it to him. He gave him those pain pills he'd been taking for his ankle, which Asher had to admit, were a blessing.

The pills helped with the cracking headache he had too. It was probably just as well he couldn't see for three days. Though the room he found himself in was small, it was blissfully dark.

On day three, he managed to stand, with Harry's help of course. And he managed to piss by himself, which was a nice change. Not that he'd ever complain about Harry ever touching his dick, but the thought of doing anything like *that* made Asher want to curl up in a ball and cry.

Except physically curling up into a ball would almost kill him as well, and even the tears would probably hurt his still swollen eyes.

He didn't dare ask to see a mirror, and he had no intention of trying to see his ribs or stomach.

He was happy with his little dark room, spending all his

time napping and trying not to move. He could hear Harry's deep voice every so often, and his laughter. He was outside, obviously. There were other voices, another man, several children, and the occasional woman's voice.

Asher couldn't follow what they talked about, but his laughter . . . the children's laughter, the man and woman cheering . . .

Asher was beginning to think he was asleep and dreaming of such things. But Harry would return every so often, smiling. He came to sit beside Asher. "How's my favourite patient?" he asked quietly. "You were asleep for a long while today."

"I'm feeling better. Not great but better."

"You look better."

Asher touched Harry's forearm, and he felt like sunshine and dust. They might have been Asher's two new favourite things. "Have I told you thank you for coming to get me?"

"Only about fifty times so far."

Asher smiled but it hurt. "Thank you."

Harry lifted Asher's hand to his lips and kissed his knuckles. "You're very welcome."

Asher wanted to keep his eyes open, as good as he could, anyway, but sleep was getting the best of him again. "Want to stay awake with you."

"Oh, baby," Harry whispered. "Go to sleep. Your body needs to heal. I'm not going anywhere. Ahmad has me fixing his roof, and Nour told me hers is next. I've already helped with the shade over the vegetable patch. I think they've been waiting a decade for someone my height to come to town."

Asher chuckled but it made everything hurt, earning himself a pained groan.

Harry reached for the pills and water. "You're overdue for one of these," he said gently. Asher took it without complaint and closed his eyes.

Harry pressed a soft kiss to the top of Asher's forehead. "Sleep, baby. I'll bring you some food soon."

ASHER FELT CONSIDERABLY BETTER the next day. Enough that he could sit up, albeit slowly, without feeling as if someone had speared him in the ribs. He managed to use the bathroom and have a bit of a bird bath to freshen up but didn't argue when Harry helped him back to bed.

At about lunch time, Harry came back in with his phone pressed to his ear. He smiled when he held the phone out. "It's for you."

Asher took the phone. "Hello?"

"Oh, my darling, I'm so relieved to hear your voice. How are you?"

Four.

"I feel like I got hit by a truck. How are you?"

"Worried for you. But I have some good news."

"What's that?"

"Are you up for travelling tomorrow?" he asked. "That big, gorgeous man of yours said you're doing better."

Asher smiled and had to cup his swollen jaw. "Did he now?"

Four was quiet then, clearly hearing Asher struggle. "He sent me photos of your face," he whispered.

"He did?"

"I wanted you to keep travelling. I wanted to bring you here where you'd be safe. He said you needed a few days. Then he sent me that photo and I could see his point."

"I didn't know he did that," Asher said weakly.

"He's uh . . . how do we say it? Protective of you."

Asher smiled again, his heart warming his whole chest. "He's been . . . I can't explain it. He's . . ."

"I get it, darling," he said sweetly. "And I can't wait to meet him in person. Tomorrow."

It took Asher a second . . . "Tomorrow? Uh, if it involves walking or anything like an overcrowded train ride from Mumbai, I just can't. I'm sure my face would be enough to concern authorities, but I hurt too much—"

"This will be much more comfortable, I promise."

Asher trusted Four, he really did, but . . . "What did Harry say?"

"He said yes, and trust me when I tell you he was very clear when he explained how he wouldn't allow you to endure any arduous travels. My darling, that man is a bear."

Asher chuckled. "He's a teddy bear."

"Oh, you do have it bad. I shall judge for myself tomorrow. You can stay here and recuperate for as long as you need. Stay forever if you want."

Asher sighed. "Tomorrow it is."

He ended the call, and a few minutes later, Harry came in with a bowl of rice and curry sauce. No meat or beans or anything he had to chew. "Something savoury," Harry said.

Asher sat himself up, nice and slow. "Oh, thank you."

Harry stood there, unsure. "Did you want me to bring the table over?"

Asher shook his head. "No. You can feed me."

Harry rolled his eyes but he relented a smile. "I think this could be a ploy for me to spoil you," he said, as he sat beside Asher on the bed. He scooped a small spoonful and gently put it to Asher's mouth. "It's a sweet curry, not spicy. My second day here, Hazeema, the woman who has been cooking for us, she made two separate meals. One for me, one for her family. I said I could eat that, there was no need to make something different. I didn't want to burden her, but she told me it was too spicy. I said I could eat spice." Harry stared at me, his eyes wide. "Well, I wasn't aware nuclear was a spice level, and I almost died. So, as it turns out, I cannot, in fact, eat what a Pakistani grandmother would call spicy food. She laughed at me a lot and I'm pretty sure she called me 'silly white boy,' which is fair enough. Not gonna lie. I will never make that mistake again."

Asher laughed, hurting his ribs and his jaw, but it felt good too. He held his side. "Don't make me laugh."

Harry pouted. "Sorry." He offered him another spoonful. "Four told you we're travelling tomorrow?"

Asher nodded as he swallowed.

"Do you think you'll be up for it? I told him yes, but if you're not ready, I'll call him back."

"I'll be okay."

Harry offered him another small spoonful and Asher took it, his eyes meeting Harry's. The kindness, the gentleness of this interaction, made Asher smile, his heart warm.

Harry looked away, his cheeks pink. Maybe Asher blushed too, but with his swollen cheeks it was hard to tell. It made the swelling under his eyes pang, so he guessed it did.

Which was ridiculous.

The hit of endorphins was dizzying and by far better than any pill for pain he could take.

He had a few more mouthfuls but had soon had enough. "Are you sure?" Harry asked.

Asher nodded. "Yeah. I'm tired again. I've never been this tired in my life."

Harry rubbed Asher's back. "I'd reckon your brain took a few real hard knocks. You were concussed pretty bad. You need to rest. It could be weeks before you're feeling better."

Asher sighed as he slowly lay back down. "Weeks . . . I don't want to be this useless for weeks."

"You're not useless," he said gently. "And you can rest when you get to Four's place."

The way he said that . . .

"Wait. Are you not coming? Harry—" He tried to sit up and regretted it immediately, crying out in pain as his ribs protested.

Harry helped him lay back down. "Just relax. You okay?"

Asher nodded but it was far from the truth. He had to breathe through the pain and Harry waited until he was settled before he spoke.

"Of course I'm coming with you," Harry said. He took Asher's hand, looking at it rather than at Asher's eyes. "Asher, I don't know what we are. You and me. I don't know the first thing about . . . *that* or where to even start, really. But

I'll stick with you until you tell me you don't want me around anymore. If that's okay with you."

Asher could have cried. He certainly couldn't speak right then, so instead, he nodded. "Yeah," he mumbled, his bottom lip trembling. "I'll stick with you too, if that's okay with you."

Harry grinned, squeezing Asher's hand. "That's very okay with me." He just about vibrated with happiness, and it made Asher smile. Harry leaned down and kissed him softly. "Get some rest. Tomorrow's a big day."

ASHER SLEPT for a few hours and the sound of Harry's laughter stirred him from sleep. Not just Harry, but children too, and a man yelling out for someone to run, run, run.

Asher wondered if he'd dreamed it until he heard more laughter.

His body ached from lying down for too long, and he needed to move. Even if just for a little while. Like Harry had said, tomorrow would be a big day of travelling, and that would involve walking to some degree.

Asher got himself upright and walked slowly to follow the sound of voices. This was his first time seeing the outside. It was late afternoon, the low-setting sun was bright enough to hurt Asher's eyes. It was a desert village, homes built of wood and clay. It seemed they were on the edge of town because from where Asher stood in the doorway, he could see a few homes either side of the one he was in, but across from them was some agricultural plots and what appeared to be a whole cricket game going on.

Harry stood in the middle with the cricket bat, and about six small kids spotted around him. One of the bigger kids bowled to him and he tapped the ball gently to one of the smaller kids. They all cheered and Harry laughed as he ran down the dusty pitch. It wasn't a real pitch, just a flat area with a set of cricket stumps at one end and an old tin pot at the bowler's end. Harry made the run easily and it was another kid's turn to bowl.

Not before another kid spotted Asher and pointed him out. Harry turned to see Asher, his cricket game forgotten, and the kid bowled at him hitting the stumps.

The cheers were loud, and an older man from the next house clapped and hollered. Harry laughed. "That's not fair! I was distracted!"

Asher found himself smiling. Smiling at the remarkable man Harry was. Sure, he could be brutal and unforgiving if he had to be . . . but there he was, playing a game of cricket with a bunch of kids, laughing in the dusty sunset. He handed the bat over to the kid that bowled him out and he came running over to Asher.

"Hey. You're up and walking."

"Sick of lying down, and I heard the laughter."

He grinned, looking back at the kids. "I don't speak Urdu and they don't speak much English, but we all speak cricket."

Asher was still smiling, his heart feeling two times too big for his chest. "You should get back to it," Asher said, nodding to where the kids were waiting for him.

Harry let his head fall back with a groan. "Relentless, I tell ya."

But he ran back over, and their game recommenced until the last of the sunlight called an end to the match. Asher stood for as long as he could, then he leaned against the wall.

He didn't want to miss watching this.

This innocent joy that had been missing from Harry's life —and Asher's—for far too long. Having fun for the sake of it, laughing freely, bringing joy to the kids' afternoon for no other reason than to just bring joy.

This is what Asher meant when he said a normal life.

Not with kids. Hell no. That was not a life for him.

But to exist without fear, without looking over his shoulder.

Would he ever get that? Did he deserve to have that after

all he'd done? Asher wasn't sure, but if he could just have a taste of it . . .

Harry walked back over to him, the grin wide on his dusty face. "You stayed out here to watch?"

"Wouldn't have missed it."

"Those kids all ganged up to beat me."

He'd most definitely let them win. "Your secret's safe with me."

Harry helped him walk back into the small bedroom when it dawned on Asher . . . something he hadn't thought of until now. "Where have you been sleeping?"

Harry tapped the mat on the floor with his foot. "Right here."

"On the floor?" Asher slowly lowered himself to sit on the bed. "Harry, I—"

"You've barely been conscious since we got here," he said quietly. "And there's no way I'm leaving you defenceless."

Oh.

Asher held up his hand. Harry took it and sat beside him. "I'm sorry I've been . . . a liability." Harry opened his mouth to argue, but Asher shook his head. "No, listen to me. Harry, in our line of work, the weak get thinned out. The injured are a liability and a weak link. We both know it. It's why you pretended your ankle didn't hurt when it clearly did. You didn't want me to think of you as a dead weight."

Harry couldn't argue that.

"But I can't hide this. Not even my face or not being able to see for three days, or all the broken ribs," Asher said. "But it's my head. It's so foggy, and I'm exhausted. If I'd have been with anyone else, they'd have either left me behind or shot me."

"My dearest Asher," Harry said sweetly. "If you'd been with anyone else, they probably would have shot you around day one or two. In Morocco or Algeria. Maybe even Spain."

Asher smiled and squeezed Harry's hand. He could appreciate the joke, but he needed to say this. "If I was with anyone else, they wouldn't have come to save me. When you realised they'd taken me, you could have taken off in the opposite direction and been ten hours away before they realised."

"I'm not anyone else," he said quietly, serious now. "And there was no way I wasn't going to find you."

"And that's why I'm grateful it's you." Asher was embarrassed to say such things out loud and maybe it was the brain-fog and tiredness talking. "If I didn't have you . . ."

"Well, let's not forget the reason they took you and beat you to a bloody pulp was *because* of me. So there's that."

Asher shook his head. "No. It was only a matter of time before something like this happened. I'm surprised they didn't just shoot me in the motel room, then wait for you to come back."

"It was about control," Harry said. "It would have been Gibson's idea to take you and lure me out, to teach me a lesson, like he was better than me. To make me beg or some bullshit."

"He was . . . bad at it. Just violent and no control. Easy to make angry and impatient."

"That's exactly how he was in my unit. I have no regrets for what I did to him." Harry shrugged. "After your first twenty-four hours, getting you here, you were so out of it and in so much pain, I wanted to kill him again."

Asher lifted their joined hands and put the back of Harry's hand to his lips then to his cheek, and he closed his eyes. "You've looked after me and cared for me like no one ever has. Not even when I was a very small boy. There have been many things absent from my life, but now I have you."

"You do," Harry whispered. "I don't have anyone either. I thought I had Parrish, but he betrayed me. All I have is you."

Asher smiled but his eyes were hard to open. "I'm so tired."

"Lie down and sleep."

"Will you share the bed with me tonight?"

"Asher, what if I hurt you. If I roll over and hurt your ribs?"

"You won't. I can't bear the thought of you on the floor, and honestly, I would really like it if you held me."

Harry smiled sadly. "Okay."

THE NEXT MORNING, Harry had left a rather sizeable sum of cash with Ahmad, Nour, and Hazeema for their troubles, he'd waved goodbye to the kids, and Ahmad drove them to the Gwarda airport, through the private gates to a hangar.

There was a private jet and a well-dressed pilot who was waiting for them. "Is that your Number Four?" Harry asked.

Asher was walking slow, the glare of the sun was giving him a headache and the truck ride hadn't been exactly pleasant, but Harry's question made him smile. "No, that's not him. I'll tell you something about my Number Four," Asher said. "Is that one, he's not a pilot. And two, he never leaves his property."

Harry frowned. "Ever?"

Asher shook his head. "No. He's agoraphobic. Well, I don't know if he's ever been diagnosed, but he can't walk outside his property gates. Has full blown anxiety attacks if he tries."

Harry hadn't expected that, and he no doubt had more questions, but the pilot greeted them. Harry spoke to him, which was basically Harry interrogating him after their last endeavour on a private plane, while Asher stared up at the steps to get into the plane.

Christ.

It may as well have been Everest.

He held onto the handrail and took one slow step at a time. He could never remember being so useless. But Harry was soon behind him, should Asher do something stupid like fall, and he helped him into his seat.

The plane was brand new and incredibly luxurious, immaculate white leather and wood veneer. But the seats . . . Asher was already having trouble keeping his eyes open. These seats were so, so very comfortable. "Oh wow."

"I'm going to buy you a recliner," Harry said, stowing away their duffle bag. "What is it with you and comfy leather chairs? Maybe I'll even buy you one of those vibrating massaging chairs."

Asher chuckled, his eyes closed. The pain pill had taken the edge off but, oh boy, was he tired.

"I'm excited to meet this Number Four of yours," Harry said. "Do I get to know his real name before I meet him? Or do I actually call him Number Four?"

"The fact that he wants to meet you is a big deal. He doesn't let many people into his house. I've only been there a few times."

"You have?"

"His new place, yes. Just a few." Asher fought to keep his eyes open. "I'm tired, Harry."

"What's his name, Asher. You gotta give me something."

Harry wasn't just excited. He was nervous. It was cute. Asher had never divulged information on Four before. Not to anyone, not for anything. But Harry was different.

"I'm going to meet the guy," Harry added. "The least you can do is tell me his name."

"It's Oh Yunho."

Harry was quiet before he sighed. "For fuck's sake, Asher. If I knew, I wouldn't have to ask. After all we've said about sticking together and trusting one another, and you say, 'oh you know,' like I already know. Which I don't. It's why I've asked you a dozen times. But if you don't wanna say, I'll just ask him myself."

Asher chuckled, almost asleep. "No. His name is Oh Yunho. Surname Oh, first name Yunho."

"Oh."

"Exactly. Oh Yunho." He was smiling though he couldn't

fight sleep another second. "We joke about his name. But Four is funny too."

"Do I want to know why he's called Four?"

Asher closed his eyes and sighed. "In Korean, the number four sounds like the word for death."

EIGHTEEN

THE FLIGHT to Thailand was about four and a half hours.
Asher slept most of the way, though Harry was happy to keep
an eye on the flight path to avoid a repeat of the Yemen
incident.

Though this plane wasn't just a paid contact via Four, or
Yunho, or whatever his name was. This plane and its pilot
were his *own* private plane and pilot. Personally vouched for,
personally sent, no expense spared.

Harry was more than curious to meet this man.

Four, or Yunho, had promised Harry that Asher would
have a safe place to recover and proper medical care, so Harry
agreed. Asher needed time, and peace and quiet, and no
stress. His face was healing okay, though the deep black and
purples were beginning to turn shades of green at the edges,
and his ribs weren't good, but his cognitive recovery was
going to need some time.

That was how hard and repeatedly those fuckers had
hit him.

A concussion so bad even four or five days later, he still
had bad headaches, brain-fog, light-sensitivity, and he *still*
needed to sleep and rest most of the day.

Knowing those assholes had done this to him made Harry

so mad he almost wanted to go back to Oman, find Gibson's corpse and head-stomp that fucker some more.

Harry knew enough about concussions that he didn't doubt Asher would be okay. He just needed time. Having multiple broken ribs on both sides of his body didn't help either.

Even thinking about Asher's injuries made Harry rage. He couldn't hurt Gibson or Hull anymore, but he sure could hurt Parrish. The man who told Gibson and Hull to do "whatever it takes."

Harry was going to make Parrish suffer.

But first, his only concern was Asher. Harry would make sure he was well cared for, then he'd work on his revenge on Parrish.

He would deliver the USB to Yunho, and whatever Yunho was going to do with that information, Harry didn't know or care. He just wanted to take Parrish down.

"What are you thinking about?" Asher asked him.

Harry hadn't even realised he'd woken up. "Oh, hey," Harry said. "Nothing much. Just Parrish, and how this is all going to end."

Asher gave him half a smile. "You know there's a saying about digging two graves on your journey for revenge."

Harry kinda shrugged. "It's how it was always going to end, wasn't it?"

"I'd rather if it didn't." Asher's gaze was soft. "I know you want him to pay for what he did to you."

"To me?" Harry shook his head. "No. I want him to pay for what he had done to you."

Asher smiled again. "That's sweet, Harry."

"But?" There definitely sounded like there was a but coming.

"But I don't want you to die for me. How can we stick together if you're dead? And you did say you'd stick with me." Then he made a face. "Unless I dreamed that. Did I dream that? Shit."

Harry laughed. "No, you didn't dream that. I said it. And you said it back to me."

"Thank fuck." Asher put his hand to his heart, but he was smiling. "And anyway, there are better ways to take him down than a bullet between his eyes."

"How?"

"You said he was a man of reputation, of rank. A family man with political ties. Men like that don't fear death. They fear losing. Take everything from him and you will watch him crumble. Ruin him, Harry."

Take away his reputation, his rank, his family and political ties . . . Hmm, that could work, but Harry really was more of a bullet-between-the-eyes kind of guy.

"Yunho will know how," Asher said. "He is a scalpel, surgically precise and clean. You, my sweet Harry, are a cleaver."

"Gee, thanks."

"Actually, I may be more of a cleaver. You're more of an axe and blunt force trauma."

Harry was about to reply—Asher was clearly feeling better after his long nap, given he was back to insulting Harry —when over the speaker, the captain advised to prepare for landing.

"I haven't seen Yunho in a long time," Asher said. "I'm looking forward to seeing him."

"How much are you looking forward to it?" Harry asked. "Do I need to give you two some private time?"

Asher laughed. "You're so jealous, it's actually sweet."

Harry rolled his eyes. There was no point in denying his jealousy. "Yeah, well, just so you know, I wouldn't be okay with that. With giving you private time. I mean, if you wanted to talk and catch up that's fine, but . . ." He shook his head. "Never mind."

Asher was apparently very amused. "I'm glad you wouldn't be okay with that because I wouldn't be okay with that either. With giving you private time with someone else. If you know what I mean."

Harry couldn't even describe the relief he felt. The joy. It made him giddy. "Good. Glad we got that sorted."

Asher laughed. "And secondly, Yunho's not like that. Well, he is. But not with me. We never went there. Never wanted to."

"What do you mean he is like that? He *is* what?"

"You'll see when you meet him."

"Great." The thing was, Harry had no idea what to expect. All he knew of Yunho was his name and that he was some kind of whiz computer hacker. That Asher had saved his life some years ago, helped him stage his own death to defect from his country.

Asher had also mentioned Korea. Not that Yunho was from there exactly, but he'd said the word four in Korean sounded the same as death. And the name Oh Yunho did sound Korean. And if Yunho had to *defect* from his country, Harry could assume, maybe, that he was from North Korea?

It didn't matter to Harry either way. He just liked to know something about a person before he put his life in their hands.

Yunho had helped them, no doubt about it. But Harry would feel a whole lot better about him once he'd met him.

The plane landed on a private runway in the humid jungle mountains of Thailand. They were then driven for half an hour to a marina where they were put on a boat—an extremely nice boat, mind you—and after sailing out into the very blue ocean for twenty minutes, an island came into view.

Harry couldn't believe what he was seeing.

It was something out of a James Bond movie.

The boat pulled into a sheltered dock that was built into the island. The lawns were manicured to perfection, island gardens were lush green, birds cawed in the trees. But from the dock, a path ran up to a grand house. Modern white stone and glass but surrounded by palms, and although Harry could barely see only a part of it, he knew it was going to be huge.

When Asher had said Yunho had money . . .

Harry helped Asher onto the dock, and as soon as Asher's

feet were on the island, a man came running from the house down toward them.

He wore old, faded jeans and a white, long sleeve over-sized grandad-collared shirt, and sandals. Harry didn't know whether to be alarmed, but by Asher's smile, he knew who it was.

Yunho.

He stopped when he saw Asher. Or more specifically, Asher's face. "My darling," Yunho said, walking to close the distance between them. He gently cupped Asher's cheeks and put his forehead to Asher's.

Harry thought for a horrible moment they were about to kiss, but no. They each closed their eyes and just breathed. "I've missed you, brother," Asher whispered.

"I was so worried," Yunho said. Then he pulled back and frowned. "Your beautiful face . . ."

"I'm okay," Asher said with a smile. Then he looked at Harry. "Harry. This is the infamous Four, Oh Yunho."

Yunho turned his attention to Harry. "We finally meet," Harry said, holding out his hand.

Yunho shook it, studying him. "I am indebted to you for saving his life."

"You saved us a few times," Harry replied. "So maybe we can call it even."

Yunho looked at Asher and gave him a smile. "He is as gorgeous as you said. And so big and strong."

Asher chuckled but looked to Harry fondly. "He is."

Having heard enough of that, Harry picked up the duffle bag, which was his cue to move along. Yunho linked his arm with Asher and they began a slow walk up to the house, Harry walking behind them. He didn't mind. It gave him a good chance to take in every detail.

The house was a mansion and straight out of a movie. Harry had to wonder how big the island was and if Yunho owned the whole thing. He suspected he might. Inside the house was all open space, from what Harry could see, white marble and million-dollar views from every window.

"I shall take you to your room," Yunho said. "It's the guest quarters on the ground floor. I didn't think you'd want to tackle the stairs."

Harry followed, bewildered at the expense of everything. But Yunho seemed very down to earth, very concerned about Asher. Harry didn't know much about clothes but he knew expensive when he saw it. Harry suspected his guess of Yunho being North Korean was correct. His dark hair was a little shaggy, and Harry put his age somewhere between thirty-five and fifty. He was a little campy, had a wide smile, sharp eyes, and an old scar that ran down the side of his neck.

The room he took them to was the size of a presidential suite in some fancy hotel. It was basically an entire apartment. In fact, the bedroom was larger than most places Harry had ever lived in, complete with the biggest bed Harry had ever seen, a full bathroom, a living area with a huge flat-screen TV.

Asher walked straight to the bed and slowly sat down. He looked beat. It had been a big day for him. "You okay?" Harry asked him. "Can I get you anything?"

He took a breath in and out and slow-blinked. "Could you please get the blinds for me. Might take some of those pain pills and rest a while, if that's okay?"

Yunho rushed to the windows, quickly closing the blinds and darkening the room considerably. "I'm so sorry, my darling," he said. "I should have asked."

Asher waved his hand. "I haven't been able to do much these last few days. Today kind of took it out of me. I just need to rest for a bit, and I'll be fine. We have so much to talk about."

Harry filled a glass with tap water and handed two pills to Asher. Then he knelt before him, unlaced his boots, and pulled them off. "Does that feel okay?"

He glanced up at Asher to find him smiling back at him. "Thank you."

Harry helped him lay down, pulled the covers over him and made sure he was comfortable. "You can rest now,"

Harry murmured, though he was sure Asher was already asleep.

"I've organised the doctor to come tomorrow," Yunho said gently. He looked fraught with worry.

Harry gave a nod. "Thank you."

He nodded toward the door. "Can we talk?"

Harry followed Yunho back out to the living room, a large room open to the ocean views with expensive furniture and artworks. Yunho sat and waited for Harry to do the same. He fidgeted with his fingers, nervous. "He is not well. To see him so vulnerable . . ."

"He is better than he was. He is strong and determined," Harry offered. "He's talking and thinking clearer than he was, so he's improving."

Yunho's expression turned grim. "I'd be remiss not to ask if you made those assholes who hurt him suffer the worst, but I saw the photographs. The police found the bodies two days ago."

"Oh? You saw photographs?"

"I was following to see if anything had been reported. Any witnesses, that kind of thing. The photographs were . . . somewhat gruesome."

Harry raised his chin. "I'm not sorry for what I did."

Yunho's gaze cut to his. "I'm glad you did it."

"Every time I see him wince or see the bruises on his back and sides, it makes me want to kill them all over again. And I'm going to make Parrish pay."

Yunho smiled, and he gave a nod. "Good."

"I'd very much like to rip the man's spine out," Harry said without an ounce of sarcasm. "But Asher seems to think there may be a better way. Something about taking everything away from him and ruining him instead. Asher said it would hurt him more. Not really my style, but he might have a point."

Now he smiled fondly. "Ah, Asher. He always was a quick learner." He studied Harry for a long moment. "You care for him," he said. Not a question but a statement, an observation.

Harry felt the man's assessment. There was no point in denying it. "I do."

Yunho seemed happy to focus on the horizon of the ocean for a long beat. "And he cares for you. I never thought I'd see the day, but the way he looked at you . . ." He sighed and smiled at Harry. "I joked with him yesterday on the phone that he had it bad for you, but I didn't realise just how true that was."

Harry's gaze lasered in on him. "Is that a problem?"

Yunho laughed. "Oh, heavens above, no. I simply never thought I'd see him look at anyone the way he looked at you just now. I've known Asher for a long time."

"He told me."

Yunho quirked a surprised eyebrow. "He did?"

"How you met. How he helped you, and how you've helped him since then."

He smiled. "He trusts you. Not a gift he gives often. Thus proving my point."

Harry inhaled deeply and sighed. "He and I have a lot in common. I can count the people I trust on one finger, and he's asleep down the hall." No, Harry didn't count Yunho in that sum, and he wasn't sorry. He'd known the man for all of five minutes. "I trust you by proxy," Harry added. "If that counts."

Yunho didn't seem one bit offended. He waved him off. "This life we lead, in the shadows, trust is something earned and seldom shared. No explanation required. But I will admit," he added, "I had concerns when things went south in Madrid. I knew you by reputation alone. Your résumé is quite impressive and I worried for Asher. After all, having two lions in one cage rarely ends well. But he told me you were different. Watching you two work together was interesting, and knowing you saved Asher was one thing. But seeing you with him, how gentle you are with him, how you care for him, is another. And if I could ever choose any one person for him, it would be a mountain of a man who would stop at nothing to protect him."

Harry didn't know how to take that. Compliments weren't something he encountered often. Hell, he wasn't even sure that *was* a compliment. "For the first two days, I wanted to kill him a dozen times. He talked non-stop, and he goaded me continuously. He just poked, poked, poked until I'd almost snap. He was relentless."

Yunho laughed and clapped his hands. "He's like a song you can't get out of your head until it drives you crazy. Then he burrows into your heart and you're never the same again." Yunho was still smiling though he grew a little teary, and Harry realised then that Yunho thought of Asher as a younger brother, or even a son. "Isn't he just the best?"

Harry nodded. "He is. He deserves good things." Harry assumed now was as good a time as any to bring this up. "We have the USB, but I'd like Asher to be the one to give it you."

"Fair enough." Yunho gave a nod before getting to his feet. "Come with me. I want to show you something."

Harry stood but looked back down the hall. "Asher . . ."

"Asher will be fine," Yunho said. "This is an island. No one can get even close without alerting us."

So Harry followed him through the house to a door with a keypad. Through that door and down a set of stairs to another door, this time with a fingerprint scanner.

Christ.

Inside was a room that put government war-rooms to shame. The far wall was filled with screens, and a long table in the middle of the room had another three screen stations.

Harry had seen the inside of national intel departments a few times early on in his career, but this . . . ? Harry thought the outside of the house was James Bond worthy. But this, now *this* was James Bond worthy. There even was a digital thermostat on the wall, which Harry assumed kept the room at the perfect temperature for all the screens and computers.

There were two other people in there, a man and woman. They both stood up when they saw Harry.

"This is Harry Harrigan," Yunho said. "Harry, this is Lucas and Aranya."

Lucas was a tall white man, with greying blond hair, about fifty years old. Aranya was Thai, maybe in her twenties, short with glasses. Her long hair was in some kind of knot on top of her head.

Harry gave them both a nod.

"Harry will be staying for a while."

"And Asher?" Lucas asked, his accent faded English, his gaze darting between Yunho and Harry's. "Is he okay?"

"He's resting," Yunho replied. He gave Harry an apologetic smile. "They saw the photo you sent of him."

One screen showed CCTV of the dock, and on another was the living room he and Yunho had been in, and one of the hallway. Asher's door was still closed. But they'd no doubt seen Harry and Asher arrive, and they'd watched Yunho and Harry talk.

Harry wasn't sure if he liked this level of security or not.

Then he noticed other screens on the wall were of various buildings, inside and out. Harry thought he recognised one in Prague? There were a few screens of profiles, complete with faces and names Harry didn't recognise. There were other screens of satellite maps and a few screens full of nothing but numbers.

It was a whole operation.

Yunho turned to Lucas. "Can you please bring up what information we have on Mr Clive Parrish."

Lucas tapped away on a keyboard, and a few seconds later, all the screens blinked and new images filled every screen on the wall. Images of Parrish spanning a decade, at least. Images of assignments, most of which Harry had completed, now with *deceased* stamped across the black and white profile faces. Screens of information, of news articles, financial transactions, phone records, names, dates. More photographs . . .

Harry looked twice. He recognised the security gate with the vehicle X-ray machine. "Is that Parrish at the oil and gas fields in Algeria?"

Yunho nodded. "Three years ago."

Lucas tapped on that image and it opened a sequence of more. "And there he is with Professor Taleb. Who, two and a half years later, he would have killed."

Harry had no idea that Parrish had met with him in Algeria. At the gas fields where all those ex-army Australians were now employed. Parrish had constructed the whole setup.

That lying piece of shit.

"A lot of his information has been deleted, scrubbed. I can't access it," Yunho said. "So I'm hoping that USB the professor's wife gave you will have tangible proof. The final nail in his coffin, if you will."

Harry hoped the USB was worth it too.

Then there was a photograph of Parrish with Traeger Mayer, dated around five years ago. Phone calls, emails, deals, energy contracts, money . . . and the assignment to have him terminated.

Harry took a deep breath and tried to calm down. "I'm beginning to lean toward my idea of ripping Parrish's spine out. While he's still alive."

Yunho stood with his hands clasped behind his back, staring at the screens on the wall. "It gets worse. Parrish's interests in the energy sector began about eight years ago. He clearly saw a profitable market and began with shares, dividends. Not just with stocks but with favours for the high rollers for a piece of their pie. He started a company called Solaris. Bought his way into the game by having threats removed. The oil and gas tycoons never got their hands dirty and paid him accordingly."

Jesus.

"Then he got greedy. And stupid," Yunho continued. "He bought into the big time, using his company and connections in Algeria and Saudi Arabia. Solaris became the middleman, actually could have been a legitimate business, well, except for the blood in the sand. But he began skimming and funnelling, just a fraction of a percent here, another fraction there, moving funds through cryptocurrency. Thought he was hiding it. He thought he was clever."

"He was skimming," Harry asked incredulously. "From oil tycoons?" Harry didn't dare guess what a fraction of a percent was when they were talking billions.

"Like I said, he got stupid." Yunho glanced at Harry. "And there are a few Australian politicians lined up behind him, it would seem. The ripples in the pond go deep."

Lucas pressed some more buttons and the screens changed again. Familiar faces, famous political faces. Harry couldn't believe it . . . yet at the same time, he wasn't surprised.

He wanted them all to pay. He'd see them all taken down, even if it killed him.

Yunho smiled. "I have a plan for Mr Parrish and his political friends I think you might like. When Asher wakes up, and if he's feeling up for it, we can discuss our best course of action."

HARRY OPENED the door to their quarters and Asher opened his eyes. He smiled as soon as he saw Harry, and it made Harry's heart skip a beat. "Hey," he said gently. "How are you feeling?"

Asher sighed out a moan. "Good."

Harry climbed up the mattress from the foot of the bed and flopped down next to Asher. "This house is insane."

Asher smiled. "Did you see the room downstairs?"

"Yep. With all the screens. I met Lucas and Aranya."

"Lucas is a great man," Asher said. "He and Yunho are lovers, if you didn't know."

Harry stopped. He had no idea. "Really?"

"About eight years now," Asher added. "They met when this house was built. Lucas was the project manager and they clicked from day one. Lucas understands Yunho and his agoraphobia. And he's been helping him run his operation since then."

Harry liked hearing this. Not just that Yunho was in a

committed relationship with someone else . . . but yes, that Yunho was in a committed relationship with someone else. "Yunho seems like a nice guy."

Asher studied Harry's face, smiling serenely. "He's the best."

"I thought I was the best."

Asher chuckled. "Did I ever say that about you?"

"Pretty sure you did. You said I was the best shot on the market."

"Now I know you're lying, because I'm the best shot on the market."

"Oh, maybe it was me who said you were the best. I can't remember now."

Asher laughed and leaned over as far as his sore ribs would allow. He pointed to his lips, and Harry happily obliged by kissing him softly.

"You must be hungry," Harry said. "Want me to go find something? Or do you want to get up?"

"I want to get up. I can't believe I fell asleep like that."

"You had a big day. After four days of barely being able to move, all the travelling today was a lot for you."

"I'm sick of being like this."

"I know, but you're getting better," Harry said, tracing a gentle hand through Asher's hair. "Every day you're better than the day before. You'll be back to yourself in no time. Annoying the shit outta me before you know it."

Asher smiled. "I hope so. Help me up?"

"Sure." Harry jumped off the bed and slowly helped Asher to his feet, only for Asher to wrap his arms around Harry. He pressed his face into Harry's chest, his neck, and held him tightly.

"Just a hug," he mumbled.

Harry slid his arms around him, gentle, careful, and held Asher in a warm embrace. It wasn't the kind that led to anything more. It was the kind of hug that fed his soul. He could feel parts of himself long thought broken starting to come back to life, to knit back together. Healing. Soothing.

"Feels so good," Asher mumbled. "Thank you."

"It does," Harry whispered. And the words I love you were right there, surprising him, scaring him. He didn't say them out loud. He almost did. He could have.

Probably should have.

He'd never said them to anyone. Yet he wanted to say them to Asher.

"You okay?" Asher asked, pulling back. "You froze up. I didn't mean to make—"

"No," Harry said quickly. He cupped Asher's tender, still-bruised face. "I just . . . Oh, Asher. I'm just really glad you're okay, and holding you now, like this, it just . . . I'm not very good with words. I have no experience in talking about shit like this." He sighed, embarrassed. "I'm just really glad you're okay. That we're okay, that we made it this far."

The corner of Asher's lips curled upward in a half smile. "I'm glad too. I'm glad I didn't shoot you in Madrid. I'm glad I decided to let you tag along."

"Tag along?"

He grinned. "Yep."

"Well, would you look at that. You're back to annoying me already."

He slowly raised his hand to cup Harry's cheek. "I have no experience in talking about shit like this either, just so you know. But I'm glad we made it this far too. And I'm glad you said you'd stick with me. Because if it weren't for you, Harry, I don't know what I would have done."

Harry pressed his lips to Asher's in a soft, warm kiss. "You'd have been fine, baby."

Harry knew he'd said the wrong word as soon as he said it. As soon as Asher's eyes lit up and his smile became a grin. He held the side of his face, his swollen jaw. "Baby?"

"It just came out. Sorry." The truth was, he'd called Asher that a few times but mostly when he was out of it. When Harry was tending to his injuries or carrying him to safety. When Harry was in protective-mode and Asher needed him . . . Now it just rolled right off his tongue.

"Did you call me baby?" Asher was so freaking happy. "I'm sorry, I think I misheard you. Could you repeat that?"

"I said," Harry enunciated slowly, "shut the fuck up."

———

YUNHO PUT out a huge platter of fruits, cheese, cold meat, and bread, and Harry was happy to see Asher pick at it for most of the afternoon. Then for dinner, he did small portions of grilled fish with mango that were amazing, and Asher devoured that too. Chewing only on one side of his mouth, but eating all the same.

He sat in the fading tropical sun on the glorious patio, talking and laughing with Yunho and Lucas. Even though they had a history that didn't involve Harry, he never once felt like a third wheel, he never felt as if he were intruding. He listened to their stories, and Asher would smile at him and touch Harry's leg or hold his hand like it was the most natural thing in the world.

He was relaxed, and even as he grew tired in the late evening, he was still happy.

Harry would do anything to see him like that all the time.

But it wasn't long before Asher's blinks were getting longer and he couldn't seem to pay attention. "Okay," Harry said, getting to his feet. "I think we need to call it a day. Come on, sleepyhead." He gently helped Asher up from his chair. He turned back to Yunho and Lucas. "Thank you for dinner, and for everything really, but the first hot shower and comfortable bed in weeks is calling."

Harry got Asher into the shower, and the sounds he'd made bordered on explicit. He scrubbed himself and let the hot water stream over his tired and aching body, and Harry didn't have the heart to hurry him along. He still couldn't brush his teeth properly; it wasn't likely he'd lose his other bottom molar on the right side of his jaw. It didn't feel loose anymore, but his jaw was still swollen and tender.

When Asher finally got into bed, he couldn't even keep his

eyes open. "That was the best shower of my life," he mumbled.

Harry kissed his freshly washed hair and left him to sleep.

And holy hell, the shower was sublime.

Washing away the dirt and dust, yes. But also the stress, the worry, the fear. The hot water and soap were wonderful, but knowing they were safe here, being able to finally breathe . . . that was the best part.

When Harry finally climbed into the bed, Asher was fast asleep. The bed was huge, the room was huge, everything was on a grand scale. And the one thing about all the days and nights he and Asher had spent together in the last few weeks was the cramped space. The shared rooms, the shared beds. And now this huge space felt too vast. He wouldn't be able to sleep, worrying where Asher was, if he was okay.

So Harry shuffled over, closer and closer. And as soon as he touched Asher, he mumbled in his sleep and snuggled into Harry's side.

That was so much better.

Harry closed his eyes with a smile, and sinking down in the most comfortable bed in the world, he had the best night's sleep he'd ever had.

NINETEEN

THE NEXT MORNING after a late breakfast, Yunho's boat arrived, carrying the doctor and boxes of other supplies. Two staff Harry hadn't seen before unloaded the boxes. It was mostly fresh food supplies that were hauled straight through to the kitchen and some other bags were left on the dining table.

The doctor was a middle-aged woman who looked over Asher's injuries, gently touching around his swollen eye sockets and along his jaw.

She didn't think anything was broken.

His ribs were a different story. She grimaced at the bruising but could only assume, without X-rays, that nothing was splintered and puncturing anything it shouldn't. His lungs were clear, his kidneys and liver were functioning adequately, no trouble passing urine. And, she said without a hint of humour, given this was day six and he hadn't died yet, she could only assume he'd be okay.

His pupils were dilating normally, which was a good sign, though he didn't appreciate the penlight shined in his eyes.

"His speech was slow and slurred on day one," Harry said. "Not that he was awake much. But he's gotten better every day. He never had a temperature, no fever, no blood in his urine. He never vomited, never had a seizure." Harry looked at Asher proudly. "He's getting back to his smartass self too, which is a good sign, right?"

Asher rolled his eyes.

"Those are good signs," she replied.

But she ran all the tests she could without him having to go to a hospital. Blood pressure, a urine test with the coloured strips to check for abnormalities, and she listened to his heart and his lungs. She also did some basic neuro assessment on his motor and sensory skills, hearing and speech, vision, coordination, and balance. She made him squeeze her hands and count backwards from ten.

Which he did in five languages until she told him he could stop.

In the end, she gave him a very bruised and sore clean bill of health. She left some more pain meds and told him to rest and recover for another four weeks.

"Four weeks?" Asher cried. "What the hell am I going to do for four weeks?"

She looked him square in the face and deadpanned. "Rest. And recover. It's in the title."

Harry snorted out a laugh and Asher stared at him. "Yunho," he called out. "Be a dear and go grab me my duffle bag. Or more specifically, my friend MAC."

Harry laughed again. "No. He doesn't need it." He sat beside him and took his hand. "I'm sorry. I'm just glad you're okay."

Yunho walked the doctor out and Asher sighed. "Four weeks, Harry," he whined. "I don't want to be slow and tired for another four weeks."

"You won't be. You are getting better every day. I know it's frustrating, but you need to take it easy."

He frowned, his brow knitting, and he worried his bottom lip. "I can't . . . I can't have . . . uh, I don't want you to think it's because I don't want to, but physically, I just hurt too much, and you know I don't mind a bit of pain, but sex right now would kill me. I can't even open my mouth properly without pain . . ."

Oh my God.

Harry squeezed Asher's hand. "Hey, listen to me. I don't care about that. I'm not here for that, Asher. When and if you're feeling better, we can worry about that. Until then, you just need to worry about you." Hearing Asher's genuine worry that he'd be disappointed in him hurt Harry's heart. "I'm here for you, not for sex."

His eyes met Harry's. "Are you sure?"

"I'm very sure. Even if you wanted to never have sex again, I'd still be here."

Asher looked kind of horrified. "I don't think we need to worry about that. God, sex with you is so good."

Harry chuckled. "But you know what I mean, right?"

Asher nodded. "Thank you."

"So," Harry hedged, "if I never wanted to have sex ever again, would you still be here?" He was only joking. Kind of. What he was really asking was would Asher do the same for him?

God, when did I become such a sap?

"I guess. Under sufferance," Asher replied, trying not to smile, but then he sighed. "Of course I would, Harry. I haven't wanted to kill you for almost two weeks. Doesn't that tell you anything? I mean, I was unconscious for some of that time, but still."

Harry leaned in and kissed him, soft and sweet, both of them smiling.

Yunho cleared his throat as he walked back in. "Sorry to interrupt," he said. He was smiling and very much not sorry. He took two bags from the dining table. "I had these delivered this morning. I was going to show you where the laundry was, but honestly, I think the clothes you're both wearing are only fit for burning."

Right, then.

Asher chuckled. "I think he's trying to tell us we smell."

"Not you exactly," Yunho amended. "But the clothes . . ."

Harry looked at his jeans. They were kinda gross. "What do you mean, these smell? It's just blood spatter and seven hours on a cargo ship with two hundred goats and then four days working in the sun with Pakistani farmers."

Asher laughed and held his side. "Ow. Was it goats? On the ship? I think I remember the smell."

Harry nodded. "We slept in one of the holding pens."

"Nice."

Yunho brought the bags to them. "I'll be downstairs if you need anything. Help yourself to whatever you want, treat my house as your own."

So they got changed into clean clothes, which Harry had to admit made him feel brand new. Yunho had good taste too, and he chose the perfect size. Now wearing shorts and shirts, they found two lounge chairs in the shaded garden over-looking the . . .

"What ocean is that?" Harry asked.

"The Andaman," Asher replied. "This island is technically part of Thailand but it's very close to the Myanmar islands."

"I can't believe he owns a freaking island."

Asher smiled sleepily. "He's very good at what he does. And he gives a great deal of funding to local schools and libraries on the bigger islands. He funds an orphanage on the mainland."

"And he's never left the island?"

"No. Not for years."

Harry sighed. It was hard to get his head around. The house was nicer than any five-star hotel, the ocean was the colour of blue jelly, the sand so white it didn't look real. But he'd never left?

Clearly whatever he'd gone through in his home country, his reason for defecting, hadn't been good.

"At least he's got the gardens and beaches he can walk here," Asher added, his eyes now closed. "He's not confined."

Confined.

Confined.

Harry was sure that was the operative word. The reason for Yunho's agoraphobia. The reason, the trauma.

God, were they all messed up?

Asher had nightmares most nights. He didn't wake up. He just mumbled in different languages and flinched a lot.

Harry wasn't sure what his own trauma was. Maybe the fact he was so detached, he could kill people without a second thought. He wanted to kill Parrish. And not just kill, he wanted him to suffer.

Maybe that was something he should think about . . .

Harry must have dozed off because he woke with a start, knowing someone was watching him. He sat up and reached for his gun, which he did not have on him.

"Woah," Lucas said, taking a few steps back. He grimaced apologetically. "Sorry, I didn't realise you were asleep."

Harry scrubbed a hand over his face. "Sorry." He noticed two things: Asher was still asleep, and Lucas was holding an iPad. "Did you need something?"

"I thought you might like to see this," Lucas said, handing the iPad over. "It's been translated."

Harry saw it was an Omani police report and began reading it.

"What is it?" Asher asked, pulling himself up to sit straighter. He was still half asleep.

"Police report," Harry said. Then he read it out loud.

"Police have confirmed the identities of seven men found dead at the abandoned military training facility south of Muscat. Five men were members of the outlawed Omani Freedom Alliance, a radical militia group linked to arms and drug running. The two other men were Australian nationals, ex-military, whose weapons have been linked to a murder in Gibraltar. Police say it was a drug deal gone wrong. The Australian government has been notified."

"The Royal Gibraltar Police have closed the Interpol request," Lucas added. "You leaving your weapon behind was smart."

"I had to make it look like they shot everyone, otherwise they'd be looking for someone who left the scene. And Gibson's gun *was* the weapon that killed the fisherman in Gibraltar. I'd hoped they'd test it."

Harry looked over to Asher to find him smiling at him. "So that's it?"

Harry shook his head. "No. Parrish still needs to pay."

"Oh." Asher reached into his pocket and pulled out the USB. He held it out for Lucas. "I hope it's useful."

Lucas took the USB and the iPad and, with a nod, went back downstairs. Asher sighed and held his hand out for Harry to help him up. "Let's take a walk on the beach."

And so they walked in the sand, and they walked with the water lapping at their feet, in the warmth of the sun.

They walked that day, and the next, and every day that week.

Sometimes Harry held Asher's hand, sometimes he didn't. Sometimes he had his arm around his shoulder, sometimes they didn't touch at all. Sometimes they talked and laughed, and sometimes they just enjoyed the sound of the ocean.

The second week, Harry noticed Asher moved a lot better, he laughed a lot more, he ate more, he slept less. They watched movies, they made out some, they cuddled on the couch, in bed. They slept wrapped around each other.

Asher rested well, he regained energy and his snarky sense of humour. He was clearly feeling better.

By week three, he was bored.

Harry understood because he was getting that way too. The island was amazing and staggeringly beautiful. The house was incredible.

But it wasn't a life for Harry.

And it wasn't for Asher either.

Weeks ago, when Harry had asked why Asher didn't just live with Yunho, if he had all the money and resources in the world, why did Asher keep doing what he did? Harry understood now.

This was Yunho and Lucas' life.

Not Asher's, and not Harry's.

Could they take a vacation there every so often? Absolutely.

But live?

No.

But they were putting together a plan for Parrish, and that was the one thing that Harry was striving for. It had to be timed well, and there were risks of course.

And if it worked, it'd be better than killing Parrish. If it failed, Harry could just kill him anyway. That was Plan B.

But Plan A was better.

And it couldn't happen without Yunho. He *was* good at what he did. Harry had sat in the *war room*, as he called it, and watched Yunho at work a few times. His hands flew over keyboards, he could access almost any network in the world. He watched stock markets, he was a maestro at crypto, and he moved enough money to make Harry feel nauseous.

He could access satellites, view footage in real time, like they did in spy movies. Phone companies, electricity grids, anywhere in the world. Any government, any department, any information.

Harry didn't even pretend to understand how any of it worked or how he stayed undetected. Harry had asked, and Yunho began to explain mirrored satellites something-or-other and dark networks something else, but Harry hadn't understood a word of it.

What he had understood was the new driver's licence to go with the new passport Yunho had had done earlier. He understood the online history Yunho had fabricated to make the new identity look believable: school and college records, a few parking tickets over the years, bank accounts, and an Australian Medicare card.

A whole new life.

Not just for him, but for Asher too.

In Australia.

It would get them into the country, anyway. Where they chose to go after Parrish was dealt with, they didn't know. Maybe they'd travel Australia for a bit. Maybe they wouldn't.

After all, neither of them knew what a 'normal life' was.

They would just try and get through each day without killing each other. Or someone else.

Harry had some reservations about going back to Australia. He hadn't been there for over a decade, after all. But his mission to see Parrish fall was all the incentive he needed.

Australia's tight gun laws were Asher's biggest peeve.

"I have to leave my babies here," he said, pouting.

"Yunho and Lucas will look after them," Harry tried. "Locked up and stored correctly in a climate-controlled room. They're in good hands."

It was Yunho's war room, but still.

"I feel very naked without them. Very vulnerable. I don't like it."

Harry gave him a hug and kept him held tight. "You know you can buy new guns when we get there."

Asher looked up at him, wide-eyed and hopeful. "I can?"

Harry nodded and kissed the tip of his nose. "Of course you can. There are just some regulations, like background checks. But you have a whole new identity now, remember?"

He rolled his eyes. "Fucking Joshua. Do I look like a Joshua?"

Harry laughed. "No." Then he whispered in his ear, "I'll always whisper Asher in your ear when I'm fucking you. No other name. Ever."

Asher groaned. "Christ." He palmed himself. "You know, I feel so much better. I think if we went real slow . . ."

Harry laughed and lifted Asher's chin so he could kiss his lips. His face was completely healed, his jaw was almost there. But his ribs were still sore. Better than they were, but nowhere near ready. "I'm sorry. That was cruel of me."

"Harry."

"Asher, baby, you're not ready for that."

That fire and rage burned in his eyes. Harry hadn't seen it in many weeks. He pushed Harry toward the bed. "Sit the fuck down."

Okay, then.

That was angry Asher, fed-up Asher. Turned-on Asher.

Harry sat on the bed and Asher undid his shorts. He

pulled his dick out, but Harry was too tall, still up too high. Asher pulled his shoulder. "Get on your knees, on the floor."

Harry went willingly. He licked his lips, opened his mouth, looked up, and waited.

"Holy fuck," Asher breathed. He fisted the base of his cock and fed it to Harry.

Harry moaned as the taste hit his tongue. It had been so long, and he wanted this just as much as Asher. If Asher set the pace, he'd be okay. So Harry gave him his mouth to do with as he wanted.

Asher held Harry's head gently and guided his cock in deep and slow. His fingers stroked Harry's cheek and he watched Harry's eyes, his lips. There was nothing fast or rough about it, just tenderness.

Harry sucked and worked him with his tongue, and Asher let his head fall back, surrendering to the pleasure. His cock swelled and surged, and Harry took him in deep. Asher's hand found Harry's hair and he grunted, crying out as he came down Harry's throat.

He grunted again as his orgasm rocked through him, though this time it wasn't exactly pleasure. Harry pulled off and got to his feet so he could catch Asher as he winced and held his side. He laughed, but it wasn't without pain.

"You okay?" Harry asked.

He groaned out another laugh, more pained this time. "Worth it."

Harry pulled up Asher's shorts and sat him on the edge of the bed, letting him catch his breath. He did laugh, but he wouldn't have found it funny if Asher wasn't still smiling. "I don't think we'll try that again for a little while."

Asher sat up straight, hissing as he did and still holding his side. "Ow. Ow."

"Was it still worth it?"

"Yes." Harry helped him up to his feet. "But, and I can't believe I'm going to say this, please don't let me make you do that again. Not for another few weeks, anyway."

Harry laughed. "Okay. Come on, we better go find Yunho."

Yunho was standing at the dining table, going over every last detail. He'd gone over it a hundred times, and the plan was not that complicated. Not for Yunho, anyway. Harry was sure Yunho could do it with his eyes closed, but his concern wasn't the plan.

It was Asher.

Asher went to him and put his arm around Yunho's waist, and he too looked at the table. "Do the words change the longer you look at them?"

Yunho sighed. "Of course not. I just . . ." He glanced at Harry, then back to the table. "I should be happy for you, Asher. And I am. This is all I ever wanted for you."

"But?"

"Are you sure I can't convince you both to stay?"

Asher shook his head and whispered, "We can't stay here."

Yunho frowned. "I won't see you again. I won't work with you again. And I'll miss you. After all we've been through, all these years."

Asher was surprised by this. He turned to face him properly. "What do you mean you won't see me again?"

"You're retiring."

"So? Retiring, not dying. That means I'll have more free time to come back to annoy you even more now. And as for not working together, it just means you can take on another gorgeous young man to replace me."

Yunho shook his head. "No. Not that anyone could replace you, my darling. But I'm done with that. I almost lost you and I don't want to go through that again. Plus, I have more than enough to keep us all busy with the finance side of it." Yunho gave a fond smile to Lucas. "It's about time we scaled back anyway. Lucas says I need to learn how to relax."

Asher laughed as he looked to Lucas. "You let me know how he gets on with that."

Lucas nodded and rolled his eyes. "About as well as you retiring, I would suspect."

Asher laughed but it was Yunho who spoke. He shook his head and put his hand on Asher's chest. "Asher has wanted a normal life for as long as I've known him." Then he gave a smile to Harry. "And now he can have that. He deserves it. And if there is one person in the world who can protect him, it's you."

Harry's chest burned, but he managed a nod. "If I don't wring his neck first."

Yunho's laugh became a sigh. "Are you both ready to go?"

Asher's eyes met Harry's and he nodded. "Yeah. We're ready."

Yunho inhaled deeply and went back to the papers on the desk. He was suddenly back in pro-mode. "Right. My jet will fly you to Darwin to refuel. This is where you will clear customs. Then you both fly onto Sydney. Once you land, I start the ball rolling and I will let you know when to pay Mr Parrish a visit."

Harry nodded. "Understood."

"It could be a couple of days," Yunho pressed. "These things could take some time. Dropping information in legitimate channels always does. We will stay in touch. You have your new phones?"

Asher nodded. "What are we supposed to do in Sydney for a few days?"

"Buy a car," Yunho said. "Look at real estate. Your new bank accounts are quite healthy."

Harry still wasn't too comfortable with what Yunho considered healthy. "Ah, yeah, about that . . ."

Yunho smirked. "When Parrish goes down, you'll both have a lot more."

Asher chuckled at Harry's expression. "I told you. It's just numbers."

"It's not the numbers that scare me," Harry said. "It's where the decimal point is."

Asher laughed. "I get to pick the new car."

Harry sighed. "There really is no point in arguing."

It had nothing to do with the fact that Harry would let Asher choose anything he wanted.

Lucas nodded through the window toward the dock. "Looks like the boat is ready."

Asher and Yunho walked out to the dock, their arms linked. Harry and Lucas gave them some privacy and fell into step a few metres behind them. "Thank you for everything," Harry said. "Asher's recovered well."

"You're welcome here anytime," Lucas said. "And just between you and me, Yunho would like it very much if Asher did visit often. And yourself, of course. He's worried he won't see him now, and he cares for him a great deal. They've been through a lot, long before I arrived."

Harry clapped Lucas on the back. "It would mean a lot to Asher as well. Yunho's the only family he has. He'd never abandon him. Plus," Harry said, aiming to lighten the mood. "That private jet is a terrible way to travel, and this place," he gestured to the tropical island around them, "I'm sure we'd hate to suffer this once or twice a year."

Lucas smiled at that. "I'm sure."

Yunho hugged Asher, and then surprising Harry, Yunho hugged him next. "Keep him safe."

"I will."

Yunho and Lucas waved them off, and Harry slung his arm around Asher as the boat left the dock. "You're not sad?" Harry asked.

"No. When I left Morocco and Algiers, I knew I would never be back," Asher said. "And I can say there's a good chance I'll never set foot in Europe again. But we'll be back here. I know we will. You and me, we'll be back every six months."

He said it with such conviction, it was hard for Harry not to believe him.

"You're confident on the *we*, you-and-me thing, huh?"

Asher smiled, his face a work of art in the tropical sunshine. "Yeah, I'm confident. Aren't you? Don't even try to tell me you don't love me, Harry. I know how to read you and how you look at me."

Harry pulled him in close and kissed the side of his head, then smiled out across the ocean. "You could be right."

Asher pulled back and shoved him. "Is that all you're going to say? I say that I love you and that's what you reply with."

"You didn't say you loved me. You said I loved you."

"Same thing."

"It absolutely is not."

"Is it a lie, then?"

"No. But that's not the point."

"So you do love me?"

"Yes, but that's not what you said."

Asher's smile became a grin. "I knew it."

Harry sighed. He wanted to rage and maybe throw Asher overboard, but he couldn't with his sore ribs and all . . . "You are unbelievable."

He laughed. "You can't declare your undying love for me and then be mad at me in the same breath. That's not how this works."

Harry patted down his pockets and looked around the boat. "Ugh. I don't even have a gun."

Asher grinned. "Lucky for me. Lucky for you too that I'm a better shot from a mile away."

Harry pulled him in close and wrapped his arms around him. "Means I have to keep you close."

Asher hugged him back, sighing into Harry's neck. "You better."

———

HARRY KEPT THINKING about something Asher had said some weeks ago, about knowing your identity in your bones, where you come from, the place you call home. And Harry had been away for so long, so estranged from anything homelike, he didn't really know if Australia was his home anymore.

Until he flew into Australian airspace, and not much later put his feet on Australian soil, that he understood.

He was home.

That sense of place, that familiarity. It warmed his chest and settled in his bones.

Home.

Sydney didn't feel right, though. Sure, it was good to be back. There were so many familiar sights but so much had changed as well.

Maybe it was Harry that had changed.

They hadn't accomplished much in the two days since they'd arrived. They were staying at a very fancy five-star hotel in the city. No more shady motels with indeterminate stains and inexplicable smells. Not anymore. Asher had chosen a car too. A Jaguar, just like the one he'd driven from Madrid to Gibraltar: black, sleek, and one Harry barely fit in. But killing time waiting for Yunho to call, Harry wanted to show Asher the sights of Sydney. They were at Bondi Beach, of all places, sitting on the grassy bank eating overpriced ice creams, watching people throw frisbees or kick a ball, surf, jog.

"Do you think people know?" Asher asked. "People like these. Do you think they know the world that we come from exists? Murder, espionage, blackmail. Being shot at, running for your life. Shooting people for money."

"In books and movies," Harry replied. "Not in real life. At least I hope not."

"I hope not too." They were quiet again until they finished their ice creams. "How does it feel?" Asher asked him. "To be back."

"Strange," he admitted. "Good, but different. Australia feels right. Sydney, not so much." He looked at Asher then. "I know what you mean now, about feeling where I come from. I mean, I think I knew before. But it sits right here in the solar plexus."

Asher smiled. "I'm glad you have that."

"I want you to have it too."

He smiled out at the Pacific Ocean. "I don't have it anywhere, Harry. No country, no home, remember?"

"Do you think you could have it here, one day, with me?"

Asher's cheeks tinted pink and he nudged his shoulder to Harry's. "I don't think my home was ever a place, Harry. I think that's what this whole mess has taught me. I spent so many years longing for a normal life, for a home. But home for me was never a place or a country or a flag. It's a person. And wherever he decides feels right for him, that'll be okay with me."

Harry stared at him, suddenly overwhelmed with emotion. "Asher . . ." His words. His heart. "I love you too."

Asher's whole face lit up and he laughed. "Was that what I said?"

"It absolutely was."

Before Asher could reply, their phones beeped in unison.

It was Yunho.

It was time.

TWENTY

SYDNEY, AUSTRALIA

CLIVE PARRISH LEFT his office in a hurry. He was late home for Linda's birthday lunch, like he'd been late to most family functions the last twenty years. But he'd promised her that he'd make time for her today. And he was trying, he really was.

He'd just tried to log in on his laptop and it failed. Password and fingerprint security. Maybe it was a software issue. Maybe he'd been in such a hurry, he'd done it wrong.

He'd just cursed and closed the laptop, taking it with him so he could check from home when he had more time.

On the way home, he stopped at the roadside florist to pick up something for Linda and to sweeten his lateness. He chose the largest bouquet the man had, tapped his card to pay, and smiled as he turned to leave.

"Sir, it's declined."

Clive stopped. "Declined? It can't be."

The guy shrugged, apologetically. "It could be a card error? Sometimes the lines go down. Here, let me try again."

"No, it's fine. I'll call them." Clive took cash out from his wallet, paid for the flowers, and went on his way, more annoyed than concerned.

God, did everything have to go wrong today?

He pulled up at the gate to his house, noting all the cars parked. Both his kids and their families were here, Linda's two sisters, and some cars he didn't recognise. Probably her friends from the book club, Clive thought with a roll of his eyes as he got out of the car. He took the stupid flowers and went inside.

The gathering was happening in the private gardens, as they mostly did when the weather was nice. Clive could hear laughter and chattering, kids playing. He plastered a smile on his face as he greeted about two dozen friends and family with kisses on cheeks and warm handshakes.

Linda gave him her 'be nice, people are watching' smile and leaned in for him to kiss her on the cheek. "You have a guest," she said. "Said he was one of your army boys. I didn't want to be rude . . ."

One of my army boys?

Clive's gaze went straight to the yard and that's when he saw him. He didn't know how he hadn't seen him before. Blood drained from his head down to his toes.

"Clive?" Linda asked. "Is everything okay?"

No.

No, it was far, far from okay.

Tim "Harry" Harrigan was standing in the backyard, a glass of fruit punch in one hand and a soccer ball in his other. He smiled at Clive.

Clive looked woodenly to his wife. "Yes, of course, dear. Just excuse me a moment."

He made a beeline across the yard toward Harry. He couldn't feel his legs. He wasn't sure how they carried him.

Just then, Charlotte ran up to Harry. He gave her the soccer ball with a huge smile and she ran off, happy. "Cute grandkids," Harry said, like they were long-lost friends. "Nice house too. How much did that set you back? Three million? More?"

"What the hell do you think you're doing here?" Clive

hissed. "In my house. With my family. My god. Have you lost your mind?"

Harry kept the smile on his face. "Don't speak to your guests like that. Where are your manners?"

Clive took more notice now. Harry was just as tall and broad as he always was. The man was huge. But his hair was flecked with silver now, and he had more scars on his face and arms than Clive remembered. The last decade had aged him more than ten years, but then again, Clive wasn't surprised.

"Oh, and about our last phone conversation," Harry said. "You never got back to me with Gibson and Hull's location, but that's okay. I found them. Did you see the photographs?"

Christ.

Yes, he had. They'd almost made him sick.

"They deserved every bit of it," Harry said. "You should have seen what they did to Asher."

Clive might have thought Harry had lost the plot if it weren't for the fierce clarity in his eyes. But still, Clive needed to regain some control. "You shouldn't have come here," he said, surprised at the conviction in his voice.

"Oh, I told you I was coming," Harry replied, sipping his drink.

Clive could barely contain his rage. He had to make himself whisper so he didn't yell for everyone to hear. "You threaten my family and think I wouldn't do the same? Imagine my surprise after a little bit of digging that you do have a family. Parents, alive and well, living in Sydney."

Harry's grin widened. "If you put a bullet in my old man's head, you'd be doing me a favour. Actually, beat the shit out of him first. Then do it. And make sure my mother watches."

Clive shook his head. "You're sick."

"I'm exactly what you trained me to be. An asset to be used and manipulated however you saw fit. Not the government, not the military. You."

"I *am* the military. I am the government," Clive said, his teeth clenched. "I make those hard calls for the betterment of this country." He sneered at Harry. "You were nothing but a kite, Harry. To be cut loose at any time. Nothing more."

Harry sighed. "I really hate that word. And you didn't just cut me loose, Parrish. You put a contract on my head, hoping to clean up your loose ends to cover your own ass."

"Your skills were no longer required. We're fighting a different war now. Terrorism is online. We fight people we cannot see. It's binary codes and hacking security systems. Hell, even the nuclear power plants, the bio security systems, are all controlled online. Banking, crypto . . . funding wars with money you can't even hold in your hand."

"You think wars are fought online? You think bad guys no longer exist on the streets? You wanna come with me to Kabul? To Syria? You want me to give you a tour? Want a recount of every contract I did for you?"

"That's not our fight anymore."

"It was never your fight," Harry said, his anger beginning to show. "You sent me in to kill innocent fucking people to fund your online chess games for money. While you sit here in your comfortable house with your comfortable wife while me and Asher take the kill-shots. And for what? You fed me bullshit about national security, and it was never about protecting this country. It was about lining your pockets with blood money."

"Keep your voice down."

"My blood. Asher's blood."

"Asher Garin," Clive scoffed. "You bring that man into this country and—" Cold realisation dawned on Clive and trickled down his spine. "He's here already? Watching us right now, isn't he?" He looked around, panicked. "Christ. My grandkids are here."

Harry smiled. "You know he can make a shot a mile out, right? He's really very good. Who you gonna send to kill us now? Who in the world is good enough? Who's left? The French and Russian schoolboys you sent to kill us in Madrid. Or the guys you have working at the gas and oil fields in Algeria? All those ex-army guys who are running your illegal skimming farm? Or you just gonna have them all killed as well, you know, to mitigate your losses?"

Clive's mouth went suddenly dry.

"I have all the names," Harry said. "From every deal you made with Professor Taleb before you had him killed. He'd made records of everything because he knew better than to trust you, even put them on a handy USB so you couldn't delete it online. His lovely wife was kind enough to give it to us after I promised to make you pay for having her husband killed. All the names, all the files, all the data of everything you've done in the last decade, all that data you thought you'd had erased. All the people you stole from. They're not the people you want to piss off, Parrish."

Clive's blood pressure was too high. His pulse pounded in his temple.

"You can't stop it," Harry said calmly. "It's too late. And I promise you, try and hurt Asher again, look twice in our direction ever again, and I will rain a shitstorm down on you like you can't even imagine. All the families you had me ruin, why stop there." Harry waved his hand back toward the house, toward Clive's family, to his grandkids. "Why stop there?"

"You piece of shit," Clive spat at him.

It only seemed to please him. Smiling, he put his hand up and raised one finger. "Uh-uh, Clive. Asher wanted me to use hand signals. See my finger? You don't want me to get to three." Then he raised a second finger. "Speak to me like that again, I dare you. One more finger, Parrish. Which grandkid are you least fond of?"

It took a long moment before Clive could speak. There was no begging, no bullshit. "What do you want?"

Harry smiled. "Oh, it's already done. I just wanted to watch your face when I told you. It's funny that you mentioned cryptocurrency." He shook his head slowly. "Funnelling all your illegal money into something that's decentralised and unregulated. You should have known better. Who can you report your illegal losses of illegal money to?"

What was he talking about?

Oh no. Clive's heart rate spiked, and fear squeezed his lungs. "What have you done?"

"Every cent of blood money you took is gone. We didn't touch your military pay. That wouldn't be fair. But I think the feds have probably frozen all your accounts by now, so I'm not sure it matters. Did you have trouble using your bankcard this afternoon?"

Clive blinked.

"We forwarded every detail we had—all the files, photographs, emails, contracts, financial records, all of it—to ASIO, the AFP, and Homeland Security. Oh, and all the major news outlets, here and overseas, and the oil and gas tycoons you stole from. Hell, I even think the Hague was notified. You know, because government officials ordering unsanctioned murders in other countries is *bad*, Clive."

Blood pounded in Clive's ears. He felt lightheaded. He wanted to wrap his hands around Harry's throat. He wanted to kill him, right here and now. But he knew better. Harry was too big, too strong, too brutal. Too good.

"I'm not sure how you expected this to end," Harry said, almost whimsically. "All your political friends in Canberra are probably shitting themselves right now."

"It was never . . . it was never supposed . . . They wanted more money. It was never enough—"

"Shut the fuck up. I don't want to hear one excuse out of your filthy mouth. It's too late. It's all over. You can expect the cops to come rolling in at any minute. Now, I dunno if it'll be the feds, or military police, or even state. Never did get the jurisdiction thing. Either way, you're screwed."

All Clive could do was shake his head. Harry was lying. This was all bullshit. He wanted money. That had to be it. "I can give you—"

"You can't bribe or pay your way out of this. You're going down. Personally, I wanted to kill you for what you did to Asher, in a spectacularly painful way, maybe do to you what they did to him. But this really was better." He sighed happily. "You'll be pleased to know a good portion of your money has gone back to Professor Taleb's wife and her three boys. And if you think you can make a plea deal, if you think you can give them me and Asher as a trade-off, think again. One, Asher Garin doesn't exist. Two, I'm not even in this country right now. And three . . ." Harry's voice dropped low, cold as steel. "You will take full responsibility for everything you have done or I will scrub every trace of your DNA off this planet. Starting with everyone that's at your house today. Understand?"

Clive thought he might vomit. His vision was going blurry. The world was spinning way too fast.

A siren sounded in the distance, and Harry cocked his ear. "Oh, right on cue."

Clive was cold all over. "I trusted you," he said, struggling to speak at all. "Ten years ago. I trusted you to do what had to be done. You were my first mistake."

"No. Your first mistake was sending Asher to kill me. Not because you wanted me dead, not because you betrayed your country. But because by giving Asher to me, you gave me a reason to live. *That* was your first mistake."

The sirens grew louder, too loud. Not a common sound in this expensive suburb. Then men were walking through his house. A team of them. Some of them in military uniforms, some of them in suits.

Linda was panicked, trying to stop them. "What is this? What are you doing? Clive, what's happening?"

All his friends and family stood, watching. Horrified.

He didn't hear a word of what the men in suits said. All he could see were the faces of his kids, his grandkids, his wife.

And Harry smiling.

Clive was escorted out through his house, through his gathered family, and when he scanned the crowd, searching for one last look at that smug son of a bitch's face, to burn it into his memory, he couldn't find him.

Tim "Harry" Harrigan was gone.

HARRY GOT into the passenger side of the car, still smiling. "Let's go."

Asher grinned at him. He'd been listening to the whole transaction, of course. "How do you feel?"

He couldn't actually describe how he felt. There were no words that captured it. "Good. I feel real good. And relieved."

"His face?"

"Priceless."

"Was it worth it?"

"Absolutely."

Asher laughed. "You told him I was watching."

"Well, he assumed that. I just didn't correct him. I did a stupid hand signal thing where I put up fingers, like if I got to three you'd take out one of his grandkids."

Asher laughed so hard he winced and held his ribs. "I heard. I almost choked on my mint."

The truth was, Asher was waiting in the car for him down the street. He was listening, of course, and watching for anyone who entered. But there was never any gun.

Harry sighed, an unspoken weight now off his shoulders. "His face when he saw me, oh my God. And the more I spoke, the greyer his face got. And to see him handcuffed, in front of his entire family, on his wife's birthday. Fucking poetry right there."

Asher laughed again and reached for Harry's hand as he drove. "We leaving Sydney now?" He looked at the GPS map on the dash screen. "Going north, yes?"

"Yep. Head for the M1."

"Do we know what we're looking for?"

Harry smiled and kissed the back of Asher's hand. "Nope. We'll know when we find it."

And find it, they did.

Two weeks later, after driving up the coast of northern New South Wales, staying in the coastal towns and cities, Harry drove them inland. Purely on a whim, for something to do. "There was a cute little town up this way, I remember as a kid," he said. The hinterland was green rainforests and farming land. Scenic, quiet, tranquil.

The town was still there, still cute. Still small. Not much but a local store, a hardware, a bakery, and a town hall. They grabbed a late lunch from the bakery and ate it in the park, in the filtered sunlight to a chorus of birds.

"Far removed from running along rooftops in Madrid," Asher said. His hair was a little longer now, curls that Harry adored. "Or passing through rebel checkpoints in the Arabian Desert."

Harry chuckled. "Seems like a lifetime ago."

The news of Clive Parrish's fall from grace was still front-running news. After all, when the Director of the Special Operations Command of Australia's Defence Force is charged with crimes like espionage, murder, fraud, treason, embezzlement, and about another dozen lesser things, it was always going to be huge. And not just him. There were five senators in jail with him.

It rattled the entire country, especially all levels of politics and military. The case itself could take years, and considering the international interest, every detail would be scrutinised.

The media had grabbed hold of one part of the information they'd been given.

Operation Milvus.

When Timothy "Harry" Harrigan's name was brought up as an agent sent overseas a decade ago, a death certificate magically appeared, dated 2016, Syria—courtesy of Yunho, of course—and a red line was drawn through Harry's name. Just like that.

He didn't mind one bit.

In fact, he felt an immense relief.

It wasn't who he was anymore, and if letting go of his past would help him shape a new future, he was okay with that.

"What's out that way?" Asher asked, pointing to a road leading out of town, opposite the way they'd come.

"No idea. Let's go find out."

The road was narrow. The scenery would go from tall trees to cleared farmland, back to forest, as it snaked its way around the mountains. It was beautiful out this way—

"Stop the car," Asher said. Then he yelled. "Stop the fucking car!"

Harry pulled off the road the best he could and slammed the brakes. "What's wrong?"

Asher got out and almost fell down the embankment. Harry had first thought maybe he was ill. He got out and raced around the front of the car to check on him. "Are you okay?"

But Asher wasn't ill. He looked around, his eyes wide, and put his hand to his mouth.

Harry had never seen him like that. "Asher, baby. What is it?"

"This road. This right here. Here!"

"What about it?"

"I've dreamed of this. I thought it was a memory, but how can it be?" His eyes were still wide, a little teary now. "This road is the place I told you about. Harry, I've dreamed of this. Of here."

Holy shit.

"When you thought you were with your parents?"

He shrugged. "I just felt loved." He shook his head and began to cry. "I knew when I was here I was safe and loved. I didn't know . . . I didn't know what love was. I just assumed . . . I wanted it to be my mother so much."

Oh, man.

Harry wrapped his arms around him while he cried and kissed the side of his head. "I got you, baby."

"It wasn't my parents. It was you who loved me."

He rubbed Asher's back. That one memory, that one feeling, was all he ever thought he had of his parents, and now he didn't even have that. "I'm sorry."

He pulled back, sniffling and wiping his face. "Don't be sorry. I'm not sad. I mean, I am, but I'm also happy. It was you, Harry. Always."

Harry cupped his face in both his hands, wiping away a stray tear with his thumb. "Always."

He nodded and more tears welled in his eyes, but he laughed. "I think I found where I'm supposed to be."

Harry kissed him. "I think so too."

EPILOGUE

THE PLACE they ended up buying was just a few kilometres up the road. It was three hundred and eighty hectares of land that wasn't much use for anything other than billy goats and hunting. Mountains, rocky cliffs, water streams, and trees.

It wasn't originally for sale, but Harry expressed interest, offered way over market value, and the deal went through without a hitch.

When he'd promised to give Asher everything he deserved, he meant it.

There wasn't even a house on it. Well, not what many people would call a house. It was a large barn-style shed made of wood and steel, mostly run down, but it had a kitchen and a bathroom. The last owners had put it there years ago, intending to build a proper house that never happened.

It was all open space, one huge room with an old pot-belly stove, and a large porch that looked down to the valley below. There were no neighbours. They were surrounded by a few kilometres of forest. The shed itself was in need of a lot of work, but it was absolutely perfect.

As soon as Asher had walked in, he looked around and

grinned. "Yunho would be horrified," he said with a laugh. "But Harry, this is it."

Twelve months on, they spent all their time building and fixing the place. They acquired some weapons, they hunted, they made target ranges on their property, and they often had competitions on accuracy, speed, and agility. They made slow love, they fucked hard, and some days they never left their bed at all. They fought too, over stupid shit like cooking and cleaning, sometimes over the shooting competitions, but for the most part, living with Asher was pure and utter perfection.

Harry had bought an old Patrol ute because the Jag wasn't built for trips to the hardware or driving along the track through their property. Personally, he preferred the old, beat-up four-wheel drive over the brand-new luxury car.

This particular day, he'd gone to town for their weekly supply run. He'd been to the grocery store and the hardware, and of course the bakery. Harry had once made the mistake of making Asher try a lamington and now he had to buy him one every week.

He carried the bags inside and saw that Asher was perched up on his favourite recliner, FaceTiming on the laptop with Yunho. They'd been back to visit him once in the last year and were planning to go again in a few months.

Harry took a small tin of mints out of the bag, walked it over to Asher, and gave Yunho a wave. "Hey."

Yunho waved on screen, and Asher grinned at Harry. There was a peacefulness in his eyes. "Is that everything out of the truck?"

"One more. I'll get it."

He continued his conversation with Yunho and Harry went back out to the ute. The last thing was a box from the front seat and he carried it carefully back inside.

"What have you got there?" Asher asked. "Did you buy me a cake?"

Harry snorted. "No. It's not a cake." He put the box on the couch beside Asher. "Open it."

Asher's eyes went wide. "Is it for me? Is it a MAC 50?"

Harry laughed. The box was nowhere near big enough for that. "Not quite."

Asher opened the box and gasped. He looked up at Harry. "Are you serious?" He smiled, stunned and teary-eyed, then gently picked up the tiny black kitten. He cradled it to his chest. "Oh my God, Yunho, look! A baby. Harry, you got me a baby."

Well, it was a baby cat, but yes. "There was a box of them at the hardware. They're eight weeks old—"

"There was a *box of them*?" Asher yelled. "And you only got one?"

"Oh no," Harry lied. "No. That's not what I said."

Yunho laughed on the screen. "I'll let you go. Good luck, Harry."

The screen went black.

Not that Asher cared. He was still staring at Harry. "There was more?"

"No. I mean, there was. But that was the last one."

"You lie."

Harry blinked, backpedalling as fast as he could. "I'm pretty sure that was the last one."

"Harry."

He ignored the death-stare and patted the little kitten that Asher was still holding to his chest. "Look at her, Asher. I saw her and I knew you'd love her. Please don't be mad."

Asher did look at her then, properly. He held her close to his nose, she meowed at him, the tiniest little meow, and he snuggled her into his neck. "She is perfect. And I'm not mad."

Harry leaned in and kissed Asher's lips. "You get to name her."

"I do?"

"Of course you do. She's yours."

"I've never had a pet before." He pouted and held her out in his hands to get a proper look at her. She was all black with blue eyes, a bit on the small side, but cute as a button. "She's so little," he whispered, then held her to his chest again. "*Mala.*"

"Mala?" Harry wasn't opposed, he just wasn't sure he'd heard him correctly.

Asher kissed the top of the kitten's head. "It means 'my little one' in Croatian."

Harry kissed the top of Asher's head. "Then it's perfect." He got up from the couch and went to the kitchen to finish putting the groceries away. "I bought some kitten food from the shop but I don't know if it's the right one. I got some litter as well, so we'll have to make her a litter box."

He looked over and Asher was still on his recliner, still holding and snuggling Mala.

"Did you want to feed her?" Harry asked. "She'll know you're her dadda if you feed her first."

Asher walked to the kitchen area, keeping Mala tucked against his chest. "I'm her dadda," he murmured. "And you're her papa. Harry, look at how beautiful she is!"

Oh hell. Harry had created a sap.

Asher was absolutely beaming. He took the kitten food and sat at the table with her and began to feed her. She was hungry. "You know," Asher said, "I should have told Yunho just to go ahead with the fake marriage certificate with the citizen papers. It would have been easier. And then little Mala here would have two daddies for real."

Harry laughed . . . until he realised exactly what Asher had said. He turned to stare at him. "What?"

Asher glanced his way but went back to feeding Mala. He shrugged. "He asked me if I wanted that. When he was sorting out the citizenship paperwork. He said he could just throw that in. I thought he was joking. I said I didn't really think you'd be up for that, so he didn't include it."

Harry stood there, the can of beans in his hand forgotten. "Asher . . ."

He shrugged again. "It's not like we're religious people who need to stand before some God to declare anything. I certainly don't care what the government thinks."

Harry put the can on the counter and sat in the seat beside him. "Would it be fake, though?"

Asher smiled as he fed Mala another piece of her kitten food. "Well, yeah. As fake as all the other documents we have. I mean, they're real. But they're just not obtained legally. So you'd be marrying Joshua."

"No, I'd be marrying Asher."

His eyes cut to Harry's, and he stared for a long moment. "What are you saying?"

He laughed, because God, was he really doing this? "I'm just saying that if Yunho gave us a marriage certificate as part of our paperwork, I wouldn't have minded. That's all." He licked his lips and swallowed. "If you want to get rings so it looks real . . . or not, I don't mind either way. And no, personally, I don't need no government or religious approval. I'd just need to know that you wanted to do it. Then it'd be real to me."

"Harry," he whispered.

"It's just a piece of paper, right?" Harry joked, trying to lighten the mood because he had a sinking feeling that Asher did not want it. "Like money is just numbers." He gave Mala a quick pat on the head and stood up.

Asher grabbed his hand.

"Not to me," he whispered. "It's not just a piece of paper to me."

Harry sat back down.

"It would be the first legitimate certificate I would have. The first real one. With my name. The real me." He frowned, teary now. "I don't exist anywhere on paper. So no, it wouldn't *just* be a piece of paper. It will be proof that I ever existed. So please don't say it like that."

"Oh, baby, I'm sorry. I didn't think." Harry scooted his chair in closer, their knees touching. He slid his hand along Asher's cheek. "It wouldn't just be a piece of paper to me either. It would be real, and if you want to make it *really* real, we can get married for real on Yunho's beach and he and Lucas would be our witnesses. But I'll be marrying you. Not

Joshua or any other fake name. The real Asher Garin. That's who I would marry. Our real names on the certificate."

Asher chuckled through his tears. "You would do that for me?"

"I would do anything for you. Anything."

"You give me this news and a baby kitten in one day?"

Harry kissed him softly. "And you gave me a reason to live, so let's call us even."

He wiped his cheek and held Mala close to his chest. "Do you think she would care if her dadda and papa are married?"

Harry chuckled. "I don't think she'd care either way."

Asher gave him a teary smile and spoke to Mala. "We better call Uncle Yunho back, yes? Tell him to organise some more paperwork."

Harry pulled him in for a hug, careful not to squish the cat. "I love you, Asher."

"Love you, Harry," he murmured. It wasn't something Asher said often, which made it all the more special to hear it now.

"I'll make us dinner, and we should make a bed for Mala."

"She sleeps with us," Asher said as he went back to the recliner and opened the laptop. "She's too little to be on her own."

Harry sighed. He thought that might be the case. But he didn't mind. Anything to make Asher happy.

Asher had wanted a normal life. And if that meant getting married and being dads to what Harry was certain was going to be one very spoiled cat, then Harry was okay with that.

He was more than okay with that. He woke up every day not believing this was his real life. Not believing that Asher was his, that they were alive and free from their pasts.

Normal lives. Everything they dreamed it would be. Quiet and peaceful. Kinda boring, even.

Kinda wonderful.

The End

ABOUT THE AUTHOR

N.R. Walker is an Australian author, who loves her genre of gay romance. She loves writing and spends far too much time doing it, but wouldn't have it any other way.

She is many things: a mother, a wife, a sister, a writer. She has pretty, pretty boys who live in her head, who don't let her sleep at night unless she gives them life with words.

She likes it when they do dirty, dirty things… but likes it even more when they fall in love.

She used to think having people in her head talking to her was weird, until one day she happened across other writers who told her it was normal.

She's been writing ever since…

ALSO BY N.R. WALKER

Bossy

Code Red

Dearest Milton James

Dearest Malachi Keogh

Christmas Wish List

Code Blue

Davo

TITLES IN AUDIO:

Cronin's Key

Cronin's Key II

Cronin's Key III

Red Dirt Heart

Red Dirt Heart 2

Red Dirt Heart 3

Red Dirt Heart 4

The Weight Of It All

Switched

Point of No Return

Breaking Point

Starting Point

Spencer Cohen Book One

Spencer Cohen Book Two

Spencer Cohen Book Three

Yanni's Story

On Davis Row

Evolved

Elements of Retrofit

Clarity of Lines

Sense of Place

SERIES COLLECTIONS (AS EBOOK BOX SETS):

Red Dirt Heart Series

Turning Point Series

Thomas Elkin Series

Spencer Cohen Series

Imago Series

Blind Faith Series

FREE READS:

Sixty Five Hours

Learning to Feel

His Grandfather's Watch (And The Story of Billy and Hale)

The Twelfth of Never (Blind Faith 3.5)

Twelve Days of Christmas (Sixty Five Hours Christmas)

Best of Both Worlds

TRANSLATED TITLES:

ITALIAN

Fiducia Cieca (Blind Faith)

Attraverso Questi Occhi (Through These Eyes)

Preso alla Sprovvista (Blindside)

Il giorno del Mai (Blind Faith 3.5)

Cuore di Terra Rossa Serie (Red Dirt Heart Series)

Natale di terra rossa (Red dirt Christmas)

Intervento di Retrofit (Elements of Retrofit)

A Chiare Linee (Clarity of Lines)

Senso D'appartenenza (Sense of Place)

Spencer Cohen Serie (including Yanni's Story)

Punto di non Ritorno (Point of No Return)

Punto di Rottura (Breaking Point)

Punto di Partenza (Starting Point)

Imago (Imago)

Il desiderio di un soldato (A Soldier's Wish)

Scambiato (Switched)

Galassie e Oceani (Galaxies and Oceans)

FRENCH

Confiance Aveugle (Blind Faith)

A travers ces yeux: Confiance Aveugle 2 (Through These Eyes)

Aveugle: Confiance Aveugle 3 (Blindside)

À Jamais (Blind Faith 3.5)

Cronin's Key Series

Au Coeur de Sutton Station (Red Dirt Heart)

Partir ou rester (Red Dirt Heart 2)

Faire Face (Red Dirt Heart 3)

Trouver sa Place (Red Dirt Heart 4)

Le Poids de Sentiments (The Weight of It All)

Un Noël à la sauce Henry (A Very Henry Christmas)

Une vie à Refaire (Switched)

Evolution (Evolved)

Galaxies & Océans

Qui Trouve, Garde (Finders Keepers)

Sens Dessus Dessous (Upside Down)

Spencer Cohen

GERMAN

Flammende Erde (Red Dirt Heart)

Lodernde Erde (Red Dirt Heart 2)

Sengende Erde (Red Dirt Heart 3)

Ungezähmte Erde (Red Dirt Heart 4)

Vier Pfoten und ein bisschen Zufall (Finders Keepers)

Ein Kleines bisschen Versuchung (The Weight of It All)

Ein Kleines Bisschen Fur Immer (A Very Henry Christmas)

Weil Leibe uns immer Bliebt (Switched)

Drei Herzen eine Leibe (Three's Company)

Über uns die Sterne, zwischen uns die Liebe (Galaxies and Oceans)

Unnahbares Herz (Blind Faith 1)

Sehendes Herz (Blind Faith 2)

Hoffnungsvolles Herz (Blind Faith 3)

Verträumtes Herz (Blind Faith 3.5)

Thomas Elkin: Verlangen in neuem Design

THAI

Sixty Five Hours (Thai translation)

Finders Keepers (Thai translation)

SPANISH

Sesenta y Cinco Horas (Sixty Five Hours)

Código Rojo (Code Red)

Código Azul (Code Blue)

Queridísimo Milton James

Queridísimo Malachi Keogh

El Peso de Todo (The Weight of it All)

Tres Muérdagos en Raya: Serie Navidad en Hartbridge

Lista De Deseos Navideños: Serie Navidad en Hartbridge

Spencer Cohen Libro Uno

Spencer Cohen Libro Dos

Davo

CHINESE

Blind Faith

CPSIA information can be obtained
at www.ICGtesting.com
Printed in the USA
BVHW081239190722
642473BV00005B/172

9 781925 886726